Heaven and Earth

Heaven and Earth

J.M. Benjamin

www.urbanbooks.net

Urban Books, LLC
300 Farmingdale Road, NY-Route 109
Farmingdale, NY 11735

Heaven and Earth

ISBN 13: 978-1-62286-590-1
ISBN 10: 1-62286-590-1

First Mass Market Printing November 2017
Printed in the United States of America

10 9 8 7 6 5 4 3 2 1

Distributed by Kensington Publishing Corp.
Submit orders to:
Customer Service
400 Hahn Road
Westminster, MD 21157-4627
Phone: 1-800-733-3000
Fax: 1-800-659-2436

Heaven and Earth

by

J.M. Benjamin

Chapter One

As Chill turned onto Remsen Avenue in his silver 645i, black top convertible BMW and parked, his eyes immediately zeroed in and locked on Twan. The lyrics of Jadakiss's raspy voice blaring through the speakers of Chill's Beemer was cut short as he shut off his car and hopped out. Chill took a quick glance down at his Black Label hooded sweatshirt, making sure the chrome .45 automatic concealed underneath it tucked in his waistband showed no indication of a bulge. Thinking that he had noticed a slight detection of his weapon's presence, Chill smoothened out his sweatshirt before making a beeline over to where Twan stood.

"Ayo, T, lem'me holla at you for a minute," Chill called out, walking up on Twan.

Twan was in the midst of puffing on a blunt when Chill rolled up on him. Instantly, he became agitated by Chill's sudden presence.

Twan was not surprised, having a good idea why Chill wanted to speak with him, but he was not in the mood, and he intended to make it known.

"What'chu wanna holla at me about?" Twan retorted aggressively. "Can't you see I'm busy?" he added, taking a pull of the blunt to show Chill that he was, in fact, disturbing his weed-smoking session. Chill disregarded Twan's words. A grin appeared across his face as he sighed. He knew confronting Twan was not going to be an easy task, but nonetheless, knew that it was long overdue.

"Ayo, Twan, why you keep stepping on my li'l man's toes out here, dawg?" Chill blurted out, catching the attention of everyone within ear distance. "I know it's enough paper out here for everybody, sun; you ain't gotta be on no cutthroat shit," Chill continued.

After receiving the disturbing phone call that had interrupted him in the middle of something important, it was Chill's intention to maintain his composure when he confronted Twan, but as he spoke, he could feel his adrenaline stirring up inside him. And Twan's reaction did little to minimize it.

"Mal, you see this shit? This li'l bitch-ass nigga gonna go run and call his daddy," Twan chimed in disgust, directing his words to one of his street colleagues by the name of Jamal he had just been sharing the weed-filled blunt with. Jamal made no reaction or gave no indication that he condoned or entertained Twan's remarks. He was cool with both Chill and Twan and remained neutral in the potential altercation, as he continued to puff on the blunt Twan had now passed him.

"Ain't nobody cut that li'l nigga throat, B," Twan barked in a DMX tone taking offense to Chill's accusation. "I told that ma'fucka that was one of my regulars," he continued in his defense, claiming the drug addict the dispute was over was a personal customer of his.

This was not the first time Chill and Twan had exchanged words over a drug sale. Chill was also not the only one whose workers had a problem with Twan's tactics in regards to how he hustled on the block, known as Remsen Avenue. He was just the only one who had stepped to Twan. Everyone else was either too afraid of the ending result of a confrontation with Twan or felt that his antics were not affecting their own cash flow. However, Chill did not fall into either category. For him, it was merely the principle of the matter. It was about respect. Something he'd felt had diminished a long time ago in the game, but because he was old school, he still gave it, so, in return, he demanded it.

"Come on, dawg. He told me how shit went down," Chill stated firmly, trying to hide his annoyance with Twan. He had believed all that was relayed to him by one of his workers over the phone prior to his arrival, despite the fact that he had known Twan longer. The only thing knowing Twan longer than his worker accounted for was the fact that Chill knew how Twan got down. He knew he was as guilty as sin and had done exactly what he was being accused of. Just as he had known Twan would deny it when confronted.

"Yo, he said that fiend nigga didn't even know you, my dude," Chill revealed, now getting fed up with all the word play between him and his childhood friend.

Twan's facial expression grew cold. "I don't give a fuck what that li'l bitch-ass nigga told you," he quickly snapped. "That was one of my ma'fuckin' customers, and he wanted to cop from me. *Like I said,*" he added, putting emphasizes on his last statement.

"Yeah, a'ight," Chill replied dryly.

"I know it a'ight, nigga," Twan said in attempts to chump Chill off.

Chill caught the sly remark but didn't feed into Twan's attempt; instead, he began to step off, seeing that he was actually fighting a lost cause. That is, until Twan's next words caused him to pause in his tracks.

"What you need to do is find you some real ma'fuckas who can hold their own out here to hustle for you and get rid of them three pussies you got on your team," Twan spat.

Chill caught the combination of blatant reproach and humor at his expense in Twan's tone, and it instantly caught his vein. For the life of him, he could not understand why his childhood friend was trying to provoke and force his hand. Chill had been in the game for a long time. He had been through his share of trials and tribulations in the process, and in his opinion, had made it through just fine on his own. No one had ever dictated or schooled him on how to move or conduct his business in the streets—or anywhere else, for that matter. He simply learned and taught himself, which is why Twan's words had bothered him so much. He did not take too kindly to someone trying to tell him how to run his operation or handle his business, especially someone who knew nothing about running one or being a team player.

Chill spun back around. He was now an arm's length away from Twan.

"Don't worry about who the fuck I got on my team or what I'm doin'," he said, gritting his teeth through clinched jaws.

"Well, nigga, then, don't be worrying about what the fuck I'm doin' then," Twan spit back. "And *back* the fuck up anyway unless you tryin'a see me fo'somethin'," he added in a high-pitched tone.

"It's whatever, yo," Chill replied with no intention of backing down.

"Whoa, whoa, yo, both you niggas chill the fuck out," a kid named Troy intervened. "Niggas tryin'a eat; fuck all that other shit. Twan, go 'head with that, man."

If looks could kill, Troy's family and closest friends would be dressed in black sobbing over his casket the way Twan had shot him a rock stare.

"Mind ya ma'fuckin' business. This don't have nothing to do with you," Twan ordered.

Troy started to respond but thought it best not to comment on Twan's remark. Not while he was without the nine millimeter he normally kept on him. His only intent was to defuse the rising altercation between his two street colleagues, but he knew that Chill was capable of handling himself in any situation. Troy also knew that both men were just alike and neither would back down, which is why he was not surprised when Chill began to speak.

"Yo, ever since you came home from Rahway, you think you run shit around here, dawg, but, yo, you ain't Deebo kid, and this ain't Friday. You can't keep tryin'a muscle dudes and think that shit gonna fly," Chill stated sternly. "Those days are over, baby."

Chill's words only fueled Twan's fire that had been slowly igniting inside him.

"You say that to say what? You threatening me or somethin'?" asked Twan, with a distorted expression on his face, chest swelling up as his right hand grazed the butt of his gun. He could feel his own adrenaline beginning to kick into overdrive at the thought of what could possibly happen next. Despite him being aware of how everyone viewed him around his hood, Twan knew that not everybody on his block feared him, and Chill was one of the ones among that small percentage. Like himself, Twan knew that Chill too had a reputation for being strapped at all times, not to mention a reputation for busting his gun when necessary.

As he towered over Chill's five feet seven, 165-pound frame, there was no doubt in his mind that Chill was packing heat. There was no way Chill would ever roll up on him the way he had without bringing backup, thought Twan.

Not unless he was just plain stupid, had a death wish, or both. Twan was sure of that. No matter what the case, he was growing tired of Chill's cockiness and was ready to put an end to the verbal sparing match. In the past, he had put bullet holes in dudes for less, but Chill was an exception because they had a history, a good one before the drug game, but as the situation progressed, Twan was beginning to block all of that out. He had been on a mission since being released from prison, and Chill was trying to come in between him and his business.

"Yo, kid, I don't threaten. All I'm sayin' is—"

"Fuck what you sayin'," Twan interrupted in a baritone voice, cutting Chill's words short. "I helped pioneer this ma'fuckin' block and damn near raised most of you jokers in the game out here. You niggas got drop-tops and all types of trucks and shit while I'm pushin' an old-ass Millenia. Bottom line, I'm doin' what the fuck I wanna do out here until I feel my paper right, and if a bitch wanna test me, then that's their ma'fuckin' funeral, smell me?" Twan growled adjusting his hammer in his waistband.

His words drew attention in his direction. Every hustler on the "ave" had heard what he had just said and felt some type of way about his statement, but no one dared to step up and voice their feelings on the matter. However, in their minds, each man plotted and anticipated the day they or someone else caught Twan slipping. Troy was the only one who was tempted to intervene for a second time but thought better of it once again, seeing the visual daggers between Twan and Chill being thrown at each other.

Twan's words tore into Chill like hot slugs. He knew this moment would someday come. He had tried his hardest to avoid a clash with his childhood friend. The fact that there was not a person within ear's distance that wasn't paying attention to what Chill and Twan were saying to each other only heightened the situation. Reputations were now at stake. Most of the other hustlers were glad that Chill had enough heart to say what they had felt but kept to themselves, while others feared the worst.

It was no secret that Twan had come home from East Jersey State Prison, which was one of the roughest prisons in New Jersey, six months prior after serving six years. He had been on a paper chase since his first day of being home. Originally, he was only supposed to have served four years for the shooting case he went to prison for, but while doing his bid, he stabbed a kid from Camden in the neck in the mess hall over a verbal dispute about a basketball game. Luckily for him, the kid survived, but the incident landed him in solitary confinement for two years and a loss of two years' good time, causing him to serve an additional two. The word had spread throughout the entire New Brunswick how Twan from "Remsen" put "work in" in the joint, and those from his hood knew that when he came home, he would be the same, if not worse, than before, and they were right. Coming home six inches taller and nearly a hundred pounds heavier, at six foot, 240 lbs, Twan tried to flex his muscles, literally, in attempts to intimidate other hustlers who he felt stood in the way of fattening his pockets. He even toted a snub-nosed .44-bulldog revolver in his waistband in plain view to let everyone know that he stayed strapped. That is why everyone knew he would not allow Chill's words to ride. His rep and status on the block depended on it.

Judging by the situation at hand, Chill felt there was no way of getting around what he had foreseen today. Feeling the tension and knowing the caliber between both men, everyone began to fade into the background in attempts to stand clear of the potential harm and imminent danger that existed. What started out as a minor confrontation was steadily erupting into something major. All eyes were locked on

Twan and Chill—from a safe distance, of course. Everyone was, in fact, so focused on the two that no one ever noticed the unidentified SUV parked a short distance up the street.

Chapter Two

The stolen navy-blue 2008 Cherokee pulled alongside the curb on Remsen Avenue and parked.

"That's him right there," the backseat passenger of the Cherokee pointed out.

"Which one?" the driver asked.

"The big, tall, dark-skinned one with the velour sweat suit on."

"It don't even matter which one he is," the front-seat passenger interjected.

"It ain't like these niggas just gonna let us walk up on their man and do something to him, then walk up outta here."

"I was thinking the same thing," said the driver.

"So what are we gonna do?" asked the backseat passenger.

"You ain't gonna do shit. You gonna stay ya ass in the truck while we handle this shit. If he see ya ass, he gonna remember you."

"Look," the driver said to the front-seat passenger, "something's about to go down over there."

The front-seat passenger immediately drew their attention to the commotion.

"Not without us, it ain't," the front-seat passenger said, snatching open the door, just before pulling down the black mask.

"Get behind the wheel and be on point," the driver instructed the backseat passenger as that individual did the same with a mask just before exiting the SUV to back up his partner.

Chapter Three

"Yo, T, you must think shit sweet, dawg," said Chill, standing his ground. "Ain't nothing pussy about me, kid, so all that shit you poppin' is extra. Ain't nobody tryin'a test you, big homie. Dudes know how you get down, but just like I know you not gonna let nobody carry you like a sucka, you gots to know that neither am I. So, what are we gonna do? Huh?" Chill attempted to reason with his friend. "We gonna shoot each other over a punk-ass hundred-dollar sale, 'cause I got my strap on me too, daddy," Chill informed Twan, lifting the Black Label hoodie up enough to reveal his .45 automatic. "And if you reach for ya joint, that's exactly what's gonna happen, my nig," Chill added, giving fair warning. He had hoped that Twan used what little sense he had, the benefit of the doubt for having and seen the bigger picture, causing him to make the right decision. The last thing Chill wanted was to catch a murder charge or be killed over a petty drug dispute, but he knew that in the streets, people had killed and died for less, so he was prepared for whatever.

Twan grilled Chill intensively while pondering over his words. He was already contemplating on drawing his weapon, and there was no doubt in his mind that when he pulled it, he wouldn't hesitate to use it. But there were two things that caused him to second-guess himself. One, was he ready to go back to the one place he despised the most? The second, would he actually be able to beat Chill to the draw? It was those two reasons, and them alone, that caused Twan to make a rational decision to let sleeping dogs lie. For the moment, anyway, but he made a mental note and a promise to himself that he would finish what Chill had started some other time.

"Fuck that hundred dollars," Twan spit, reaching into his pocket.

A small load had been lifted off Chill's shoulders. At first, he thought Twan was going for his gun and was about to reach for his own until he saw that was not the case. Instead, Twan pulled out a knot of cash.

"Here, take this shit," he then said, tossing a hundred-dollar bill in Chill's direction.

Insulted by the gesture, Chill instantly replied, "Man, I don't want ya money, kid."

In all honesty, it wasn't about the money at all with Chill, but Twan did not get it. He now also felt insulted by Chill's decline and his demeanor changed.

"Oh, my paper ain't good e—"

"*Boc! Boc! Boc! Boc!*"

"*Brrrgah! Brrrgah! Brrrgah!*"

"What the—*Boom! Boom! Boom!*"

"Aagh!"

"*Brrrgah! Brrrgah!*"

"Oh shit!"

"*Boc! Boc! Boc! Boc!*"

"Get in!"

"*Boom! Boom! Boom! Click! Click!*"

"Somebody call a ma'fuckin' ambulance!" shouted Troy.

The sound of Troy's voice caused Chill to end his pursuit.

"Yo, who the fuck was that?" an out-of-breath Chill asked, making his way back to where shots had moments ago erupted, with his .45 still in hand. He had just chased and unloaded his weapon into the navy-blue Cherokee as the two masked gunmen jumped in and sped away. He watched as the Cherokee's taillights vanished up the street.

"I don't know, but Twan's hit," a bewildered Troy yelled out.

By now, everyone had come out of their hiding places and gathered around Twan. His body lay helplessly on the ground as blood spilled out the side of his mouth and oozed out of his bullet-riddled body. Numerous shots ripped into his flesh before he even had the chance to pull his own weapon. He could hear the voices surrounding him asking the questions among each other of "who" and "why," with no avail. The only one that was able to provide them with answers was Twan himself, but the blood that began to clog his throat passage prevented him from speaking out as he lay there fighting for his life. He made an attempt to speak but had only managed to grunt inaudibly. He could not believe—or rather, didn't *want* to believe—that this was his final fate. During his time in prison, he had heard many stories about so many others being released after serving years and years on lockdown, going home in search of their ghetto forty acres and a government mule, only to have their lives cut short from making the mistake of underestimating a person's capabilities. Now, here it was, he was faced with the same type of statistical situation from making that same fatal error.

As his life began to flash before his very eyes, the only thing Twan could think of that would have been the cause of him lying on the cold concrete fighting death was what had taken place the other day. And now, it was because of his egotistical way of thinking that he had gotten more than what he'd bargained for. Twan was almost certain that because he had reacted first without thinking, all over a bruised ego, he was now being met with an untimely demise.

That being his last thought, Twan's eyes began to dilate in the back of his head as his body began to convulse. Death had opened its door and embraced him before the ambulance arrived.

Chapter Four

"Le Le, slow the fuck down," Earth commanded from the backseat of the Cherokee, pulling off her mask. "You gonna get us knocked the fuck off."

Glancing at the speedometer, Le Le did as she was told. She hadn't realized she was doing 80 mph down Remsen Avenue. Her only concern at that time was getting her two girlfriends out of harm's way after the gun battle erupted on the notorious block. There was no way she would have been able to live with herself if something was to have happened to either of them. After all, it was because of her they had gone around there in the first place.

"Are y'all all right?" Le Le asked, looking back at them through the rearview mirror.

"Yeah, we good," Heaven assured her. "But I can't say the same for that nigga," she added.

"So y'all get 'em, then?"

"What the fuck you mean did we get 'em? Of course, we did," Earth stated irritably.

"Cool out," Heaven said. She knew where her friend's hostility was coming from and didn't blame her, but now was not the time for either of them to lose a level head. Still, Earth would not let it go.

"Nah, fuck that," Earth retorted. "We wouldn't even be in this predicament if it weren't for this bitch. I told ya dumb ass before about showing off for mu'fuckas," she spat, directing her words at Le Le.

"I wasn't tryin'a—"

"Just shut the fuck up and drive," Earth said, cutting her short.

Heaven knew better than to intervene when Earth was reprimanding one of their workers. Not only were she and Earth partners in crime, but more so, they had been friends even longer, so Heaven knew her girl all too well. There was no doubt in her mind that if she attempted to pacify the situation or aid Le Le in any type of way, specifically trying to calm her road dawg, it would only add fuel to the fire. Earth had been that way for as long as Heaven could remember, extending back to their days when the two had first met at Edna Mahan Correctional Facility for

Women in Clinton, New Jersey. As Earth continued to verbally scold and chastise Le Le, Heaven
could not help but to reflect on her partner's and
her first encounter.

*"Listen up for your name. State your number
when your name is called."*

*It had been six long and stressful months
in Middlesex County Adult Corrections Center
and Heavenly Devine Jacobs was finally being
shipped out to prison. As crazy as it sounded,
she was more than ecstatic to be leaving the
county jail transferring to prison. Her first time
ever being locked up, Heavenly had copped
out to a plea agreement of seven years with a
three and a half year stipulation, meaning she
would have to serve at least that before she was
eligible for parole—all for the sake of love. At
least, that's what she had thought at the time.*

Growing up in New Brunswick, New Jersey,
raised by her father, who was known to be one of
the biggest heroin dealers in town, and a mother
who was deemed one of the finest females in all
of Franklin, Heavenly's childhood was that of
a ghetto fairy tale. At birth, she had inherited
her mother's God-given beauty, but as she grew
older, she gravitated and inherited her father's
taste for the streets and money. By the time she

was fifteen, Heavenly, who had shortened her name to Heaven, had every baller, young and old alike, that laid eyes on her, wanting her, but only those who had paper, and plenty of it, could afford the luxury. Even then, Heaven made it hard for them because her father saw to it that she didn't want for anything. That is, until a fateful day occurred, changing Heaven's life forever. When she was eighteen, Heaven's parents were murdered during a home invasion over money and drugs, while Heaven was away in Cancun for Spring Break.

Having practically been left with nothing, Heaven instantly switched into survival mode, using her knowledge of the game and her most valuable assets to get ahead in life. In no time, she had secured the position of wifey with a known money getter from the uptown area of her town. Initially, Heaven's intent was to do what she had to do in order to survive, but as time progressed, she found herself falling in love with the hustler. It was that same love that caused her to take the weight for a quarter of a kilo of cocaine and an eighth of a kilo of heroin that was found during a raid in an apartment in her name. Heaven was convinced that he had loved her just the same, if not more, which is why she didn't hesitate to step up to the plate and wear the drugs when he had asked her to. Her boyfriend had constantly showed his love and support while she awaited sentencing. During that time, he made sure her commissary was strapped, collect calls were accepted, visits were never missed, and letters and cards were sent daily. He had done everything any woman in Heaven's position would want a man to do for them—all the way up to the time Heaven had signed and was sentenced on her plea. The entire time Heaven assumed that her man was keeping it real with her like she was with him, but that whole time he was actually keeping it real fake. Before the ink had dried on the papers she had signed, like a thief in the night, he had vanished, never to be seen or heard from again, leaving Heaven with a lengthy prison sentence and a hardened heart.

"Heavenly Jacobs."

"400441," Heavenly replied.

This was the number given to her after sentencing, a number that she had memorized and would remember for the rest of her life. In the six-month period she had been confined, incarceration had already begun to impact her life. It was her every intent to leave out better and

smarter than when she had come in. Only in
Heaven's case, she was set on becoming a better
and smarter criminal. She peered out of the
gated window of the New Jersey Department
of Corrections bus as it arrived and came to a
halt at the state correctional facility for women.
When it was her turn to exit what was called the
"Blue Bird," an eerie feeling swept through her.

No more than five minutes inside the female
prison, women of all shades of color, weight,
and heights, filled the dayroom area. When
she and others entered the housing unit that
would be her place of residency for the next
three years or so, she knew she was going
to have problems. She heard someone cat-
call "Fresh meat," as she and five other women
carefully walked down the tier in search of
their assigned cells. Other women began to
pour out into the dayroom from their living
quarters hearing the "fresh meat" call.

It was apparent that two of the females that
had been shipped with Heaven had been to the
facility before. Heaven noticed that they were
giving handshakes and hugs to a few of the
women and overheard one of them ask what
they had done this time to return. While she
continued down the tier in search of her cell,

Heaven noticed three manly looking females eyeing her from afar, but did her best to maintain her poker face and pretend as if she hadn't.

After only a week at the facility, the same trio, who Heaven now realized were female studs, tried to run up in her cell with the intention of conducting a gang rape. Heaven was no slouch when it came to throwing her hands. Her father had taught her how to defend herself at a young age, but based on their sizes, she was not sure if she could fight off all three butch chicks at once. Ready to protect her womanhood or die trying, Heaven positioned her back against the cell wall, threw her hands up, and got in a fighting stance. The three would-be attackers all smiled.

"Bitch, we can do this the easy way or the hard way," the biggest of the three said in a deep tone, unfazed by Heaven's attempt to fend for herself. The other two manly looking females barricaded the entrance of the cell with their huge and grotesque bodies, while their partner prepared to make her move. Just as the gorilla of a woman was about to launch her attack on Heaven, a shadow entered the six-by-nine cell from behind.

Heaven had also noticed the sudden dimness but couldn't see the cause through the women.

When the three women all turned and directed their attention toward the cell entrance, their eyes widened at the sight. Earth stood just outside of the doorway in her white wife beater, gray sweatpants, and beige state boots tightly tied, twirling two razor blades around in her mouth with her tongue. She had watched from day one when the long-haired voluptuously shaped redbone had come into the institution, and Teresa and her clique immediately began scoping her out. Normally, Earth didn't get involved in other people's affairs, but there was something about the new girl that drew her in, besides the fact that she had a weakness for light-skinned women.

Well aware of Earth's reputation with the two infamous blades she always kept in her mouth, the two girls who posed as blockers for the intended rape stood down. Neither of the two wanted any problems with Earth, but Teresa's ego and pride took control over her intellect. She could not let Earth punk her, especially not in front of her two lovers.

"Yo, this don't have nuthin' to do with you, E; you don't know nuthin', you don't see nuthin', won't be nuthin', ya dig?" Teresa spat boldly.

Earth snickered to herself. Teresa's words held no weight. She had known her for years, even outside the prison walls. They were both from Plainfield; Earth from the projects, Teresa from Third Street. Earth believed Teresa to be a coward, who preyed on who she felt to be weak on the streets and had been displaying the same behavior at the facility since Earth had arrived some years earlier. The two didn't get along on the outside, and the same applied on the inside. Up until now, Teresa had stayed out of Earth's way and never gave her a reason to pull her card or go up against her. Today, Earth welcomed the challenge.

The last female who had made the mistake of going up against her had received more zippers on her face than Edward Scissorhands, resulting in Earth serving nine months in solitary confinement. Without uttering so much as one word, the two other females cautiously began to bail out of the cell like a row of ducks, not even attempting to glance over at Earth out of fear of triggering her off. They saw what was evolving between Earth and Teresa. Though they were lovers of Teresa, they knew the three of them, combined, were no match for Earth. On several occasions, they were all too familiar with her work with both her hands and the razors she was legendary in the facility for.

Neither woman wanted to risk leaving prison with any additional marks or scars, and they knew the possibility was great if they sided with Teresa against Earth.

Noticing that Teresa's two flunkies had no intentions on intervening in what was about to transpire, Earth had already envisioned the cut she intended to carve into Teresa's face. She could see in her eyes that Teresa was ready to make her move, so, she too intended to make hers. Just as Earth was about to spit out her blades and commence to dicing, Heaven landed a right hook that connected with Teresa's jaw. Though the punch didn't send her to the canvas, it was effective enough to give Heaven the upper hand. Seeing that Teresa was dazed, Heaven grabbed a fistful of her cornrows and threw what seemed like a hundred punches in succession into her face.

"New Boot, chill," Earth repeated for the umpteenth time, but her words fell on deaf ears. It took four officers and a direct hit of pepper spray to the face for Heaven to discontinue the beat down she had been giving Teresa. Heaven received ninety days in lockup and returned to her initial unit while Teresa was transferred to another.

Not knowing her motives at the time, as soon as Heaven spotted Earth, she approached her.

"Thanks, but I could've handled that."

"I'm sure you could've, and you did," was all Earth replied before walking off.

Two days had gone by before either of the two said anything else to the other. It was actually Heaven who broke the ice by thanking Earth again, this time introducing herself. Within a few months, Heaven and Earth had become comrades and formed a bond as thick as thieves. No one could utter a word, look at, or even breathe funny around Heaven without facing consequences at the hands of Earth. She had beat a female from Elizabeth unconscious just for commenting to someone that she felt Heaven thought she was better than everybody else. Earth ended up serving another six months in lockup for that. The incident caused everyone, including the officers, to believe that Heaven and Earth were lovers, since Earth was a lesbian and so overprotective of Heaven. But that was far from being the case. They were more like sisters than anything else, and whenever Earth was not on lock, their discussions and plans extended far beyond sexuality, and even then, they managed to stay in touch, plotting and planning through letters and messages passed on by cool officers and trustees who frequented and worked the administrative-segregation unit. As beautiful as Heaven was, and despite the fact that Earth had a thing for thick redbones, she had the utmost respect for her new friend and never came at her on that order. It was that same respect that had spilled over into the street.

Earth was still launching her verbal attack on Le Le when Heaven snapped out of her daze.

"You understand what the fuck I'm saying?" was all Heaven had caught of the conversation as she returned to the present.

"Yeah," Le Le answered childlike.

Heaven was glad that whatever lecture Earth had given Le Le while she reminisced was slowly defusing itself. All she wanted to do now was get home, take a long, hot bath, and blow an "L" before climbing into her queen-sized bed. Heaven saw Earth massaging her temples and became concerned. "E, what's wrong?" she asked.

"Nothing. This bitch gave me a headache, that's all."

Heaven couldn't help but smile. Earth was always accusing someone of giving her a headache or blowing her high when she smoked weed. Some of the things Earth did and said had

Heaven believing that Earth was intended to be born a boy. She was just as much, if not more, of a dude than any man Heaven knew in her book.

"I know what you thinking too, bitch," Earth directed her words to Heaven.

"What?" Heaven replied knowingly with a slight grin on her face.

"Yeah, a'ight," Earth shot back stone-faced, but on the inside, she concealed her smile, not wanting Le Le to feel any comfort or relief in the matter. She felt no remorse for the way she had come down so hard on her worker. She simply didn't tolerate or accept nonsense. As of lately, Le Le had been creating lots of it and had to be checked, as far as she was concerned. That's just the way she was.

Eartha Monae Davis was from Plainfield. She grew up on the west end of the city in the Second Street, three-story housing projects. She had never known her father, nor did she care to. In her eyes, her mother, who was a full-blooded lesbian, had compensated for his absence. Her mother never offered any information on who he was or his whereabouts, and Earth had never bothered to ask. Because of her mother's sexual preference, Earth was exposed to, and introduced to, a different type of lifestyle than most young girls. For as long as she could remember,

Earth could not recall a male figure entering the household of her and her mother's. Not even when her mother conducted her weed transactions or entertained company in their apartment. The only faces she ever saw were those of pretty, light-skinned, tender-looking females who always appeared to be younger than her mother was. She would often wake in the middle of the night and run into women in the nude while on her way to the bathroom. Those were the only type her mother allowed to stay the night. Earth became both immune and accustomed to seeing this type of behavior in her home.

Like her mother, Earth was tall and panther black, though her body had yet to develop. Earth was considered around her projects to be one of the fellas, due to her tomboyish ways, indulging in sports and even fights with not only girls but also boys when the occasion arose, but at age fourteen, Earth's body made a drastic transformation, developing in places little boys and even older ones began to notice. But not only had the boys started to notice, the girls had also; one in particular. A young, attractive, nineteen-year-old girl Earth's mother let move in with them. She had been Earth's mother's latest lover.

On a few occasions, Earth had noticed the girl everyone referred to as Honey, looking at her strangely, but never paid the stares any mind. Instead, she brushed them off as meaningless, in spite of the fact that she was aware of Honey's sexual preference. That is, until one day while she was taking a shower. Honey had climbed in with her. Growing up with the type of mother she had, Earth was not afraid of the sudden intrusion but was somewhat surprised—not behind Honey's actions, but her boldness. Everyone in the projects and almost the whole Plainfield knew the reputation of Earth's mother. She was known for being violent, with a bad temper to match. Earth knew that if her mother had caught Honey in the shower with her daughter that day, Honey would have died where she stood, but Earth did not intend to tell her mother, or anyone else, for that matter. She herself had become bicurious, struggling with her own sexual identity, and Honey had sparked something inside of her that day. She was actually mesmerized by the beauty of Honey's nakedness. It was the first time she had paid close attention to a naked woman's body.

While Earth stood there motionless admiring Honey's curvaceous physique, with washcloth still in hand, Honey approached her. As their eyes connected, Honey moved in and pressed her lips up against Earth's. The combination of the softness and wetness of her lips sent chills through Earth's entire young body, and the electricity of Honey's erect nipples pressed up against her own breasts, causing her inner thighs to moisten. Although the feeling was foreign to Earth, it also felt nice. Earth had kissed boys on occasions and let them touch her in sacred places, but none of it had ever felt like what she was feeling at that particular moment. While their kisses and touches were rough, Honey's lips and touch were soft and smooth. Honey continued to kiss Earth gently, parting her mouth open with her tongue while she fondled and caressed her virgin clit. She knew just where and how to touch her in order to send her young and tender flesh to a place it had never been before. After bringing Earth to what became her first real orgasm, Honey took the washcloth out of her hands and bathed her while licking every inch of her that the cloth came in contact with. It was from that day forward that Earth discovered that she preferred the touch of a woman to a man's.

Later, when Earth was twenty-one, she caught an attempted murder charge for shooting her boyfriend in the chest with his own gun after he had caught her in bed with another woman and tried to kill them both. She received seven years for that.

Earth already had four years in the system when she and Heaven met. Their friendship had been a blessing in disguise for Earth, being as though she did not want to reside in Plainfield once she was released. Five months out of prison and before Heaven's release, with the money she had saved, Earth was able to purchase an apartment in the Ville section of New Brunswick and waited for her road dawg to come home. The moment Heaven's feet touched free soil, they began to take steps to execute the plans they had discussed back at Edna Mahan. That was seven and a half years ago, and since then, the two had been rolling together like the black Thelma and Louise.

"Le Le, turn down Townsend," Heaven instructed once Earth had finished giving their worker the third degree. "Then hook a right on Commercial. We gotta get the hell outta this Jeep."

"Yeah, no doubt. I know this shit full of bullet holes," Earth added. "That bitch-ass nigga who was in the middle of the street was shootin' a fuckin' cannon."

"I know, right?" Le Le joined. "That shit scared the fuck outta me."

"Anything scare ya ass," Earth retorted dryly. She still refused to let up off of Le Le.

"Just do like Heaven said."

Le Le didn't say another word. Instead, she did as she was told. Once she came up on the intended street, she turned onto Commercial Avenue until she reached George's Road, and then veered to the right.

"Pull over," Earth commanded just as they came up on a silver Cadillac CTS.

Earth jumped out with the jimmy to her side and made her way over to the parked luxury car.

"Le Le, wipe down the front," Heaven said as she began wiping down the backseat area of the stolen Cherokee.

The sound of the CTS's engine caught both Heaven and Le Le's attention. Earth started the new getaway car in record-breaking time. They both exited the Cherokee and hopped into the Caddy.

"Take the bridge and jump on Route 1," Heaven told Earth. Instantly, Earth knew the intended destination. On many occasions, they had taken Route 1 after an altercation or caper that required their burners. They normally disposed of their weapons before heading to Heaven's place. Despite Heaven and her both having cribs in the heart of New Brunswick, they both had main houses out of town as well. Earth's was in Piscataway Heights, while Heaven's was in a suburban area in Franklin Township.

Earth turned on the car radio and found her favorite station, Power 105.1.

"I'll bust ya head, boy," were the lyrics from 50 Cent that came blaring out of the speakers as Earth navigated the Cadillac out of the parking space.

Chapter Five

Chill drove around town aimlessly in search of the Cherokee that had just lit his block up like the New Year's ball in Times Square. He was still heated behind the fact that someone had come into his hood and violated. Not only by shooting up the strip but also slaying one of his comrades in the process. Though he and Twan were feuding moments prior to his demise, Chill still had love for his childhood friend and fellow hustler and would ride with him against all others outside of their hood, which was exactly the reason why he was on the hunt for the shooters.

After the shooting and realizing that Twan was dead, the majority of the crowd quickly began to thin out, leaving Twan where he lay. No one wanted to be around when the police arrived on the scene out of fear of being labeled a snitch or implicated in the incident. As the crowd of hustlers, friends, and innocent bystanders began to disperse, Chill hopped in his silver BMW and peeled off.

Five minutes later, Chill noticed what appeared to be a navy-blue SUV resembling the
one he was looking for parked on George's
Road as he turned onto the street. As he slowly
rode past the SUV, the .45 caliber bullet holes
on the side of the truck confirmed that it was, in
fact, the navy-blue Cherokee he had been looking for, causing him to reach under his seat
and retrieve his fully loaded Glock 9. Chill then
pulled past the Cherokee and made a U-turn
in order to park four car lengths ahead of the
Cherokee on the opposite side of the street.
Exiting his BMW, he tucked his Glock in his
waistband and concealed it under his butter
soft leather. Looking around for any indica-
tions that there was danger near or any sight of
the occupants of the Cherokee, Chill cautiously
approached the Jeep. Once he came close
enough to the SUV, it was obvious to him that
the Cherokee had been abandoned.

Chill moved in for a closer look inside the
vehicle. He put his hands up to the front passenger's window and peered in. The first thing
he noticed was the altered steering column and
instantly drew the conclusion that the Cherokee
had been stolen, and most likely, the assailants
were long gone by now, but there was no doubt
in Chill's mind that whoever had committed the

shooting was from New Brunswick and couldn't have gone but so far.

Since New Brunswick was small, Chill had either hustled or had people all throughout the city and had ways of finding out things. So, it was just a matter of time before he got the scoop on the violators, and when he did, Chill promised himself that he'd see to it that someone stood accountable for both the murder of his man Twan and the violation of his hood.

Chapter Six

"I'm a movement by myself/but I'm a force when we're together/Mami, I'm good all by myself/but, baby, you make me better/you make me better . . ."

Keya slithered down, and then off, the pole in the middle of Earth's bedroom and made her way onto the king-size bed after displaying a sexual acrobatic performance. She began to dance provocatively over the top of Earth while staring into her eyes as the fabulous track featuring Ne-Yo filled the dimly lit, surround sound bedroom. Earth used the stereo's remote to increase the volume of her Panasonic 51 disc CD changer while she puffed on a stick of Sour Diesel as she lay back enjoying the performance. She stuffed some of the remaining $200 in singles into the front part of her lover's thong that she hadn't used to make it rain while Keya was performing her pole dance. Keya stuck her middle finger in her mouth, then slid it into her thong and began playing with herself. Earth could see her knuckle prints protruding through the thong's fabric as Keya fondled her sex as she continued her dance. The way she was gyrating her entire body to the lyrics and beat of the song was making Earth horny. Each time Keya dropped down over her in a straddling position caused Earth to become more and more aroused.

Keya was a hell of a dancer and knew how to shake her moneymaker. Her specialty was making both of her ass cheeks clap, and then pop them individually. It was a sight to see and the same moves that had caught Earth's attention six months ago at a local establishment not too far from her hometown called Liquid Assets in South Plainfield. As Earth continued to blow on the high-powered weed watching Keya in a lust-filled and intoxicated daze, she reflected back on the night she and Keya had made each other's acquaintance.

Liquid Assets strip club always had something going on, but Lollipop Thursdays with DJ Rit Rat and Melle Mel was a definite night to be in the building. It was the closest Earth had come to visiting where she was from in many years. She was attracted to women with voluptuous bodies and believed this to be one of the best places to find them. Some of the hottest chicks in the tristate area and beyond came out either to perform on stage or to watch the show, while hustlers popped bottles, sipped Hennessey, Rémy Martin, and tipped big.

That particular night, Earth had stumbled across a locked doors party full of money shakers, sponsored by a known adult magazine. It was apparent to Earth when she pulled up to the hot spot that the place was flooded with local ballers judging by the rides parked outside. She recognized a few cars from New Brunswick and couldn't help but smirk seeing how they got around. One of the whips she spotted was a drop-top 6 series BMW that belonged to an acquaintance of hers by the name of Sup from the projects, and she knew the owners of the black 500 SL and the pearl-black Dodge Magnum from uptown. As she continued her scan of the small parking lot, she also recognized a few whips that belonged to some Bloods from the town she was from. Although trouble usually followed them wherever they dwelled, resulting in them getting into altercations, Earth was not in the least bit worried. Most of the gang members were either her family or close associates and had her back.

Earth parked, then hopped out of her G-5 Benz truck and headed for the entrance of the club. She noticed her boy Chubb's pearl Cadillac Escalade XL also parked up in the parking lot and knew that it was going to be a peaceful evening for her because Chubb's reputation in her town for being an official heat holder was legendary. Not that Earth wasn't a part of the "Gun Clappers Club," but tonight, she just wanted to chill, minus the drama.

Earlier, she had tried to get Heaven to come out with her, but she had refused, claiming to be drained from the streets that day. Although she was not bisexual or lesbian, Earth knew that Heaven enjoyed going to and watching some of the girls dance but not on a regular basis like her.

As she entered the spot, if one hadn't known, you would have sworn Earth was just another dude coming to get his freak on, especially when she was dressed the way she was that evening. Earth sported a North Face with a pair of Antik Denim jeans and shirt to match, and a pair of construction Tims boots and a Yankee fitted. They were charging twenty dollars at the door due to the erotic magazine presence, but Earth was friends with the owner John, so she never paid to get in.

Once inside, she was not at all surprised at the capacity of the bar. It never failed. Thursdays you could guarantee L A's, as it was referred to, being wall-to-wall packed. As soon as she entered the building, Earth gave her homegirl Tiaa who worked the door a hug, then made her way through the crowded bar, giving head nods to the congratulators and shooting ice grills at the haters. She was eager to get her drink on as she smoothly diddy bopped off of Lil Wayne's "A Milli" track through the body-infested club.

After finally reaching the bar, four shots of Rémy and two Coronas later, Earth was ready to direct her undivided attention toward the dancers as she nursed on the bottle of Rosé she'd ordered. Scanning the stage of half-naked women, in all shapes, sizes, and colors, Earth immediately zeroed in on one of the dancers in particular who had caught her eye.

She had known most of the others up in there that night from frequenting the surrounding strip clubs in Jersey, Philly, and the New York area, but had never seen this one before. She wondered if the fresh face was a part of the infamous Knock Out Queens who burned the stages up in some of the hottest exotic clubs. Earth ordered another bottle of Rosé just to stunt and sipped lightly on it, feeling the alcohol starting to take effect as she studied the new girl who was now showing off her flexibility and acrobatic skills on the stage pole. Earth couldn't help but to take in every inch of the stripper. She was a sundae mixture of ice cream and caramel, but the perspiration, which glistened over her entire body, made her appear to be more golden than she really was. She stood at a medium height of five foot nine, and her breasts were shapely built, slightly exposed on the outer and inner parts of the gold bikini top she wore, while her nipples protruded through the material. Her waist was petite, but her hips and thighs were muscular and thick like a track runner, and her bottom was firmly shaped. In the face, she resembled Kimora Lee Simmons, only darker, with cotton-candy lips, high mountain cheekbones, and deep, slanted, dark eyes as if she were of Asian descent.

Earth continued to watch the honey-toned dancer for the next twenty-five minutes until she exited the stage. Occasionally, the two of them made direct eye contact. They stared at each other for five minutes straight as Earth continued to nurse the champagne and watch the dancer prop her leg up on the bar and make her glutes do a routine dance of their own for a paying customer. As if he'd read her mind,

Earth learned from DJ Rit Rat that the girl's stage name was Lite. As he announced her exit, she and the DJ exchanged acknowledging head nods. Earth was contemplating on seeking out the sexy stripper after losing sight of her in the midst of the crowded club, but before she had the chance to make her decision, she saw the girl slither through the crowd, heading in her direction.

"You wanna lap dance?" Lite asked seductively walking up on Earth.

"Nah," Earth replied.

Disappointed, Lite flashed a fake smile and attempted to walk away, only to be stopped in her tracks by a hand. She turned back in the direction where Earth sat, and again, the two made eye contact. Earth, smiling, leaned in closer. "I didn't say I wasn't gonna tip you, though."

Earlier, she wondered whether Lite had thought she was a dude from afar when they acknowledged each other, but close up, there was no mistaking her gender regardless of how much her attire made her appear masculine, so Earth was positive that Lite was into females. Lite's next words only confirmed it. "You's a fly bitch," she said pressing her body up against Earth. Earth just smiled and sucked her teeth as if something was caught in them. Lite began to slow grind her inner thighs into Earth's pelvis as Lil Wayne's track "Lollipop" played in the background. Earth grabbed her by the waist and matched her rhythm.

"Do you like this?" Lite leaned in and whispered in Earth's ear.

"Do you?" Earth shot back in the same whisper tone, sliding her hands down to Lite's ass cheeks, palming them.

"Uh-huh," Lite replied licking her lips.

Earth then reached into her front right pocket and pulled out a stack of bills. Lite pretended not to notice, but Earth had already peeped the way her eyes had lit up. She could practically see the dollar signs in Lite's pupils, not to mention the fact that her grinding became extra hard. She knew that Lite was already thinking and plotting on ways to get as much as she could of the money Earth possessed in her hand, especially after seeing the big faces that dominated the bankroll. Earth decided to make it easier for her.

"What's ya name?"

"Lite."

"Nah, what's ya name?"

Lite looked at her with attitude. Earth remained stone-faced.

"Keya, why?" she decided to answer with hands on her hips. Earth disregarded her question.

"How much you think you gonna make before the night out?" Earth asked aloud.

"Huh?" Lite answered dumbfounded while continuing the dance.

"You heard me."

"Tsk. Why?" she asked with even more attitude, trying to sound feisty and offended, but Earth brushed her tone off and maintained her coolness. "Just answer the question and you'll find out."

"Tsk!"

At the sound of Lite sucking her teeth for a second time, Earth was instantly turned off. She grabbed Lite's arms in an attempt to release her hold from around her neck, but before she could, Lite clinched her grip tighter. "I don't know, about another $300 to $400," she blurted out, curious to find out Earth's reasons for inquiring.

"Okay, let me go ahead and give you that so we can get up outta here then," Earth said calmly.

"What?" Lite asked. "What makes you think I roll like that?"

"I don't; I just asked."

Her words caused a huge Kool-Aid smile to appear on Lite's face. In all honesty, at one point or another, against her better judgment, Lite had rolled like that to make ends meet. She did not believe that she would make any more than another $100 or $200 in addition to the $600 she had made already. Here it was, she was being offered nearly twice that. She had left with men for less, so she had no problem with leaving with a woman, especially since she was bisexual. Without hesitation, she said, "All right, let me go get my things."

"Don't keep me waiting long. I'll be parked out front in a green Benz truck."

Earth gave a few daps and head nods to those worth acknowledging, threw her hand up in the air in the DJ's direction as her name was announced by her hometown friend DJ Rit Rat, and made her exit out of the club. Since that evening, Keya and Earth had spent many nights together enjoying each other's company the way they were doing now.

"You know I love you, right?" Keya purred, laying her head on Earth's chest after they had just finished making passionate love.

"Yeah, you love me, all right. You love my paper," Earth slyly remarked.

Keya's head instantly shot up. "See? Why you gotta say some fucked-up shit like that?" Keya spit, now pushing off Earth's chest.

"'Cause it's true," Earth replied nonchalantly.

"You know what, E? Fuck you!" Keya screamed, hopping out of bed.

"I already did," Earth retorted.

Keya gave Earth the middle finger as she heatedly gathered up her clothing. "I already did that too," Earth sarcastically stated, rolling over to retrieve the half blunt and lighter she had on the nightstand.

"I hate ya punk ass," snapped Keya, hurrying into her powder-blue laced thong.

"One minute you love me, the next minute you hate me. Make up ya mind," Earth replied.

"E, why are you actin' all shitty to me all of a sudden?" Keya questioned in a whining manner.

For a minute, there was a brief pause. Earth lit the blunt, inhaled a mouthful of smoke, and then clouded the air with its residue.

"You really wanna know why, Lite?" Earth asked dryly, addressing Keya by her stage name, knowing that would irritate her.

"Oh, it's Lite now, huh? Tsk! Ma'fucka, it ain't been Lite in six months, so what's changed?" she spit with venom.

"Nothin', that's the fuckin' problem," Earth shot back. "You still doin' the same bullshit you been doin' from six months ago."

"Oh, I get it now," Keya said, understanding. "Here we go with the bullshit again."

"Whatever," Earth stated in an uncaring manner.

"No, it's not whatever. I told ya ass before that if you wanted me to stop dancing, then make me wifey and not ya bitch, but you the one that wanna be this muthafuckin' gangsta and act like you don't know how to love and shit," Keya lased out, her New York accent now coming out. "Soooo, I'ma keep doin' me until you start actin' right. If you not gonna take care of me exclusively, then I'm gonna keep suckin' and fuckin' ma'fuckas until—"

"*Bam!*"

"Ma'fucka, no, you—"

"*Umph!*"

Keya never saw Earth fly off the bed, let alone throw the right hook that connected on her jaw while in midsentence, sending her straight to the floor. Semi-dazed, Keya attempted to lash out verbally, only to have her words cut short again with a kick in the midsection by Earth, causing her to instantly curl into a fetal position.

"Bitch, don't you ever disrespect me in my own ma'fuckin' house again like that," Earth roared. "I don't give a fuck who or what you do, but don't try to throw that shit up in my face like I'm some ma'fuckin' lame or something. I'll kill ya dumb ass up in here, you hear me?"

Earth could see the fear in Keya's eyes as she launched her assault and was unmoved. She also saw the blood that was beginning to trickle out of Keya's mouth from one of the blows she had just delivered. "Bitch, get the fuck up off of my floor 'fore you fuck up my carpet, and I really have to hurt ya silly ass," Earth ordered.

"Matter of fact, get your ass outta my fuckin' house before you make me break your ma'fuckin' neck."

Keya could not believe what had just happened. She was stricken with both fear and hatred toward the woman she had professed her love to and wanted nothing more than to get as far away as she possibly could from her. After the first time the two of them left the club together, Keya had done her homework on Earth and found out more than she would have ever imagined, but the news of Earth being both a baller and a gangster did not deter her but rather intrigued her. Initially, she had set out to get as much money as she could out of Earth, but in the process of trying to do so, she fell in love with the female hustler. Now, here it was, all the love she thought she'd felt for Earth had quickly been replaced with hate. Slowly, Keya rose, never taking her eyes off Earth who stood in front of her motionless. Neither of the two uttered a word, but their eyes spoke volumes. Earth's telling Keya it was officially over, while Keya's said it was far from it. Keya snatched up the three-quarter chinchilla she had worn over to Earth's home and made her way to the door with nothing but revenge on her mind.

Chapter Seven

"Whaddup, ma?" Le Le greeted Shell, pulling up in her red 350 ZX blasting the Remy Ma track "Conceited."

"Qué pasa, mami chula?" Shell replied as she made her way over to the Z.

Shell was a deep, brown-skinned, medium-height mixture of black and Dominican, with a body stacked like a thoroughbred horse. Her short cut with the teased burgundy highlights accentuated her round, smooth face, quarter-sized eyes, and lusciously petite lips only heightened her beauty. Her sex appeal and street persona drove men crazy. She was the ideal woman for anyone who was in search of a down-ass chick, but Shell did not need a man, or a woman, for that matter, to do anything for her, nor did she want them to. She had been doing for herself since age thirteen, and now at the ripe age of twenty-eight, she was still holding herself down, thanks to Heaven and

Earth. Meeting them nearly eight years ago at the Greek Fest in Philly at Fairmount Park was what Shell considered a blessing in disguise. Instantly, she'd hit it off with the two, and when opportunity was offered, Shell took advantage of it and had been on Heaven and Earth's team ever since.

"You out here kinda early," Le Le stated.

"Any money comin'?"

"It was, but then shit slowed up," Shell replied. "I made like $900, but I guess that was that early-morning rush," she added.

"I feel you. Let me park up. I'm coming out."

"A'ight."

"So what happened yesterday?" Shell asked. She was aware of the situation with Le Le and the kid from Remsen and had heard about someone getting shot on the block but didn't know if the person who'd violated Le Le and the person who'd gotten shot were one and the same.

"What'chu think?" Le Le replied dryly.

"Damn, bitch, what's with the attitude?" Shell snapped, taking offense to Le Le's response.

"My bad girl, I didn't mean to sound like that," Le Le apologized. "It's just that after that shit jumped off, Earth got all up in my shit, like I provoked that ma'fucka to do what he did to me."

"So they did get the right dude, then?"

"Yeah, with his bitch ass. I wish I could've been the one to do it, but Earth wouldn't even let me get out of the Jeep. She get on my nerves sometimes with all that he-man shit," Le Le chimed in disgust.

"*Tranquila, mami,*" Shell interjected. "That's family right there. I understand where you coming from, but you know how Earth is. She don't be meaning no harm; she just be looking out for our best interest and don't want to see us fucking up or have something happen to us. It's rough enough out here hustlin', but then on top of that, we females," she went on to explain. "You know dude ain't feelin' that on the real. The only reason we really getting it off is because of all the work Heaven and Earth put in around here to see to it that we got somewhere to eat, and there's never a time when you can say that Earth never had your back, right? Wrong or indifferent. True, she may bark you out if you're in the wrong, but she never left any of us for dead."

"Tsk! Yeah, but—" Le Le attempted to protest.

"But nothing," Shell cut her off. "Come on, Le, you sound real crazy right now. I mean, I ain't tryin'a say that shit with that joker was your fault because nothing you could've done or said constitutes that ma'fucka putting his hands on you, but the way I heard it, you was shittin' on ole boy extra hard, and knowing you, I can only imagine with your conceited ass."

Shell's words drew a laugh out of Le Le. Shell had hit the hammer on the nail. Le Le knew that day the wannabe balla approached her, she had deliberately gone out of her way to belittle and shine on him. That day, Le Le had been looking exceptionally good. She had just gotten eight neat cornrows going to the back put in her hair and was sporting a powder-blue BEBE velour sweat suit that hugged her 34-26-32 measurements like a glove and a crisp pair of white-on-white Air Force One Nikes.

When the dark-skinned bald-headed giant had first stepped out of the ancient Mazda Millenia on sight, Le Le was not feeling him, and she made it known from the door that she was uninterested, as she had done with so many other brothers in the past who thought they had a chance. Le Le had no idea that the brother who had introduced himself as Twan would react the way he had to her cold shoulder. She knew she had gone too far when she told him she had enough money to buy him, but she was too far gone to care.

When the incident had first occurred, Heaven was the first person Le Le had reached out to, knowing that she could have a fair shot at telling her side of the story. And she was right. Heaven had heard her out without judgment or prejudice, but when Heaven pulled up in her blue CLK 430 on the block Earth was riding shotgun, Le Le could see Earth looking stone-faced through the passenger-side window of the Benz and knew what was 'bout to happen next. Le Le prepared herself for the verbal reprimand Earth was about to hand down to her as Earth spilled out of the CLK with the ice-cold expression plastered across her face. Le Le knew she had a reaming out coming and secretly felt that she deserved it, so she took it on the chin the way she always did when Earth got on her about something, but Le Le did not understand why Earth felt the need to drag the matter out and bring it up again two days later. Although Le Le was in agreement with all Shell had said in regards to Earth's methods and motives behind her madness, she still couldn't help but to feel some type of way about how hard Earth had come down on her. Rather than going back and forth with her friend, knowing that Shell could not understand, especially when she could do no wrong in Earth's eyes, Le Le decided to downplay the subject and let the matter go.

"You're right, Shell, maybe I'm overreacting, but you ain't had to put me out there like that, talking about I'm conceited," Le Le added with a smile.

"Bitch, you are."

The two of them broke out into laughter.

"So . . ." Le Le replied in between laughs.

A few hours had gone by with Le Le and Shell having the block all to themselves until another one of their partners came appearing out of nowhere.

"Hey, y'all," greeted Sonya.

"Girl, where the hell did you come from?" Le Le asked, startled.

"From up the street," Sonya replied. "I walked down. I ain't parkin' my shit all on the ave. like that, so it can get all hot. I just got my joint," she added in regards to the new Infinity SUV she had recently brought.

"*Cómo estás?*" Shell greeted rather than asking.

"*Tato, y tu?*" Sonya responded in Spanish the way Shell had taught her.

"You know a bitch living. I can't complain."

"I heard that. What's up? What's the paper flow lookin' like?"

"It's kinda slow compared to normal," Le Le said. "I been out here for about three hours and only made a G note. Shell's been out here all morning and only made about $1,300."

"Damn, where the hell is all the money at?" Sonya spit.

"I know, right?" Shell retorted.

"Let me go put this shit up 'fore the boys roll up on my ass, but what's up, y'all? Wanna get a dice game started?"

"That's what's up," Le Le replied.

"Bring it on, *mamá*," Shell followed.

"There it is, then; I'll be right back."

Sonya was notorious for gambling. That was one of her side hustles that kept her ahead of some of the other females around her way, but at times had also been one of her downfalls. Depending on how you looked at it or who was doing the looking, Sonya's gambling habit really caused her more harm than good. Wherever there was a dice game in town or even out of town, if Sonya came across it, she wanted in. Because of her beauty and only standing at the max height of four foot eleven, Sonya toted a very big gun, which she had no problem pulling out and using if she felt threatened, cheated, or disrespected. Every so often, someone would make the mistake of playing her for weak, so she'd have to prove just how thorough she was when she stepped outside her hood. Not only was she cute in the face, she had ass for days and tits to match. She was built like a mini stallion. Her dark, silky skin and light brown eyes mesmerized men. Those factors contributed to a few occasions when peaceful games ended in ugly altercations, ultimately bringing heat back to Seaman Street, where everyone knew she was from.

Le Le ran across the street to the Puerto Rican bodega and purchased two sets of dice along with two Phillies blunt cigars. Moments later, she, Shell, and Sonya were engulfed in an intensive crap game while rotating the blunt of Purple Haze throughout the three-female cipher.

"All bets good," announced Sonya.

"I'm laying twenty dollars." Le Le peeled a twenty-dollar bill from her money stack and let it fall to the pavement.

"I got twenty," Shell followed.

"Bet," Sonya confirmed just before she released the dice. One die landed on the number four while the other stopped spinning and landed on a deuce.

"Point six," she said, then bent down and retrieved the dice.

"Fifty more you don't hit your point," Le Le increased her bet.

"Bet to you," Sonya pointed at her while shaking the two dice in her other hand.

"Fifty more you don't either," Shell joined in confidence betting against Sonya rolling the intended number.

"Bet to you too. Jump Judy," Sonya yelled as she twist her wrist, then released the dice and snapped her fingers twice.

The dice revealed the numbers three and two, so Sonya picked them up and began shaking them once again.

"I'm doubling up," Le Le said, tossing another twenty and fifty-dollar bill onto the ground.

"Now strike 'em," Sonya commanded the dice. The first die landed on a three while the other continued to spin on its tip.

"Quattro," Shell called out, stomping her foot at the spinning die, hoping for the number four.

"Chill," Sonya, said to her. "Let my shit breathe." As the three of them continued to stare, seconds later, the spinning die came to a halt.

"Yeah, crap out. Pay me mines," Le Le exclaimed, seeing the die land on the number four.

"*Dame mi plata, tigre!*" Shell said, telling Sonya in Spanish to pay her, her money.

Somewhat heated for crapping out, Sonya chucked off the $140 she had lost to Le Le for her initial bet and side bet, then handed Shell her seventy dollars.

They were all so caught up in the dice game that they hadn't noticed the crowd of spectators forming around them. There were at least eight drug fiend customers who didn't want to inter-rupt the game the three women were playing. Le Le was the first to notice.

"What's up, y'all?"

"Hey, Le," a few of them replied. "Y'all doin' something?" one of the fiends asked.

"Yeah, how many you want?" Sonya asked. Like a domino effect, everyone began to call out the number of drugs they intended to purchase. In total, there was over $400 in sales waiting to be served. Le Le, Shell, and Sonya split the transactions three ways and resumed their game, never noticing the two dudes who had just hopped out of the burgundy Chevy Tahoe.

"Bets down," Sonya instructed. Le Le and Shell dropped their monies to the ground. Nine was the point Sonya had now rolled.

"Yo, ma, I lay $300 to $200 you don't buck that Nina," a short, stocky, light-skinned bald-headed male stated from behind them. Between his clean-shaved head and the lengthy and expensive-looking diamond chain with the bracelet to match that he wore, the kid was giv-ing the sun a run for its money. He was the pas-senger of the Tahoe. His words drew the atten-tion of Le Le, Shell, and Sonya.

Not recognizing either of the two dudes, Sonya shook the dice and rolled. Instantly, a five and a two revealed itself on the dice, causing her to crap out once again. She was fuming on the inside from the interruption of the dude that caused her to lose focus of her intended number, but she kept her composure.

"Yo, can me and my man get in?" the same male asked.

That was all Sonya could take. "Ayo, playa, can't you see this is a private game? Ya money ain't no good here," she dismissed him.

"What?" he questioned with a puzzled expression on his face.

"You heard what I said. Your fuckin' money ain't no good here," Sonya repeated more aggressive than the first time she had made her statement.

"What the fuck you mean my paper ain't no good here, bitch? My money good everywhere."

The unknown male's last remark caused both Le Le and Shell to direct their full attention toward the two unknown men. They both had a bad feeling about the situation, especially knowing Sonya.

"*Bitch?* Your mamma's a bitch," Sonya shot back. She already knew where the confrontation was headed. This was not the first time she had been in this type of predicament. Her only regret now was that she had stashed her gun. Luckily, she still had something to defend herself with in her possession.

"King, you hear this li'l broad?" the light-skinned kid laughed to his dark-skinned friend who stood there expressionless. But before the dark-skinned kid could respond, what happened next was all unexpected.

"Swoosh!"

"Agh!"

"Bitch, *clack-clack.*"

"Boom! Boom! Boom!"

"Pop! Pop! Pa-Pop!"

"Shit! *Boc! Boc! Boc!*

Without so much as a blink, Sonya spit the razor blade Earth showed her how to carry in her mouth and sliced the light-skinned kid across the face with it, opening up the right side of his cheek like a can of tuna. The blow caused the light-skinned kid's blood to gush out onto her own face. Not seeing the attack but hearing his man scream out in agony caused the dark-skinned kid to reach for his gun. Shell had already managed to run for her own, but the dark-skinned kid had drawn and cocked his hammer back with the intention of gunning Sonya down. Shots rang out. Sonya closed her eyes, ready to meet her Maker. As the shots ended, Sonya realized that she was still standing.

When she opened her eyes, she saw the Tahoe peeling off and Earth, Heaven, and Shell all standing around with their guns still in hands. Tears of joy began to trickle down her face. It was times like this when she really appreciated and was grateful for friends like her girls. That day, she made a promise to herself that she would try her hardest to give up gambling—or at least try to stop getting into altercations while doing so.

Meanwhile, Sonya was not the only one who was making a promise that day. As the dark-skinned kid known as King rushed his man Original to Saint Francis Hospital, he vowed to even the score with the chicks who had just minutes ago outnumbered and outgunned them.

Chapter Eight

It had been nearly a month since the altercation over the dice game had transpired with the two unknown men. Heaven and Earth had thought it best that everyone play the block close and the situation by ear for a week or so until they found out who the two dudes in the Tahoe were and the heat had died down around the way. They also thought it best for them all to stay strapped at all times. It was better to get caught with it than without it was their motto. Shell, Sonya, and Le Le were given specific instructions not to go out to any clubs, parties, or any other functions or gatherings for a while. It had really been Heaven's idea for everyone to fall back from going out, out of safety for the team. Earth backed her partner's decision totally. Very seldom did she go against or challenge something Heaven said or did. As hard as it was for her, Earth herself had stopped going to the strip clubs or any place she could get her freak on. She knew of many cases where jokers had been caught slipping with their pants down, literally, and was not trying to add her name to that long list. Instead, she stayed home watching her personal collection of triple X adult videos. It was times like this that she wished she and Keya were still in contact. After all, she did miss her despite what she had said and how she had treated Keya. As she lay there watching the latest Lacy adult video thinking about Keya, Earth's house phone rang.

Rather than answer it, she let the answering machine pick it up.

"Earth, pick up the phone. It's Heaven."

Hearing her partner's voice, Earth reached over and snatched up the receiver. "What's good, sis?"

"Everything's decent on my end, how 'bout you?"

"Bored as hell, that's about it."

"I can't tell. What'chu watchin'?" Heaven could hear the sexual noises in the background.

Earth laughed. "That new Lacy video. This bitch is serious with her shit. I'll bust her ass, though."

"You're a freak. You shot out," Heaven laughed.

"Whatever, I'm serious. What's really, though?"

"I was calling to tell you that those two dudes wasn't Bloods or Crips that Sonya had beef with."

"I figured that," Earth retorted. "'Cause if they was, we would've already been at war with either gang by now."

"Yeah, I thought the same thing too, but I still didn't find out who they were, though."

"Then that means they wasn't nobody, then," Earth replied.

"Not necessarily, but they ain't somebody that gotta keep us from doing us," Heaven said. "That's why I called up the girls and told them we going to Dolce's tonight."

"*That's* what's up," Earth responded. Although Earth was not into dressing up regularly, she always enjoyed herself whenever she did in order to get inside the prestigious establishment. Dolce's, in Elizabeth on Broad Street, was a cool out spot for the mature crowd on Sundays, the "grown and sexy" Earth referred to it as, but on Tuesday nights, you would think you were in one of the top nightclubs in New York City the way the crowd came out. The dress code alone kept the young knuckleheads out of the club, who thought a button-up, jeans, and Tims was dressing up. This was where you would find the heavyweights in the game, from ballers to pimps, flossing from head to toe, popping Rosé and

Moët bottles like they were spring water. Even the wannabes went up in there and stepped their "Ball 'til You Fall" game up whenever they went to the popular hangout. There was no other place in North Jersey you could find off the chain on a Tuesday night like Dolce's.

"A'ight. We all riding together, so I'll pick you up in about an hour," Heaven said.

"I'll be ready," replied Earth.

Chapter Nine

"Peace, god, what's the deal?" King greeted Original with a pound handshake and hug as he entered his man's apartment with a gym bag hanging from his shoulder.

"Everything's copacetic, lord," Original replied in a mild tone. His words were somewhat slurred.

The 135 stitches he had received on the side of his face nearly a month ago had made it a little difficult to talk, causing his speech to be altered. The doctor had told him to take it easy and minimize the movement of his mouth as much as he possibly could, out of concern that he may rip the stitches, reopening the facial wound. This made Original extremely self-conscious, causing him to restrain from lengthy conversation, or any conversation, for that matter, and forcing him to go on a liquid diet. Since that day on East State Street, Original had laid up in his crib watching movies on his DVD digital theater system and playing Xbox on the fifty-inch plasma television. This was the first time he had seen his man King since then.

Upon entering the apartment, King couldn't help but notice the filth of Original's crib. This was unlike his man. Original was normally a neat type of dude who kept his home and appearance intact. King could only assume that the permanent scar on Original's once-favorable look to the ladies was the cause of the drastic change. King felt bad for his man and not a day had gone by without him playing the tapes back in his head about that day, wondering whether there was something he could have done differently to prevent what had happened to Original. King knew that his man had a reputation for being arrogant and overbearing toward women, which is why he knew he should not have stopped when Original told him to pull over, especially since they were from out of town and weren't totally familiar with the New Brunswick area. Initially, they had come from their hometown of Newark to New Brunswick to conduct a drug transaction with a dude Original had served prison time with. After the completion of the drug deal at that time, King knew it was a bad idea to agree to Original's request, traveling with the thirty-two Gs they had in the book bag and the total combined amount of seven grand they had in their pockets. The last thing they needed, thought King, was to be robbed, or worse, to get approached by the police and take a loss for nearly forty thousand in cash, all because Original wanted to get in a dice game with a bunch of chicks, but it was not for King to question his man's decisions. After all, Original was the brains behind the organization. King was simply the muscle.

"Yo, how ya shit healing up, beloved?" King asked. He didn't want to stare at the still fresh-looking scar, but the wound was inescapable as it stood out to King in 3-D.

"It's healing," Original replied, keeping his words short. It was apparent that he had already acquired a complex about the scar. King noticed how Original had sat on the futon as if to shield the right side of his face.

"What did the doctor say?" King continued to pry.

"A couple more weeks," Original stated, trying to hide his annoyance. He was not in the mood to be answering questions. Especially ones about something he tried to forget about each day.

"What's good in the hood, though?" Original asked, changing the subject.

"Since you been MIA, I been moving a couple of ounces here and there," King replied in reference to the quantity of cocaine he had sold.

"But shit ain't the same without you though, god. Ma'fuckas be asking for you. You know a lot of cats don't fuck with me. They only dealt with me on the strength of you, so they be actin' type shook when I come through."

Original just shook his head in agreement. He understood exactly what King was going through. King was not at all a drug dealer; he was a gunman, but Original respected the fact that he had stepped up to the plate in his absence.

"What'chu tell 'em about me?" Original asked inquisitively.

"I ain't tell 'em shit. It ain't any of their business, feel me?"

"No doubt," Original replied admirably.

"Yo, it ain't much, but it's like twenty-four grand up in this bag," King then said, handing Original the gym bag. "Altogether, it was thirty-five, but I took eleven for my cut. I still got four birds and a little over a half of one left. I know if I would've shot out to New Brunswick, I would've moved more, but I ain't been out there since shit popped off 'cause I didn't know if them bitches knew ya mans and 'em or what and some funny shit jumped off. I wasn't trustin' it, feel me."

"I feel you." Original nodded. Hearing King mentioning the word "New Brunswick" triggered off something inside of him. The veins in his neck began to pulsate at the thought of the last time he was in the town. Furthermore, Original couldn't believe how he had let a situation concerning a bunch of females throw him off his square. In the past, he had been stabbed and even shot by someone in the streets, and without hesitation, he had sought revenge. That was simply one of the rules of the game, and Original viewed himself as being one of the ones that played by the rules. That being the case, Original knew that like any other altercation or drama that resulted in any harm or disrespect against his street credibility and reputation, regardless of gender, the situation had to be rectified.

King could see that Original was disturbed by the mentioning of New Brunswick and appeared to be in deep thought. "Yo, god, what's on your mind?"

"New Brunswick," was Original's response.

"There it is, then," a now-hyped King retorted. "Just say the word and it's a wrap for them broads." Original managed to crack half a smile behind his man's eagerness.

"In due time," Original told him. "In due time," he repeated.

Chapter Ten

Just as they figured, Dolce's was rocking when they stepped inside. The way they were all dressed, you would have never known that these five enticing-looking women who entered the club were some of the most dangerous among their kind. Sexy and deadly would be the words best to describe Heaven, Earth, and their crew. Each one of them sported a different style of cut chinchilla. Heaven rocked a matching ear cover piece over her Doobie. Underneath her fur, she wore a bone-colored sweater dress that dipped just enough in the front to show off the right amount of cleavage and wrapped itself around her every curve. She also wore a pair of four-inch mocha knee-high boots that accented the shades of brown in her long-haired floor-length fur. Earth rocked a black-on-black top and a pair of Seven jeans with black-and-white Manolo Blahnik shoes. The attire managed to take the edge off of her normal thuggish persona. Shell sported a winter-white catsuit with a diamond belt that fell just right around her tiny waist, and a pair of multicolored pointed toe shoes made by Jimmy Choo. Both her right and left arms were draped in an assortment of bangles and bracelets that accented each color in the $300 Jimmy Choos. Sonya wore a pair of black-and-white leggings and a black flirty cropped lace top that moved every time she did, revealing the star tattoos that ran across her midsection. Her size seven feet were covered with a pair of three-inch black bootie boots by Zigi Soho. Le Le wore a nearly see-through gold-colored minidress made by Donna Karan. It was lace and had gold and crystal jewels hanging from everywhere but not enough to hide anything. She rocked a pair of peep toe four-inch heels by Jessica Simpson's shoe line.

As they headed toward the bar, the onlooking women envied while the men lusted. The five of them were indeed a sight to see, but to show that they were more than what the flesh revealed, as soon as they reached the bar, Heaven ordered five bottles of Rosé, along with five double shots of Rémy, five Amaretto sours and a bottle of Patrón. After moments had gone by and drinks had been downed, all five of them officially had their buzz on. The champagne and liquor mixed with weed they had smoked on the way to the club had taken effect.

"Let's flick it up," suggested Shell.

"Yeah, we haven't been out in a while. Let's take some pictures," Sonya agreed. Both Heaven and Earth looked at each other. They were very cautious when it came to taking photos. But given that it had been awhile since they had all taken a group picture, and they both knew how much it meant to their crew to capture moments such as tonight, as if on cue, Earth spotted one of the cameramen who was working the dance floor and motioned for him to come over to the VIP section. He noticed her and walked over to where they sat.

"What's up, ladies?" the well-dressed light-skinned brother with the camera asked over the music.

"Yo, we wanna take some pictures," Earth told him.

"Where y'all wanna take 'em at?"

"Right here."

"Got you."

Within seconds, the cameraman began to do his thing. Onlookers stared as he snapped what seemed like a hundred different shots of Heaven and Earth and their crew. Each pose was different as they raised up drinks and bottles. He had even managed to catch a few with Earth tossing a stack of singles in the air. Once he was done shooting, he turned the camera around to them. They all leaned in to get a look as his high-tech digital camera replayed the photos back for them.

"Them shits is hot," Sonya yelled out.

"You like 'em?" the cameraman asked.

"Definitely," Heaven answered for them all.

"Which ones you like?" he then asked.

"I like all of 'em," Le Le joined.

"Yeah, we like 'em all," Earth followed. "How many you take?"

The cameraman looked at his screen. "Thirty-four," he answered.

"How much you'll give me all of 'em for?"

The cameraman could not believe his ears. He was used to people who he took photos of liking them all, but he had never had anyone wanting to outright buy so many at one time, especially not women. He knew they were not your average chicks. He did a quick calculation in his head. "I normally charge ten dollars a picture, but since you're getting them all, give me two eighty and I'll print 'em out and frame 'em for you."

Without hesitation, Earth pulled out her stack of money and peeled off three crisp one hundred-dollar bills. "Don't worry about it, playa, we respect hustlers," she said, tipping the cameraman.

"I appreciate that," he said pocketing the money. He pulled out a business card. "If y'all every need a photographer, my name's Gavin." He handed Earth the business card. "I take pictures at Club Abyss, 78 Lounge, and at The Cavalier's Ballroom sometimes too."

"That's what's up," Earth retorted.

"Thanks. I'll be back with your flicks."

Everyone resumed his or her drinking session.

"Oh, this my shit right here," Le Le shouted as the club's DJ filled the air with the sounds of Cassidy's cut, "I'm a Hustla." "Come on, let's go dance," she said to Shell and Sonya.

"Fuck it, come on," Sonya replied.

"Yeah, fuck it," Shell followed. "Y'all comin'?" she then directed to Heaven and Earth.

"Do you, ma," Heaven answered for the both of them, seeing that Earth was preoccupied with her bottle of nectar.

"E, I'm shooting to the bathroom. I'll be right back," Heaven then stated as her three-crew members made their way toward the dance floor.

"I'll be here," Earth said through sips.

As the songs in the air changed, so did Earth's alcohol level. She thought the liquor and cham-pagne were playing tricks on her, thinking she had heard her name being called over the blar-ing music. Earth turned toward the direction in which she had thought her name was being called. Her vision was semiblurred due to the intoxicants. Realizing she had actually heard correctly, she had to squint her eyes to make out the identity of the individual. As her perception began to clear, the only thoughts on her mind was, she hoped it wasn't an enemy of hers and wished that she had somehow smuggled her gun into the club, but once she'd zeroed in on who the person was sitting next to her, Earth began to be at ease. After all, the redbone beauty was harmless. "Melissa," Earth said in confirmation.

"Hey, E, long time no see," Melissa spoke.

"What's good, sexy?" Earth said, instantly sobering up. Melissa was an old flame from Earth's hometown. She was actually one of Earth's first lovers, not to mention the prettiest one Earth had ever been with, after her first introduction to bisexuality. Melissa was five foot seven and built like Jessica Rabbit. She had green eyes and naturally cherry-red luscious lips that looked like she could suck a blow pop down to the gum in just one try. It was those same lips that drove Earth up the wall and had her fighting both men and women over Melissa. One of the reasons Earth had stopped dealing with Melissa was because she enjoyed, or rather favored, dick over pussy, not to mention she'd gotten pregnant by a nigga.

"Damn, I see you been taking care of yourself," Earth complimented. "How's the baby?"

"He's good, with his bad ass."

"That's what's up. Who you here with?" Earth asked, now moving closer to Melissa. Surprisingly, Earth could smell the familiar White Diamond fragrance that she used to love on Melissa emanating off her body.

"Me and a couple of my girlfriends, and, no, not like that," Melissa added before Earth had the chance to comment.

"I wasn't gonna say nothin'," Earth smiled.

"Yeah, right," Melissa smiled back. "Who are you here with?"

"My peoples."

"Anybody I have to worry about?" Melissa asked seductively.

"Nah."

"Good."

"What's up? What'chu drinkin'?" Earth offered.

"Vodka and orange juice."

"A'ight. Yo, let me get a Vodka and orange juice," Earth ordered, getting the female bartender's attention.

Once the drink arrived, Earth passed it to Melissa.

"Thank you."

"You can thank me later," Earth slyly remarked.

"E, you still crazy," Melissa smiled through her drink.

The two of them began to chat, making small talk. Earth hadn't talked to a female so flirtatious since she and Keya had been messing around, and she enjoyed how the conversation was going between them. She was positive that before the night was over, she and Melissa would find themselves in bed together. She envisioned Melissa's juicy lips between her inner thighs and her own mouth reciprocating head between Melissa's. The thought had Earth on fire, and she was ready to make her move.

"So what's up? You rode up here with your girls?"

"No. I drove my own car. I met them here," Melissa answered, already knowing where Earth's line of questioning was going.

"So what's up with me and you for the night?" Earth asked confidently.

Melissa smiled. "That could be arranged," she answered.

"There it is, then; let's get up outta here."

"Okay, but give me a minute. Let me go tell my girlfriends I'm leaving," Melissa shot back.

"I'll be right here."

Earth watched as Melissa sashayed her way through the crowd and licked her lips. She hadn't been with anyone since Keya and was in dire need of a tune-up. While Earth waited for Melissa, she scanned the crowded room in search of Heaven. It just dawned on her that Heaven had been in the bathroom for a long time. Cursing herself for losing focus and not being more on point, Earth rose up off the barstool. Just as she was about to go on a search for her partner, she saw Heaven in what seemed like a deep conversation off to the far right with someone she recognized from being from the Ville in New Brunswick. It was apparent that Heaven was in no danger Earth concluded, especially since she was talking to one of the biggest cowards in New Brunswick, according to her. She wondered what the two were talking about, but saw no sense in intruding. Although Earth got along with a few dudes from Henry Street where the guy named Rock was from, she didn't particularly care for him. When it had spread that someone from Plainfield, a female at that, was getting money in the Exit 9 town, he had been one of the main ones talking about banning her from the town. It wasn't until they had found the main instigator in Joyce Kilmer Park with a shot to the head and his male member stuffed in his mouth that he left well enough alone. Since then, Earth waited for the day he'd give her a reason to end his life.

Earth scanned the dance floor for Le Le, Shell, or Sonya to tell one of them to let Heaven know that she was leaving. As she looked, she couldn't locate any of her workers. She did locate someone else, though, and the sight of that person caused her blood pressure to reach a volcanic level. Without even thinking or batting an eye, Earth flew off the stool and proceeded to push her way through the partygoers until she was in range of what disturbed her and made her react the way she had.

"What the fuck you doin'?" Earth roared, snatching Keya by the arm.

Keya had been so caught up in grinding her ass into Mustafa's dick to the sounds of "Blow the Whistle" that she hadn't seen Earth roll up on her. She was totally caught by surprise.

"Get ya hands off me," Keya yelled, pulling away from Earth. By now, the dance floor had magically parted like the Red Sea. It was evident what was going on, and for those who recognized all parties, none of them wanted any part of the possibilities.

"Yo, who the fuck is this dyke-looking bitch?" Mustafa asked heatedly. He was upset behind the fact that Earth had just interrupted his groove. His girl Keya had him harder than a ton of bricks until the unknown female showed up.

"She's nobody, babe," Keya said holding Mustafa back, standing in between him and Earth.

"You wasn't saying that when I was eating ya pussy," Earth blurted out.

"Fuck you!" Keya screamed, spitting in Earth's face.

"Crack!"

As before, Earth immediately counteracted off the disrespect by Keya and threw a right hook, sending her straight to floor.

"You stupid bitch," Mustafa barked just as he launched at Earth.

"Crack!"

"You the stupid bitch!" Sonya yelled.

Before Mustafa could throw a punch, Sonya had clonked him in the back of the head with the Rosé bottle she had been sipping on. By then, the bouncers were making their way through the crowd, only to find Keya getting up off the floor in a daze and Mustafa lying unconscious with blood spilling out of the back of his head. Earth and the rest of her squad had already dispersed.

"Shell, Heaven was over by the bathroom talking to that nigga Rock from the Ville. Go get her and tell her we'll be out front," Earth instructed Shell.

"Okay."

As they were making their way toward the exit, Earth saw Melissa approaching. "E, what's up? Is everything all right?" Melissa asked noticing the look on Earth's face change. From afar, she had noticed some commotion on the dance floor. Melissa remembered how bad of a temper Earth had back in the day and wondered if she had anything to do with the sudden interruption in the club.

"Everything's good. Go pull your car out front. I'll meet you out there," Earth coolly replied.

Le Le and Sonja looked at each other, but neither said a word. It was no secret to them how Earth got down, so the situation was evident. The exchanges in glances were due to the beauty of Melissa.

"Tell Heaven I'll holla at her later and fill her in on everything," Earth told Le Le once they had reached the front of the club.

As soon as she walked outside, Earth heard the horn honking. She made her way over to Melissa's white 5 series BMW and hopped in.

A few minutes later, Keya helped Mustafa into his emerald-green Escalade and pulled off.

"Babe, you gonna be okay?" Keya asked.

"What the fuck you think?" Mustafa shot back from the passenger seat while compressing a towel to the back of his head.

"Don't yell at me, Mu," Keya whined.

"What? I'm sitting here with my ma'fuckin' head busted open over some dyke shit, and you talking about don't yell at you? You buggin' the fuck out. Just get me to the hospital, yo, so I can get my shit stitched up. Then I want you to tell me everything you know about that bitch you used to fuck with," he commanded.

Keya drove in silence, but she'd heard loud and clear what Mustafa had just said to her. She intended to drive him to the nearest hospital, just as she intends to tell him all he needed to know. She knew he had status in his hometown of Elizabeth and was someone not to be taken lightly. Keya sensed an opportunity. The time had finally come to get her revenge for what Earth had done to her nearly a month ago. As she drove, the only thing on her mind was how payback was a bitch.

Chapter Eleven

"Yo," an out of breath Earth answered.

"Yeah, it's me. What's wrong with you? You fuckin' or something?" Heaven asked.

"No, bitch, I couldn't find my phone," Earth snapped, looking around realizing that Melissa was gone. The two of them had endured a wild and enjoyable evening last night, and Earth was looking forward to a repeat occurrence this morning.

"Anyway, where you at?"

"I'm outside, you ready?"

"Almost, I'll be out in a sec."

"A'ight."

Moments later, Earth came out of the house toting a Nike gym bag and jumped in Heaven's X5 BMW truck.

"What's good?" Earth greeted.

"You tell me," Heaven replied, pulling off.

"Man, last night was crazy," Earth sighed.

"I heard. What the hell happened with you and Keya?"

"Fuck that bitch," Earth answered dryly.

"So what happened?"

"Nothing really. She tried to style in front of some dude, so I knocked her dumb ass out. And then he tried to play super-save-a-ho, and Sonya clonked his silly ass with a bottle."

Heaven stared at her partner for a brief moment.

"I thought you didn't fuck with Keya anymore."

"I don't."

"So why were you so worried about who she was with or what she was doing, then?" Heaven questioned. "Besides, it looked to me like you were doing you anyway."

"What?"

"You heard me. I saw you with that light-skinned chick all night. Who was that?"

"Who? Melissa? Oh, that wasn't about nothing. We grew up together," Earth replied.

"She's from Plainfield too," she added, trying to downplay her booty call last night.

"Uh-huh," Heaven grunted, not buying Earth's story.

"Uh-huh what? What about *you?*" Earth asked, still derailing Heaven's question.

"Me what?"

"I seen Rock all up in ya face. What was that about?"

"Oh shit!" Heaven exclaimed. "I'm glad you reminded me. I knew there was something I had to tell you."

"What?" Heaven's tone alarmed Earth.

"Did you hear about some joker from South Trenton that's been going around robbing and shit?"

"Nah, why would I, and what happened?"

"Nothing yet, but last night, Rock comes up to me and asks could he holla at me on the one-on-one for a minute. At first, I'm like, what the fuck this clown wanna talk to me about, 'cause you know we don't really fuck with them jokers from Henry Street like that, but I guess he peeps my vibe or something 'cause he says it's important, and it's 'bout me and you. So anyway, we slide off to the side, and he starts asking me have we been having any problems around the way, and the first thing that came to mind is all the shit we been getting into lately, but still I play the role and tell him no. That's when he goes into it about the cat from South Trenton doing stickups, saying that he heard from his man that heard from another dude that overheard that kid talking about running down on some bitches that supposed to be doing their numbers out in New Brunswick, and when he heard it, we were the first ones to come to his mind. I mean, I know we ain't the only bitches getting doe out here but better safe than sorry, feel me?" Heaven ended.

"Yeah, I feel you," Earth replied.

She had listened attentively as Heaven had run down the story told to her by Rock.

"You didn't get a name?"

"Rock said he didn't know it."

"That ma'fucka knew," Earth retorted. "I bet you if you would've told him he was gonna get some ass, he would've remembered."

"Where'd that come from?" Heaven asked, surprised by Earth's statement.

"Com'on, sis, I'm saying, why else would a nigga tell you all that? It ain't like you and him cool or nothin'. I mean, that's good looking on our part that he slipped you all that, but I'm sure that he did that on the strength of thinking he was gonna get some pussy for that."

"Well, he didn't, and he ain't, so fuck 'em," Heaven spat with attitude.

"I know that. Don't take it out on me," Earth joked seeing how upset her statement had made Heaven.

"Whatever, E."

"Yeah, anyway, so how you wanna handle this shit, just in case he was talking about us?" Earth asked, changing the subject.

"First, we gotta find out who he is. Then we'll take it from there," Heaven answered.

"I'm with that. Damn, we stay in some shit."

"I know, right?" Heaven agreed.

"I don't know how we able to eat with all this beefin' shit that been poppin' up. I think ma'fuckas can't accept the fact that some females outdoing their low-budget asses," Earth stated.

"Maybe," was all Heaven said.

"That has to be it. But fuck 'em. What they gonna do? Either tell on us or try to lay us down."

"E, don't talk like that," Heaven said in a serious tone.

"It is what it is, but anyway, what's up with them bitches around the way?" Earth asked, again changing the subject.

"Everything's good. They're good. I left Sonya in charge and gave her the burner. I told her to call one of us if anything goes wrong and hold Le Le and Shell down while they're out moving the rest of the work. We had a little over a half of bird left, so I just bagged all of it up when I got in from Dolce's 'cause I knew we had a lot to do this morning."

"That's what's up. Hopefully, Le Le stupid ass can stay the fuck outta some shit while we gone."

"E, why you so hard on Le Le? Leave her alone," Heaven said in Le Le's defense.

"Yeah, I'ma leave her alone, all right. Alone in the ma'fuckin' dirt somewhere she keep doing dumb shit to bring heat down on us."

"What about the shit Sonya pulled last month?" Heaven reminded her.

"At least Le Le's situation was handled off the block."

"Yeah, but Sonya's a trooper. She handles her B-I when she gets into something. That nigga we pushed from Remsen should have never left the block when he smacked her up and robbed her. It was guns around there, and Le Le scary ass could've got to one in time," Earth stated.

"Then the bitch got the nerve to act like she wanted to put some work in when we went around there. She would've fucked around and got all our asses murdered," she added.

"All I'm saying is to ease up on her, sis. She's a good worker, and she's loyal to us. And we both know that good help is hard to find nowadays. We lose her and it forces us back on the block. And I know you're not tryin'a catch another case," Heaven pointed out.

"If it's in the script, then there's not shit I can do about it," Earth replied, not wanting to give Le Le any type of credit. In all reality, Earth knew just as well as Heaven had, that she did not want to return to jail under *any* circumstances.

Just then, Earth's thoughts were interrupted by the sounds of rap artist Lil' Kim's lyrics. She increased the volume of Heaven's stereo.

"This bitch Kim is gangsta," Earth said in admiration as she nodded her head to the flow of the song.

"Yeah, she definitely stood up," agreed Heaven.

"Out of all them ma'fuckas, she the only one who held it down. Niggas ain't shit," Earth chimed in disgust.

"For real, they were supposed to have been her manz and 'em. And she took care of them dudes when Big died."

"She's that queen bitch for real, for real," Earth announced. "That's the type of bitches we need on our team—straight riders," she ended.

"I feel you, but we got some riders, tho," Heaven said in her team's defense.

"I'm not saying we don't; I'm just saying *technically,* we don't know if Shell and them built for that jail shit because they never did bids before.

We know what it's like, so we know what we're up against. It ain't about nothing to us if we had to go lay down for a minute," Earth explained in regards to her and Heaven's past incarceration.

"I mean, Shell and Sonya, if it came down to it, I could see them wearing their weight, but Le Le's scary ass, I could see her folding if they came at her with some football numbers. That's just how I feel. And on the real," Earth continued, "we know better than to be fucking with anybody that never tasted prison life before. We've just been lucky, that's all."

"Maybe," was the only response Heaven could conjure up. But she knew that Earth was 100 percent right.

"I got a couple of chicks in mind to put on the team, tho; I just gotta fill 'em out a little more."

"Yeah, we could use a few more," Heaven agreed.

"I got us. Did you call the connect and put the order in already?" Earth asked, changing the subject.

"Yeah, I told him we wanted four large pies with extra sauce instead of the three we usually get," Heaven replied in regards to the four kilos of coke she and Earth intended to buy from their New York connect.

"That's what's up."

As they jumped onto the highway, Heaven popped in one of her favorite artist's CDs and turned the volume up to the maximum. The X5 sounded like a club as she and Earth cruised down Route 78 East listening to Young Jeezy's new CD, heading for the George Washington Bridge to meet with their Dominican connect uptown.

Meanwhile, back in New Brunswick, Blaze sat in the stolen black Buick trying to look inconspicuous while observing the massive drug flow on Seamen Street. He had been scoping out the block for three consecutive days now, in hopes to get a tail on the two chicks named Heaven and Earth he was squatting on but to no avail. Out of spite and frustration of not getting any closer to the duo he had been turned on to, Blaze was tempted to run up on the three females he'd been watching all morning clock a few Gs and lay them all down but thought better of it, because that would be too easy. Besides, why settle for the small fish when there were bigger fish he could catch? Blaze reasoned with himself.

He had been told that the two chicks that would soon be his latest vics were seeing major paper, and he knew that the three female hustlers he watched now were only workers for the female duo Heaven and Earth, and that's who he wanted. Blaze had been content with the stickups and home invasions he had been doing throughout his part of town of North and South Trenton, coming up on twenty to thirty thousand-dollar licks. But when someone pulled his coat to a bunch of females, two in particular, doing astronomical numbers and getting more money than the average dude out in New Brunswick, that piqued Blaze's interest. He couldn't pass up the sweet opportunity and took his show on the road.

He was told to proceed with caution because the one named Earth was known to be ruthless when it came to busting her gun, so Blaze had already made up his mind, once he located and got the drop on the two females, she would be the first to go. The last way he wanted to go out was by some female he told himself. He would not be able to rest in hell if he went out like that. His ego and pride, not to mention his reputation as a gangster, convinced him that he'd rather take his own life than have it stolen at the hands of a woman. The more Blaze thought about it, the angrier he became. If there was ever any doubt before, there was none now. As soon as he landed a lead on the whereabouts of the two named Heaven and Earth, he would take them for everything they possessed—including their lives.

After staking out the block for what seemed like the entire day to him and seeing that Heaven and Earth were not showing up, Blaze started up his hooptie and drove off.

Chapter Twelve

"Bang! Bang! Bang!"

"Who the fuck bangin' on the damn door like that?" Earth barked.

Both Heaven and Shell had puzzled expressions on their faces. Since they had come back from New York, Heaven and Earth had given specific instructions to Le Le and Sonya not to disturb or interrupt them while they, along with Shell, cooked and bottled up the product they had only hours ago purchased from the city. Aside from the two of them, Shell was the only other one allowed to take part in this particular part of the operation for two important reasons. One, she herself had skills when it came to cooking up the product, and two, her bottling skills were better than Heaven and Earth's put together.

Shell had been exposed to drugs since she first entered the world. Her father and all of her uncles were coke dealers, and even some of her cousins on her father's side of the family. Over the years, the men in her family who indulged in the illegal drug trade had either gone off to prison for an eternity, were murdered, or were deported back to their native country of Dominican Republic, including Shell's father who had not only been deported but was serving life in a Dominican prison. Heaven and Earth's connect was, in fact, a mutual acquaintance of Shell's father and uncles, who played a major part in their more-than-fair prices they paid for their product, thanks to Shell. It was one of the reasons Earth had favored Shell over Sonya and Le Le. Earth had often expressed to Shell that had she been a redbone, she would have made her wifey.

Heaven favored her simply because she seemed sharper than her other two workers.

"Tsk! This bitch," Earth chimed, looking through the peephole.

"Who is it?" Heaven asked.

"Who you think?" she answered unlocking and snatching open the door. "What the fuck do you want?" Earth questioned, pulling Le Le inside the apartment.

Shell just shook her head. She already had a feeling who was at the door. Le Le was the only one out of the clique who was always doing or saying something at the wrong place and time.

"We ran out," Le Le began to explain. "And Sonya sent me up—"

"What the fuck you mean Sonya sent you up here?" Earth finished Le Le's sentence, becoming angrier. "Bitch, who do you work for? Huh? Sonya don't call no ma'fuckin' shots around this bitch. What the fuck did we tell your stupid ass before we came up here?"

"Gosh, Earth, I was only—*Umph!*"

"Who you talkin' to like that!"

"E, chill," Heaven intervened, jumping up, seeing her partner throw a punch into Le Le's midsection, causing her to belly over.

"Heaven, don't grab me. You know I don't like that shit," Earth spit, instinctively knocking Heaven's hands away. By now, Le Le was on one knee gasping for air. Shell had gotten up and gone to her aid but was warned against it.

"Don't help her ass," Earth said to her. "Let that bitch choke."

Against her better judgment, Shell stopped in her tracks. The last thing she wanted to do was go against her boss. Although she wasn't in total agreement with Earth's method toward Le Le, Shell knew that Le Le had brought what happened on herself. Shell continued to stand there feeling sorry for her friend. She knew that in the game, there was no room for mistakes or weakness, each one of those costly, and Le Le was capable and possessed them both. If it meant siding with Le Le or Earth when it came to what was best for her or the team, there was no doubt that Shell would choose Earth's side, which is exactly what she was doing now.

Heaven knew how Earth felt about people putting their hands on her, especially when she was upset, but Heaven could not allow her partner to handle Le Le in the order she knew she would had Heaven not stopped her. "E, for me, let that go," Heaven tried to reason, keeping a barrier between Le Le and Earth.

"Heaven, you don't have to stand there. I'm not going to do nothing to her ass. I did what I was gonna do, but she better watch her ma'fuckin' tone when she talk to me," Earth stated. "You hear me?" she then directed to Le Le over Heaven's shoulder.

Le Le nodded her head to imply she had heard Earth loud and clear out of fear of what she would possibly do had she not.

"Shell, help her up," Heaven instructed.

"Yeah, and make sure you give her twenty-five of them clips we bottled up 'cause her ass gonna do some hustling tonight," Earth added.

Shell helped Le Le off the floor and into the kitchen to get her a drink of water.

"Stupid bitch," Earth mumbled as she and Heaven went back to their seats to finish bottling up one of the intended kilos and bagging up another in ounces before the interruption. Heaven didn't say a word. She just looked at her partner for a moment and shook her head. Then she picked up the razor blade and proceeded with shaving the rock cocaine.

Chapter Thirteen

"Excuse me, shorty, you doing something?" a man asked Le Le rolling down the passenger-side window of the champagne-colored '87 model Honda Accord.

"Yeah, what's up?"

"Can me and my boy get a clip for seventy-five?" the crack addict asked, wanting ten vials of crack for twenty-five dollars short. What the addict hadn't known was that Le Le had been out on the block by herself trying to get rid of the twenty-five clips of crack that Earth ordered her to move before she could end her shift, and if she had ten bottles remaining, she would have gladly given it to him just to rid herself of one of the clips, but the fact was, she did not.

"Nah, I'll give you nine, tho," Le Le propositioned offering what she had left.

It was nearing 11:00 p.m., not really late, but late for her. The way Shell, Sonya, and she had it set up, Le Le's shift was technically over three hours ago, and would actually be beginning again four hours from now when she brought the dope package out to catch the early-morning rush. So, Le Le was hoping the addict accepted so that she could call it a night.

"Damn, sis, that's the best you can do?" the addict complained.

"Yeah, nigga, take it or leave it," Le Le responded as if it made no difference to her.

The addict turned to his partner who was driving. Le Le could see that they were debating whether to take her up on her offer or try their luck somewhere else.

Intuition kicking in, Le Le began to walk off in case the two men tried something funny, although she had backup stashed just a few feet away from her. She was not, however, in the mood for any unnecessary drama.

"A'ight, yo, we'll take it," the addict shouted, seeing Le Le's sudden departure.

Relieved by the two men's decision, Le Le made her way over to the garbage can and retrieved the brown paper bag containing her last nine vials. "Good lookin' out," the passenger thanked Le Le just before his partner pulled off.

Le Le then pulled out her cell phone. "Shell, where you at? Well, I'm done, and I'm about to bounce. Okay. Yeah, I'ma just get a couple hours in, and I'll be back out. A'ight, bye."

After hanging up, Le Le snatched up the trey-eight revolver she had stashed, tucked it in the lower part of her back, and began to make her way to her car. She hit the alarm button on her keychain. Just then, she heard a male's voice in the distance. "Leann."

Hearing the name caused Le Le to stop in her tracks. There was only one person in the world that had referred to her by her birth-given first name, but Le Le knew it could not have been whom she thought—or could it be? she wondered. When Le Le turned around, the figure approaching her had her baffled. She did not recognize the giant of a man in the distance, but as he neared, his smile was unmistakable.

"Omg!" Le Le gasped. "Monty?"

"What's up, girl?" Monty greeted her wrapping his pythons around Le Le's waist, lifting her off the ground.

Monty was Le Le's ex-boyfriend; it had been ten years since the two had seen each other. They had been like Bonnie and Clyde before Monty had caught thirty years in prison for a murder he had maintained his innocence on. Le Le had stood in his corner throughout his entire trial, but when he lost, Monty told her it was best to forget about him and move on with her life. It was during that time Le Le had met Heaven and Earth. She met the two while trying to boost anything she could get her hands on at the mall. Taking an immediate interest in Le Le, Heaven and Earth approached her, offering Le Le an opportunity outside of petty thievery.

As soon as Le Le began seeing a nice amount of money, she saw to it that Monty was well taken care of in prison, at least for a few years, until he got into trouble and was transferred to another facility. Nearly most of her earnings while hustling for Heaven and Earth had gone to him up until the time they lost contact. No one had any inclination about how Le Le spent her money or even about her incarcerated lover, for that matter, and that's the way Le Le had preferred it. He was a life and memories outside of her relationship with her crew, and now seeing Monty at that moment had caused feelings Le Le had buried for what seemed like an eternity to resurface.

"How?" was all Le Le had managed to get out.

Monty smiled. "I finally won my appeal and got a reversal. The appellate division found the evidence they claimed to have on me inconclusive. They granted me an immediate release."

As Monty talked, tears began to roll down Le Le's face. She still couldn't believe that the love of her life was standing before her. Without hesitation, Le Le enveloped Monty in a tight embrace and kissed him.

"Whoa, baby girl, I'm home now, and I ain't goin' nowhere. We got all the time in the world," he smiled, breaking their lip-lock. "Come on now, wipe your face; no more tears," he said, wiping her cheeks.

"How'd you know where to find me?" she asked through sniffles.

"Just 'cause I wasn't out here doesn't mean I didn't keep my ears to the streets. All these years I've always known where you were. I just chose not to reach out," Monty admitted.

"I was always confident that this day would come, so I patiently waited, and I never stopped loving you either," he added, kissing Le Le gently on the forehead.

"I never stopped lovin' you," she softly replied.

"I know," he said sincerely. "That's why I came back for you." Monty put his arm around Le Le and continued walking with her toward her car. "Let's get up outta here. We got a lot of catchin' up to do," he then said, dropping his hand down to Le Le's backside.

Same ole Monty, Le Le thought with a smile as she deactivated the alarm on her Z for a second time.

Chapter Fourteen

"Goddamn, I missed this dick, daddy," Le Le grunted as Monty pumped away vigorously from behind while she took all of his length in the doggie-style position.

Le Le could not believe she was here with the love of her life. She had dated others since she and Monty had lost contact, but none ever touched her heart as he had. Now, lying here with him, she understood why. It was love that made the difference. His touch, his voice, and even the way he smelled made her wet, and her heart feel things it had never felt for no other.

"You missed this shit, huh?" he joined in the bedroom talk, switching his hands from her petite waist onto her voluptuous backside. He spread her caramel ass cheeks apart and raised them up giving him full access to her dripping sex.

"Yes," she cooed through clinched teeth. "Right there." Each stroke sent a new emotional spark through her body, igniting and confirming old feelings.

Monty continued to pound Le Le's tight and juicy cave like there was no tomorrow. Ten years of frustration had built up in him as he watched his tool insert and exert between Le Le's inner thighs. No more imaginary sex he told himself, remembering the times he had masturbated to the likes of J-Lo, Esther Baxter, Halle Berry, and Buffie the Body magazine photos, to name a few. Today and every day thereafter, Monty intended to enjoy the real thing. Unable to withstand the pleasurable feeling any longer with the help of Le Le now throwing it back at him, Monty felt his fluids building up.

"Le Le, I-I'ma about to co—"

Before he could get the final word out, Le Le pulled away from him and spun around. She was just in time to catch Monty's juices in her mouth. As she clinched her jaws around his sex and allowed the heavy fluid to fill her mouth, Le Le looked up at Monty to determine if she had done her job. As she studied Monty's facial expressions and scrutinize his body language, she noticed that Monty's upper body and some of his lower had many new battle scars. She attributed them to fighting in jail, and then, for a split second as she relaxed her throat in order to allow the come to move down into her abdomen, she wondered if she should have made Monty wear a condom, but instantly dismissed the notion. Le Le told herself that Monty was too much of a killer to allow or even to indulge in something like that, and then she carried on with her assault.

"Sheeit," he yelled out as he sprayed the inside of her mouth with his fluids. His knees nearly buckled from her performance. He couldn't help but place a hand atop her head to brace himself as she licked and swallowed every last drop of his semen. This was not the Le Le he remembered, but he was glad to meet her. He stared down at her as their eyes met, and with a devilish grin on her face, she purred, "Welcome home, baby."

And a beautiful welcome it was, thought Monty, knowing she had no idea just how much of a part she would play in his homecoming.

Chapter Fifteen

"Yo, what's up?"

"E, where you at, boo?" Melissa asked.

"I'm on Seventh coming up on Arbor School," Earth replied.

"Oh. Well, hurry up. I thought you got lost or something. The food's getting all cold, and I'm getting cold too," Melissa seductively stated.

"I'll be there in a few. Don't worry. I'll warm everything back up when I get there," Earth slyly remarked. "And I do mean *everything*."

"Umm, that's what's up. I'll be waiting, daddy," Melissa cooed.

Earth made a left turn at the light onto Rock Avenue as she hung up with Melissa. It had been some years since she had really hung and chilled in Plainfield, and she couldn't resist riding down the infamous Third Street Strip. This was the only strip in her town that from the beginning to the end, every block was actually drug infested.

Earth's head nodded with the rhythm and lyrics of Jay-Z's track, "The City Is Mine" as she turned onto West Third Street. Now floating down Third in her triple-black S500 Coupe, Earth smiled at the sight of the Elk's Mohawk Lodge on the corner of Third and Rushmore. On many occasions, she had partied, left with a nice redbone, or sometime got into beefs up in the monumental establishment with an occasional hater.

When she was growing up and first started running the streets, the area known as the Hilltop used to be flooded with hustlers like P-Love and Billheem, day in and day out, remembered Earth, but tonight, the area was a ghost town. Stopping at the corner of Third and Clinton now waiting on traffic to pass by, Earth observed a group of what she believed to be hustlers off to her left. The corner of South Second and Clinton was body infested. Before she had left Plainfield, the block had been run by her cousin Goldie. The last Earth had heard, he had blown trial and was now in prison.

As Earth came up on Halsey Street, she saw heads turning. She knew they were wondering who was pushing the Benz, but Earth's 5 percent tint made it difficult for them. She didn't recognize any of the faces as she drove by. Everyone appeared to be young. Earth knew the older heads from the known money-getting block. Names like Bo-Dee, Folge, OE, Malik, and Marcus Benjamin before he was killed during a carjacking came to Earth's mind.

As she approached Third and Monroe, she was not surprised to see the heavy human traffic flow. For as long as she could remember, Monroe had always been a live spot. This was the block hustlers like Master Love and a female name Wompa had established their legendary names long ago. As she got closer to the notorious block, it dawned on Earth that predominantly everyone out there had some form of the color red on. Instantly, Earth realized that Monroe Avenue had become a Bloods' set. One kid tried to flag her down, but she paid him no mind. To her left, Earth noticed that the once-popular block called Pond Place was now deserted. Back when crack had first come to town, a kid named Tizz was making noise around there before he had relocated to the New Projects. Pond Place was definitely the place to be back in the day she recalled.

As Earth rode past the next two blocks, she just shook her head. Both Third and Prescott and Third and Stebbins were blocks that had lost some legendary street icons to either the system or cemetery. Earth had read in the papers how Rodney Mac, who was originally from the Old Projects, and Opie from Prescott, had received life in the feds while Ronnie and Eric Mac had received lengthy sentences. All brothers and cousins. Earth could only imagine what their family must have been going through.

The death of Shap from Stebbins was very tragic and emotional for many remembered Earth, including herself. Shap's mother, Ms. Elsie, and Earth's mom were close, so Shap was like family to her. His death in 1991 had triggered off a riot on Third Street after he had been struck and killed on his motorcycle by a speeding driver. It was said that the Stebbins Place hustlers caught the driver, who was West Indian, pulled him out of the car, and retaliated. Earth couldn't help but laugh, remembering getting into a beef with one of the younger Carters from the block. It was Hassan, a cousin to the Carter family, who had squashed the altercation. It had just dawned on her that her friend Hassan Carter had been locked up for nearly twenty years for murder when he was only a teenager.

Earth crossed the intersection of Third and Grant and wondered if after all these years the Hawthorne family still owned the house on the corner. It was because of some of the younger Hawthornes that Grant Avenue was such a popular spot. As Earth rode past Spooner Avenue, she saw two luxury vehicles parked back to back on the corner and knew they had to belong to the female duo Paulette and Niecy. They were two chicks in the game that Earth had always admired and respected. They reminded her of herself and Heaven. Unsurprisingly, the next block was flooded with young dealers doing what they do. Third and Muhlenberg had always been full of hustlers on the rise recalled Earth. Melissa had told her about a young legend named Hollywood being stabbed and killed at Chez Maree, a local club on the North Plainfield side of Watchung Avenue. Earth knew Hollywood was the cousin of her childhood friend Money Kev.

She had heard about the death of Rashaun who was the brother of her friend Obie. Melissa had also told Earth about how the murder rate in Plainfield had tripled its initial record within the last year due to gang and drug-related incidents. Earth was not in the least bit surprised, though. For the past seven to eight years, that had been the case all throughout New Jersey and the rest of the East Coast. Drugs and violence had always gone hand in hand, even before Earth had been born, but what amazed her was how the West

Coast origin of Bloods and Crips gangs was so heavily adopted on the East Coast as of lately. Earth knew that what she and Heaven were involved in was far from being righteous, and she never tried to justify her lifestyle but felt that the sudden uprising and embrace of gang affiliation was the leading contributor to the rapid demise of black youth.

Now reaching Third and Plainfield Avenue, Earth stared ahead at the small housing projects known as the Old Projects, a.k.a. "The Bricks." Although she was from the New Projects, many of nights Earth recalled hanging out in the smaller development where her homegirl Lisa Silas was from. Besides, most of Earth's family had lived in the Bricks when she was a kid, including her mother's mother. She had one of the largest families, if not the largest, in her hometown. Last names like Benjamin, Bennett, Banks, Spann, Best, Sterling, Casey, and Darby dominated her city and made it seem as if she was related to the entire Plainfield.

Earth reminisced on how she use to go night swimming at the Plainfield Avenue Pool with some of her cousins, skate in the tennis court, and just hang out in the field and basketball court watching the older heads getting their hustle and dice game on. Even back then, Earth knew that she would grow up and get money. Her project was known for selling crack when she got into the game, and the Bricks was known for dope, so Earth hustled back and forth selling them both. It was in the Bricks Earth had befriended ghetto superstars like Bisquit, Al-Mateen, Amazing, Path, and Devine, who Earth had heard through Melissa had recently been caught by the feds in New Mexico. From what her cousin Wanda Best had told her when they were down in Clinton, her younger cousin Azzie controlled a great deal of the project's flow until the feds had run down on him after a female agent went undercover to set him up.

Earth was tempted to ride around her old stomping grounds but thought better of it. She knew there was a possibility she'd get caught up if she ran into some of her old street colleagues, especially her peoples Biggs, who she had heard had come home and turned it up in the game. Knowing she wouldn't hear the end of Melissa's mouth, Earth hooked a left onto Plainfield Avenue. Coming under the bridge, she then bucked a right onto West Second Street where the projects she had been born and raised in were located. The first thing she spotted were the two telephones that sat on the corner. She smiled. The two phones had been there for as long as she could remember. The numbers remained the same since she was a kid. Earth wondered if they had been changed after all these years. She came up on the first two buildings of the housing projects, 544 and 540. She remembered the buildings being the only two that no one ever tried to hustle out of until a brother a few years younger than her that resided in the 540 building entered the game and turned it up.

Earth noticed all the heads in the middle section of her projects where buildings 536 and 532 were located. Once upon a time, one of her childhood friends controlled the majority of money flow that came through there, but after a big raid in the town, he was convicted of being responsible for supplying nearly thirty drug houses. After he served his time, Earth heard he had given up the game. She didn't recognize any of the new faces but was sure that they had to have been the younger brothers and cousins of the pioneers of the New Projects. It had always been that way, thought Earth as she came up on the building she had been raised in and hustled out of. Seeing 528 and 524 known as "the front" brought back many memories for her. She had lived in building 524. Her living room window faced the outside of the front. Earth would stare out the window for hours, watching her young cousins Pete, Squirm, and Raheem compete with other money getters like the Godley and the Smith brothers while raking in numerous dollars daily. Earth laughed to herself remembering how the older hustlers complained over how hard her cousin Squirm, the younger of the two brothers, hustled. She watched as he hustled circles around some of the dealers and their workers. By the time Earth had gotten into the game, her two cousins had already taken their hustle game to another level and started getting paper down in the dirty. The last Earth had heard was that her cousin Squirm had served time in the feds and had written a few books that were published while Pete had retired from the game completely.

Passing Second and Elmwood Place, Earth glanced to her left and noticed a dice game going on in the middle of the block where building 120 and 116 were located as she rode by. At one point, everybody had hustled in the area known as "the back." Two of Earth's other longtime friends and project legends were from building 120. She knew they had to be hood rich by now or else close to it. As for building 116, that was once the building of all buildings, remembered

Earth. It was the one the duo Krush and Wajdee had on fire. The two had dominated the early and mid-eighties around the projects. They were passing out packages to any and everybody back in the day as if it were government cheese. Earth couldn't help but think about how they, along with others, were major contributors to why the Second Street Housing Projects had been deemed the Crack Capital of Plainfield.

Reaching the corner of West Second and Liberty Street at the bridge, Earth slowed down, then zoomed past and up the street headed for Melissa's Meadowbrook Village. Earth couldn't believe they had converted the once-roughest housing projects in town into condos. These were the same projects where a black female officer was gunned down in the back in the early eighties, which had been the final incident that caused the city to evict residents and condemn the vicious development. When Earth had gone off to prison, the area was abandoned, so this would be her first time seeing the reconstructed area.

A lot had changed in the town based on what Melissa had been telling her. It was hard for her to imagine the once-known money-getting block Arlington Avenue was no longer a place you'd see a heavy traffic flow of addicts and fiends.

Aside from the projects, they were the deepest hood in town. That was one of the few blocks Earth had actually been cool with the majority of the hustlers. She had gone to school with many of the younger hustlers.

As she got closer to Melissa's house, Earth thought of how her good friend Chuck's cousin Termite, who should have been the first Shaquille O'Neal before Shaq emerged, was killed, all over a beef that erupted over the decrease of the price of heroin. She shook her head as she reminisced about the frivolous deaths over the past twenty or so years since she'd been in the game. Now on West Front Street making her way to Melissa's, the track "I'm in Love with a Stripper" by T-Pain came over the radio. Instantly Earth thought of Keya. She changed the station immediately. Keya was now a thing of the past. Melissa was now the present and possibly the future, thought Earth as she crushed through the downtown area of Plainfield.

Chapter Sixteen

Heaven waited for the Caucasian woman to back out of the parking space in her Chrysler 300 so she could park. Heaven admired the pearl-white luxury car as the woman pulled out. She herself had wanted one of the Chryslers, but so many people had purchased them that she had changed her mind. Besides, people in the hood were referring to them as the poor man's GT Bentley, and for one, she was far from being poor; two, she already had a GT. So why settle for less when you can afford the best was her logic. It was not Heaven's intent to go to the Jersey Garden's Mall in Elizabeth today, but when she had gotten a call from a girlfriend of hers from Newark named Rashida, placing an order for some work, she decided to do a little spending afterward. Rashida was from Chancellor Avenue in the Weequahic section. She was one of the few females Heaven had known that was getting a nice piece of dough in the game.

Heaven had met Rashida at a club in East Orange called Bogie's back in the early nineties when she and Earth used to frequent the spot back when it was the Sunday hot spot. The two of them had somewhat met after practically going head to head in a dice game up in the club. Later that night when everyone had switched locations from Bogie's to the White Castles on Elizabeth Avenue in Newark, Heaven had noticed the white 5 series BMW with the chrome BBS rims pulled into the parking lot. At the time, Heaven also had a white 5 series Beamer with gold BBS rims, so the similar whip caught her attention. Curious about who the owner was, Heaven watched as the driver-side door opened and the same female she had just previously been involved in an intense dice game materialized. Also recognizing Heaven, Rashida approached her and complimented Heaven on her spotless BMW, and Heaven then returned the compliment.

Later, Heaven found out that the true difference between the two luxury vehicles was not only the color tone of their rims but that she had owned hers and Rashida's belonged to her boyfriend. That night, the two had exchanged info and Heaven had thought nothing else about it, until one day Rashida had called her out of the blue. She had explained to Heaven how her boyfriend had been locked up and she needed to make some money to bail him out. After discussing it over with Earth, Heaven let Rashida come to New Brunswick and hustle up enough paper to bail out her man. Rashida and her man had long ago broken up, but she and Heaven remained friends. This is why Rashida remained loyal when she got into the game for herself, vowing to only deal with Heaven and Earth as her connect.

Heaven parked her X5 BMW SUV and made her way inside the largest mall in New Jersey. Six outfits, three pairs of footwear, and a leather jacket later, she was exiting Jersey Garden Mall. As Heaven made her way to her truck, she disarmed her alarm, and as she did, a voice caught her attention.

"Excuse me, miss, are you about to pull out?" the baritone voiced asked.

When Heaven turned to see who the owner of the deep voice was, she saw a handsome bronze complexion peering out at her from the silver Dodge Magnum wagon sitting on twenty-four-inch chrome slippers. She was all too ready to give whoever it was behind her attitude because she was not in the mood for any lame pickup lines or come-ons, but something in this man's face told her that his motives were sincere. He was simply looking for a parking space.

"Yeah, I'm on my way out," Heaven replied softly.

"A'ight, that's what's up."

Heaven couldn't help but notice the Magnum driver looked as if he had just come from the barbershop. His dark, deeply rooted wavy hair was lined up without flaw and seemed to overlap at the same time like an incoming tide of an ocean. His shape-up was razor sharp to a tee as his jawbone was lined with facial hair that ran into his neatly trimmed goatee.

Sensing that she might have been staring far too long, Heaven snapped out of her daydreaming state and made her way to her Beamer truck. The man's smile only confirmed what she had thought she was doing, which was admiring him.

"Nice truck," he complimented.

"Thank you," Heaven responded closing and locking the hatch back. She then made her way to the driver's side of the X5 and stepped in slowly. She could literally feel the handsome, brown-skinned brother's eyes on her voluptuous backside and wanted to give him an eyeful. She was tempted to turn around and catch him in the act as a means to embarrass him, but she didn't take him for being the type of man to be easily embarrassed. Instead, Heaven waited until she was in her truck before looking back.

She pretended to be adjusting her rearview mirror when the Magnum driver's face came into view. To let her know he was checking her out also, the Magnum driver flashed another smile intentionally.

Although occasionally Heaven enjoyed a flirtatious moment, especially with someone who was nice on the eyes, she knew it was time to put an end to the charade. The way things were going in her life, the last thing she needed was to add a man to the equation. She had no desire to pursue or let any man pursue her at this time in her life. With that on her mind, Heaven started up her truck and began pulling out. Once she backed out, she waited until the Magnum pulled in before she drove off. Just as she passed by, Heaven noticed out of the corner of her eye that the Magnum driver was trying to get her attention. She pretended not to see him and kept going. Out of force of habit, Heaven took one more glance out of her rearview mirror. When she looked, there was something vaguely familiar about the Magnum driver standing there in the middle of the parking lot. Heaven had noticed it before but brushed it off. Now she was certain she and the handsome brother had crossed paths before, but she couldn't put her finger on where.

Chill cursed himself for slow rolling on pushing up on the attractive light-skinned sister. Normally, he would've made his move right off the bat with someone as fine as the X5 driver, but something about her made him move with caution. He could tell that she was feeling him and that the chemistry was there, but there was just something that prevented him from acting on it. Someone as bad as her, pushing a BMW truck, had to have a man he figured. Still, there was no denying what had just taken place. He made one last failed attempt to acquaint himself with the beautiful female stranger, and now she was gone. He hated letting the woman slip away so easily, but as he made his way to the entrance of the mall, his only thought was that if it was meant to be, then it would be.

Chapter Seventeen

"E, I'm starving. Let's go get something to eat," Melissa suggested as she lay seductively on her side in the nude next to Earth. She and Earth had just ended a sexual frenzy moments prior.

"All that eatin' you just did and you still ain't full?" Earth joked. "Babe, you greedy. I'm full after all of that pie I just ate," Earth continued jokingly in reference to the oral pleasure the two of them had previously performed on each other, sliding her hands between Melissa's legs.

"E, you nasty," Melissa chimed, mushing Earth upside the head. "Stop," she then said, removing Earth's hand, knowing if she let it stay what would come next. "I'm for real. Let's go to the Waffle House. Please," she begged submissively.

"Damn, Mel," Earth griped, addressing Melissa by the nickname only she called her. "We just can't order no pizza or something? I don't feel like getting up and getting dressed. I just wanna chill with my chick, sex you up, puff on something, get some rest, then wake up and do it all over again," Earth said with a devilish grin plastered across her face, reaching over to grab Melissa by the inner thigh for a second time.

"Tsk! Get off me," Melissa pouted, attempting to pull away with attitude.

Earth smiled. She knew Melissa was fronting. Earth knew that Melissa loved when she touched her like that. After all, it was her spot. Most of the time, that's all it took to turn Melissa on and have her inner thighs moisten.

"Oh, you don't want me touchin' you now?" Earth asked teasingly.

"No!" Melissa replied in a failed attempt to give Earth more attitude.

"So you don't want me touchin' you like this?" Earth rhetorically asked, finding her way to Melissa's clit, as she began to massage it with two fingers.

"*Sss!* E, stop," Melissa purred. "You *know* that's my spot."

"It is?" Earth whispered, fully aware as she continued gently massaging Melissa's G-spot. Melissa now lay flat on her back with her muscular legs spread eagle while Earth explored her sex. She moaned in ecstasy as she felt the wetness of Earth's lips on her breasts as Earth furthered her probe. Earth's breathe tickled Melissa's flesh, sending chills through her entire body as she accelerated her pace of fondling. Earth was driving Melissa wild. She was now licking her own lips and caressing her own breasts while Earth made her way south, kissing, licking, and sucking on her midriff. Each time Melissa felt Earth's teeth gently press down on her flesh she flinched, unable to control her reflexes, causing the muscles in her clit to contract.

Just when she thought she couldn't withstand the pleasurable torture Earth was performing on her, Melissa began to feel her love juices building up inside of her, and as if on cue, the floodgates opened and released themselves.

"Aaagh, she-iit!" Melissa cried out as Earth continued to massage her clit, knowing that she had brought Melissa to an intense climax.

She could feel Melissa's love cream pouring onto her fingers. Melissa moaned and bit down on her bottom lip. Earth's fingers gyrated her clit as she slid up and greeted Melissa with a passionate kiss. She then placed her middle finger in Melissa's mouth letting her taste her own sex.

"Umm," Melissa cooed. "*Now* can we go get something to eat?" she then asked seductively.

Earth removed her hand from between Melissa's legs and lay back on the queen-size bed.

"*Pss!*" she exclaimed reaching over to retrieve the already-rolled up blunt of Hydro.

"E!" Melissa continued to sigh.

Earth lit the L, inhaled its smoke and smiled, then exhaled the potent weed's residue.

"A'ight, a'ight, with ya spoiled ass," Earth gave in. "Let's knock this L out first."

Now Melissa was smiling. She knew she had won and was pleased.

"Thank you, baby," she softly replied in a childlike manner, taking the blunt from Earth.

Moments later, Earth turned left onto Park Avenue off of East Second Street. As they approached the infamous late-night area, she glanced over at Melissa and shook her head. Earth had expected as much, looking ahead.

"What?" Melissa asked dumbfounded, pretending not to know why Earth had shot her such a look, but in all honesty, Melissa knew. The same thoughts had crossed her mind as they turned on to the street of their intended destination.

"Nothin'," Earth answered dryly. The only thing on Earth's mind now was the fact that she was glad she had gone with her first instinct and traveled to her old stomping grounds with her .40 cal., seeing the body-infested area before them now. She knew it was a bad idea agreeing to bring Melissa up to the area historically known for its trouble during the early hours of the evening. The power of the pussy thought Earth as she internally cursed herself for allowing Melissa to persuade her.

"You wanna go somewhere else?" Melissa asked, seeing the disturbed look on Earth's face. She too now regretted her request to eat at the popular in-town after-hour spot legendary for its violence over the years.

"Nah, we good," Earth replied, pulling alongside the curb of Red Towers Restaurant as she crossed the light of West Fifth Street. Her mind was telling her to keep going, but her ego and pride convinced her to stop. It was times like this when Earth really felt that she was intended to be a dude at birth, but in the midst of the formation, was changed to a female.

Throwing the Benz in park, Earth couldn't help but reflect back to the good ole days of 1988 and '89 when the monumental spots The Diner and Red Towers were the places to be after a function or an event. Back when shootings and deaths were minimum, hating on another that was doing their thing didn't exist, cars were customized inside and out, stereo systems could be heard from blocks and blocks away, and guys and girls sported and rocked gold like they were kings and queens from the pyramid days. Those were the days, thought Earth while exiting the coupe.

All eyes were on Earth and Melissa immediately upon exiting the luxury vehicle. Earth caught the stares but paid them no attention. Everyone really began to lock in on the two when Melissa came from around the passenger side of the CLS and hooked her arm around Earth's. Guys' stares turned into mean mugs while chicks threw visual daggers and rolled eyes. With her red St. Louis Cardinals fitted, multicolored LRG jacket, baggy True Religion jeans, and white-on-white Uptowns on, Earth knew that it was difficult to distinguish her gender, so she was certain that she was being mistaken for a dude, which created the majority of the funny stares. Being from Plainfield herself, she knew how funny people in the streets were about out-of-towners coming to their neck of the woods. They did not take too kindly to it, especially if it was a male coming to visit a female from the town. Earth herself had joined in an occasional beat down of an out-of-towner at The Diner or local hangout back in the day on both males and females. But despite Plainfield being her birthplace and original stomping grounds, she continued to let the crowd assume she was a foreigner as well as mistaking her gender. She could care less about the opinions they all were formulating.

As she and Melissa waited for incoming traffic to pass to cross the street, Earth noticed a clique of females having a conversation with two guys off to her far left. Although she didn't know them, she had seen them before. She remembered as if it were yesterday when she had seen the four chicks in the Cinderella strip club out in Elizabeth the night she had escorted Lite out there to dance. She wondered if they remembered her or if they had even noticed her presence. A familiar feeling began to overcome Earth. A feeling that had been a part of her since she was a youngin'. It was the same feeling she had gotten when danger was near, something she had named her "spider senses."

As she and Melissa floated across the street, Earth felt the crowd's eyes on her. At that moment, she knew she had two choices. One, she could keep it moving and not entertain what she knew would come behind looking in the clique's direction, or two, match their stares and let the chips fall where they may. Without hesitation, Earth chose the option she normally would under any similar circumstance. As she turned her head in the crowd's direction, there was no doubt in her mind whether she had been remembered as she and one of the girls with whom she had a minor verbal spar and altercation over a spilled drink made eye contact.

Earth recalled the manly looking heavyset chick next to her receiving a lap dance at the bar from one of the dancers while Lite slow grinded on her. Unable to control herself from the dance, Earth remembered the girl bumping her and knocking over her own drink, but credited the spill to Earth, demanding that she replace the cranberry and Rémy. Earth saw that the girl was more than tipsy and had brushed the statement off, returning back to her session with Lite. However, she was interrupted with a tap on the shoulder. Knowing who was the cause of the interruption, without even bothering to turn around, Earth grabbed the pudgy hand and squeezed the girl's fat fingers tightly, then spun around.

Before anything could jump off, the girl's female entourage had observed the commotion and peacefully escorted their partner out of the strip club, knowing that she was drunk and most likely the instigator. As they were literally dragging their girl out of the club, Earth was able to hear the loose threat the heavyset female had thrown her way. Judging by the constant stares from the particular crowd, it was apparent to

Earth that this may well be the night that the girl intended to cash in on her threat. It was also apparent to her that the same burly chick was intoxicated again. Earth went on full alert. She stopped in her tracks and watched as the girl drunkenly staggered in her direction with her crew trailing. They too seemed to have had one too many, thought Earth.

"E, let's just go," Melissa suggested, now tugging on Earth's arm.

"Just go get in the car," Earth said, hitting the alarm to the Benz while keeping her eyes locked on the intoxicated women.

"What's really good now, bitch, you in *my* hood now," Earth heard the drunken girl slur.

Seeing the potential altercation arising, people began to pour out of the two after-hour spots and spill out into the streets. That was one thing about Plainfield, thought Earth. They loved drama and loved beef even more.

Earth continued to stand there as the drunken girl approached. Once the girl was within three feet of Earth, she threw up her fist in the air in attack mode. Still, Earth didn't budge. She remained calm, contemplating on how she intended to handle the situation. By now, both dudes and chicks began to yell out, hyping up the situation.

"Beat dat bitch ass," her girls called out in unison.

"What the fuck she fightin' a dude for?" Earth heard someone among the crowd of people asked.

"Represent, Tee-Tee," others screamed.

The fact that the raw Hennessy she had been downing the entire night at Richmond Beer Gardens strip club had her thinking she was Queen Kong, Tee-Tee made her move.

"Bitch!" she yelled as the right hook she intended to land on Earth's face was launched. Earth smiled as she sidestepped the weak punch that was televised. The throw reminded her of *The Matrix* as she watched it go by as the girl stumbled and fell to the ground. As she looked, she saw Melissa still standing there. The look on her face told Earth that more trouble was behind her. When she turned, Earth saw the remainder of Tee-Tee's crew headed her way.

"Bitch, you think you just gonna come to the muthafuckin' Field and get that shit off on our homegirl?" another rough but slimmer-looking chick shouted.

"We gonna beat cha ass," another joined. Growing tired of the situation, before the three approaching girls could reach where she stood,

Earth pulled the .40 caliber from behind her back and cocked it. The facial expressions on the three hood rat-looking females were priceless, thought Earth as she pointed the barrel of the gun in their direction. Instantly, those in fear scattered and scurried, while others who were used to seeing weapons drawn stood at bay.

"E, no," Melissa cried.

"Shut the fuck up and get in the funkin' car," Earth barked without looking back. Her demeanor had switched from calm to deadly.

Melissa did as she was told as tears began to form in her eyes. The last thing she wanted was for something to happen to her lover, but what she didn't know was Earth was the one in full control.

"You li'l bitches think you gangstas," Earth spit. "You dirty bitches ain't gangstas," she roared, becoming angered at what the four apparently young girls thought they were going to do to her.

"You don't rep the Field, you bum-ass bitches. *I'm* from the Field too," Earth announced, feeling the need to let everyone know in case someone decided to play super-save-a-ho just because they thought someone from out of town had the hometown hostages at gunpoint.

"We're sorry, we didn't kn—" one of the girls tried to apologize for her crew's stupid behavior, but Earth cut her short.

"I don't wanna hear that shit," she spat. She was beyond reasoning. She wanted to do more than just inflict fear into the females who intended to bring her harm. She wanted to embarrass and humiliate them for their disrespect toward her. Earth waved her gun at each female that stood before her. "You low-budget bitches take all of that country shit you wearing off," she ordered.

Each girl gave Earth a puzzling look as if she was speaking a language foreign to them, then looked back and forth at each other.

"*Bwow!*" The echoing sound came out of nowhere. "You heard what the fuck I said," Earth barked. The shot she let off was within inches of the women, sobering them all instantly. Wide-eyed, each woman began to rapidly peel out of their weekend party outfits. At one point, Tee-Tee was thinking of ways to sneak attack Earth from behind but hearing the shot that Earth had let off only confirmed that it would be a costly mistake.

Thinking better of it, Tee-Tee remained in her position under the parked SUV as she watched her three partners strip naked in the middle of the street. Onlookers couldn't help but stare as the three females, in tears, peeled out of their clothing. Some of the men and women shot heckles and laughed at the mismatched and worn-out panty and bra sets the females wore while others made comments about stretch marks, scars, and the body shapes of the trio. Earth also watched while admiring one of the young girl's body in spite of her rage. She was tempted to further her humiliation by gun fucking them all in front of everyone but decided against it. Now was not the time to go overboard any more than she already had. Instead, she had other plans.

"Now, back the fuck up!"

The three girls did as they were told. Earth then walked over and scooped up all the debris of clothing.

"Oh, shit, that's Earth, from my hood," one of the older heads laughed, recognizing his friend. He was now glad he hadn't pulled out his own .40 cal to assist the young girls. It was his intent to bed one of the girls for the night until the incident transpired.

Earth knew the voice without having to see the face. She knew it belonged to a childhood friend from the housing projects where she had lived. There was no time for socializing or strolling down memory lane, she thought. She was surprised she had managed to get all that she had just done off without any police showing up. With weapon still drawn, Earth backed up to her Benz counting her blessings, not wanting to wear out her welcome any longer. She then threw the clothes in the backseat of her car and hopped in the driver's seat. Everyone was still standing around watching, each person in their own thought having their own opinion of what had just taken place. When Earth got in the car, she didn't have to look over at Melissa to know she was fuming. *Serves her right,* thought Earth, placing some of the blame on Mel for the situation that could have gotten ugly and gone against her favor had she not been strapped. Just as she peeled off, Earth rolled down her passenger window as she made a quick U-turn and screeched to a halt.

"Krush, let them dizzy bitches know who I am!" and then she was gone.

Chapter Eighteen

Three weeks later, Heaven and Earth went out to their favorite eating spot to celebrate their peaceful weeks around their hood. Despite the countless altercations they had been involved in, things around their way were mellow, and it was back to business as usual.

"Damn, a bitch full off them steak and eggs," Earth complimented as she and Heaven exited the late-night diner.

"You ain't never lied," Heaven agreed, feeling the same way about the blueberry waffles with ice cream she had just eaten. "I could use a blunt right about now."

"You ain't said nothing," Earth shot back, pulling out a fluffy dime bag of Haze and a Dutch Master cigar from the inside pocket of her Rocawear leather. "I'll drive while you roll up," she told Heaven.

Heaven shot her a funny look. "What?" she said as if Earth had lost her mind. It was no secret; Heaven had never let anyone drive her

GT Bentley, not even her road dawg, Earth. That was her baby, her pride and joy, and she had vowed never to let anyone behind the wheel as long as she owned it. "Girl, you buggin'!" Heaven exclaimed. "You know how I am about my baby."

"Bitch, ain't nobody gonna crash ya shit up," Earth spit. "Besides, we're only five minutes away from your crib. Gimme the keys and stop playin'."

Heaven listened while Earth talked but was still skeptical. Earth was right; they were only a few minutes away from her house, but anything could happen in five minutes. Especially when Heaven knew that Earth was known to be a reckless driver. In three years, Earth had crashed one car, a truck, and totaled another one. And Heaven did not want to include her prized possession in that ratio.

"Heaven, throw me the keys. I promise I'll do under the limit and even put on my seat belt," Earth promised as if to read Heaven's mind. Against her better judgment and with extreme reluctance, Heaven tossed her Bentley keys to Earth. In exchange, Earth handed her the bag of marijuana and a cigar.

Earth disarmed the alarm and climbed into the driver's seat. She immediately began to adjust the butter soft seat to a comfortable position while Heaven hopped in the passenger side.

"What other CDs you got in here?" Earth asked, searching through her console.

"I got Jay-Z's *Blueprint 3*."

"Oh yeah? Where's that at?"

"It's already in there," Heaven replied.

"A'ight. I wanna hear the first track."

"That shit hard, right?"

"Hell yeah," Earth answered putting the key into the ignition.

Earth reached for the stereo dial and increased the volume before backing out while Heaven rolled up the fluffy bag of weed.

"What we talkin' about? Real shit, or we talkin' about rhymes. You talkin' about millions, or you talkin' about mine?" were the words that came blaring out of the GT's speakers. Earth began to nod her head to Jay-Z's metaphor as she rapped along.

"What we talkin' about? Fiction, or we talkin' about fact?" Jay-Z continued as Heaven joined in with him and Earth.

Between both of them being engrossed in the song, Earth focused on backing out of the parking lot and Heaven preoccupied with the drying process of the blunt with her cigarette lighter, neither of the two ever noticed the two 750 CBR motorcycles approaching from the left side—until it was too late.

"Brrrgaah! Brrrgaah! Brrrgaah!"
"Brrrgaah! Brrrgaah! Brrrgaah!"

The GT Bentley slammed into the back of a parked car as the bullets tore into Earth from the shooters' .40 cal., causing her to lose control of the wheel while Heaven's own body was pumped with hot slugs.

They never knew what hit them as they sat slumped over and motionless in the GT Bentley.

Chapter Nineteen

One week later . . .

"Omg, I think I just seen her eyelids move," Le Le screamed.

"You sure?" Shell and Sonya both asked in unison, hopping out of their chairs.

"Yeah."

"Shell, go and get the nurse," Sonya instructed.

"Okay," Shell replied, already making her way toward the nurses' station.

It had been a long and stressful seven days for the three women ever since they had found out about the incident that night at The Diner involving Heaven and Earth. Day in and day out, they had been at the hospital faithfully. The word had spread throughout all of New Brunswick like wildfire about Heaven's Bentley being shot up with both her and Earth inside. Many had come to pay their respects, but that had soon fizzled out after a week. Neither Heaven nor

Earth had any immediate family that was worth notifying, aside for Le Le, Shell, and Sonya. All they had were one another.

For the past week, Seamen Street and Lee Avenue had been officially shut down. At least, the part that was run by Heaven and Earth. Not out of fear of not being able to maintain because, if the occasion arose, each one of them felt that they would step up the game and handle their business, whether on the money tip or beef. For them, it was out of love, loyalty, and most importantly, respect. None of them would ever think about going against the grain by making their own moves or any decisions in regards to their block without consulting with either Heaven and Earth or both of them. Besides, they all had enough paper to hold them down until that was the case. Now, here it was, there was a possibility that they had gotten a breakthrough.

"Sweetheart, can you hear me?" the nurse asked but received no response. Trying a different approach, she said, "If you can hear me blink your eyes."

Still there was nothing.

"Young lady, are you sure you saw something?" the nurse asked Le Le.

"Yes, I'm sure," Le Le retorted with attitude.

"Well, there is nothing now."

"Oh shit," Sonya shouted, drawing everyone's attention to her.

"What?" Shell asked.

"Yeah, what?" Le Le followed.

"Look," she said pointing to the bed.

"I'll go call the doctor," the nurse offered seeing her patient's eyelids flutter.

"I told y'all," Le Le said. "Heaven?" she called out. "Can you hear me?"

"Heaven, it's us, your girls," Shell said with teary eyes.

"Heaven, please open your eyes," Sonya sighed, her eyes becoming teary-eyed as well.

By now, all three girls had tears cascading down their faces as Heaven's eyelids continued to fight with the decision to open or not. You could see tears beginning to trickle down Heaven's face as she battled with herself to overcome the challenge. As she fought, Le Le, Shell, and Sonya continued with their words of encouragement in hopes that Heaven heard them.

"*Vamos, despierta. Abre los ojos,*" Shell cried, pleading for Heaven to open her eyes and wake up.

"Yeah, you can do it," Le Le followed up with.

"Please, wake up," Sonya said in the same tearful manner. Then, as if to answer their prayers and pleas, miraculously, Heaven's eyes opened.

The cries and sounds of joy could be heard throughout the entire hospital wing when Le Le, Shell, and Sonya saw Heaven's eyes fly open. One would have thought a stadium full of NFL football fans had a team that just won the Super Bowl by the sounds that came from Heaven's bedside in the hospital room.

"What's going on?" Heaven managed to ask in a husky tone, still somewhat in a daze of confusion and pain.

"Are you all right?" Le Le asked through her sobs.

"Yeah, where the hell am I?" Heaven replied glancing around the room. Noticing all of the machinery and seeing the tubes running from the equipment to her, it dawned on her after she had asked.

"You're in the hospital, ma," Shell answered.

"What happened?"

"You were shot," Sonya said. "Once in the abdomen, your chest, and a graze to the head."

"Huh?" she said confused. But as she tried to shift her body and lift up, the pain she felt confirmed the half. "Agh," she moaned.

"*Tranquilo,*" Shell said, reaching out to help Heaven sit up.

"I got it," Heaven replied, straining to gain position.

"Where was I when I got hit?"

"You and Earth were leaving The Diner," Sonya told her.

Hearing the restaurant and her partner's name, Heaven's mind began to race.

"Where's Earth?" she asked. Le Le, Shell, and Sonya all looked at one another in silence.

"Did you hear me? Agh," Heaven asked raising her voice in pain. "Where the fuck is Earth at?"

"Heaven," Le Le started as tears began to resurface in her eyes. "Earth didn't—" "No, Le, don't tell me that," Heaven cried out already thinking the worst. The night at The Diner was now all coming back to her. She remembered the two of them leaving their favorite restaurant and how Earth had convinced her to let her drive her GT Bentley while she rolled up a blunt. The last thing she recalled was the two motorcycles with two riders, each one speeding off after they had unloaded on the car just before she had lost consciousness. "No-nooo-nooo, that shit can't be true," Heaven said in disbelief.

She did not want to believe that her partner in crime, her road dawg, sister, and most importantly, best friend, was gone. After all they had been through and survived together, thought Heaven. How could it come down to this?

"Who was it?"

"We don't know," the three of them said.

"What the fuck you mean you don't know?" she barked. "How long I been here?"

"About a week," Le Le answered.

"And we been here since day one," Sonya added. Heaven could see the exhaustion in their faces as they stood there by her bedside and knew that Sonya's words were true. Had things been different she would have been more compassionate toward them, but right now, there was no room for her to show any sign of weakness or become soft. Her right hand had just been brutally murdered, and it was now up to her to see to it that street justice be served.

"Look, I appreciate y'all holdin' me down and all while I was laid up, but you should've been out there with your ear to the ground tryin'a find out who the fuck violated. Y'all ain't doin' me or Earth any good up in here right now. I'm, I'ma be a'ight. When I get up outta this bitch, I'ma—"

"Praise God," Heaven's nurse strolled in with the doctor causing Heaven to cut her conversation short.

"Ms. Jacobs it's good to see you're awake," the doctor said approaching with a smile. "How are you feeling?"

"Fine," Heaven replied. "A little sore, though."

"That's understandable, considering you went through a rough ride. You gave your friends here a good scare."

"I heard," Heaven passively retorted.

"Well, not to worry, the hard part is over. It only gets better from here," the elderly, gray-haired African American doctor assured her. "Now, young ladies, if you'll excuse me, I need to examine my patient." He directed his words to Le Le, Shell, and Sonya.

"No problem, Doc," Sonya answered for all of them.

Each one of them then went over to Heaven and kissed her good-bye as she lay there motion-less; rather speaking it, she gave each one a look that indicated that she wanted them to carry out her initial statement. Moments later, they were out the door.

As the doctor conducted his examination, Heaven was conducting her own examination in her mind, playing back the chain of events inside her head that had occurred prior to her being wounded and Earth's demise. Every beef or alteration that they had been in for the past few months bounced around in her mind. The shooting out on Remsen Avenue, when she and Earth had gunned down the dude who had

smacked up and robbed Le Le, the guy who
Sonya had cut in the face and she and Earth
had shot at over a dice game, then Earth's altercation with Keya up in Dolce's over some jeal-
ousy shit that led to some dude getting busted
in the head with a Rosé bottle. And lastly, the
dude Rock had told her about that same night
from South Trenton who was overheard talking
about running down on some chicks from New
Brunswick who he believed to be them. With all
of these incidents weighing heavy on Heaven's
mental, the thought had given her a migraine.
Due to the pain she was in, combined with the
anesthesia they had given her, Heaven was in
no condition to think straight. As she began
to drift back off into a slumber while the doctor continued his exam, the only thought on
Heaven's mind was revenge.

Chapter Twenty

"Brrrgaaah—Brrrgaaah."

The sounds of the rapid gunfire woke Heaven out of the nightmare that had just moments ago had her tossing and turning. When she opened her eyes, she was somewhat startled by the two unfamiliar bodies standing by her bedside. Now regaining her visual focus, it was apparent to Heaven that the male-female duo were not doctors, and she instantly became disturbed by their presence. Judging by their attire, it was obvious to her that they were the police. Mentally, Heaven began to prepare herself for the interrogation that she knew was to come but was in no mood for as she put on her game face.

"Ms. Jacobs, glad to have you back with us. I'm Detective Saleski," the excessively overweight Caucasian male expressed, trying his hardest to sound sincere.

His partner, who was African American, revealed a sympathetic smile. "And I'm Detective Crawford," she joined in.

"We're from the New Brunswick Homicide Division," Detective Saleski continued, extending his business card in Heaven's direction. Heaven gave the card a blank stare before hesitantly reaching out to accept it. She didn't even bother to look at it, already knowing that she would never use it, not only because it was the code of the streets, but also because she had other plans on her mind for whomever violated.

Detective Saleski noticed the disinterest in his card and was not in the least bit surprised. He had expected as much. He knew the history on the female tag team, more so Heaven, stemming back to juvenile days, because she was from New Brunswick. He reviewed Heaven's criminal record and saw that she had several run-ins with the law before the age of eighteen. When her partner Earth arrived on the scene, Detective Saleski had asked the local informants around town about the female duo and found out more than he had bargained for. At first, he couldn't believe some of the stories he had heard about the pretty young women, but in his sixteen years in law enforcement, nowadays, nothing surprised him. The only thing that did surprise Detective Saleski about the two was the fact that prior to the present incident, neither of their names had come across his desk, especially Eartha Davis's. Having had some connects with the Plainfield Police Department, after hearing about the two, he had researched Earth's extracurricular in the streets. From what was told to him by his good friend and colleague Frank Wilson of Plainfield's police department, Eartha Davis, just like her mother, was a rough customer. It made sense to Detective Saleski. Brains and bronze, he thought, knowing that Heavenly Jacobs and Earth Davis were made for each other. According to another of his colleagues, Paul Schuster, of the narcotics force, and locals, whenever opportunity presented itself, Heaven and Earth had always expressed their disdain for New Brunswick's finest, which is why when he and his partner were assigned to the case and he heard the involved parties, he knew that it would be like pulling teeth. But still, he had a job to do, and he intended to do just that. Despite his personal feelings, today, he told himself that Heavenly Jacobs was not the accused; she was the victim.

"My partner and I were assigned to the shooting that took place a week ago involving you and the deceased Ms. Eartha Davis up at The Diner," Detective Saleski stated.

Hearing her road dawg being referred to as the "deceased" caused the pit of Heaven's stomach to boil. The thought of her right hand being gone was still overwhelming to her. She fought back the tears of anger that were building up inside of her. She refused to let the Caucasian detective or the woman see her vulnerability, allowing them to pass judgment. Like her partner in crime, Heaven was a thoroughbred, and she intended to maintain as just that. Detective Saleski saw right through the façade that Heaven was portraying. He had seen it countless times, and it always amazed him. People from the streets pretended to be so hard, and when a tragedy occurs, rather than seeking help, they feel compelled to keep up their front. The detective continued with his job as he tried to minimize the growing tension.

"Ms. Jacobs, we understand that this is a bad time for you, losing your friend and all, and on behalf of my partner and I, let me apologize for the inconvenience. I know that the situation is still fresh, but the fact of the matter is, I need to ask you a few questions about the incident so my partner and I can do what we do best. Do you understand that?"

Heaven listened, giving no response or even indication that she had heard him. She was in no mood to be answering anything, and even if she was, she wouldn't, especially when it was the authorities who were doing the questioning. Police and Heaven had never seen eye to eye. She had lived a lawless life, having no respect or regards for any authoritative figure. She couldn't even stand being in the same vicinity with a cop, but aside from her personal views, Heaven knew that her encounter with the detectives was inevitable based on what had happened to her and Earth. She wanted nothing more than for justice to be served to the perpetrators and her partner's murderers be punished, but street justice was on her mind. She wanted to be the arrester, judge, jury, and executer. But for now, Heaven knew that she had to play her cards close to her chest on this one, careful not to expose her hand or anything that could possibly be used against her at a later date. She cautioned her words in her mind before she finally decided to acknowledge the detective's question. "There's nothing that I can really tell you," she began clearing her throat, "that you probably don't already know," she ended in a raspy tone.

Her throat was parched from the medication being fed to her through the intravenous tube in her arm. Her response didn't come as a shock to the detective, although he was hoping for a miracle. Getting Heaven to cooperate with him and his partner was not going to be a walk in the park he knew.

"Ms. Jacobs, like I stated earlier, I realize that this a difficult time for you right now," he compassionately said. "And it's apparent to me and my partner that you've suffered a great loss. We're not here as the bad guys; we're here to help put away whoever did this to you and your friend, and the only way that we can do that is with your cooperation. We'd just like to hear in your own words what you remember or can recall about that evening . . . Anything that may point us in the right direction and help us solve this case in as fast of a manner as possible."

Heaven pretended to be listening to the detective, but her mind was actually somewhere else. As painful as it was for her, Heaven was preoccupied with playing back the tapes inside her head of what had happened just a couple of weeks ago, trying to make sense of things, but so many thoughts flowed through her mind that she could not gather them altogether. Images of the last time Heaven had seen her partner in crime alive invaded her thoughts the most, but she couldn't help but dwell on the two motorcycles with double riders on each bike that had changed her life forever. She tried to lock in on the scenery in her mind as the same scene played. All she could remember was the two bikes speeding away just before she closed her eyes. A glimpse of something else flashed in and out of her mind, but she could not make out what exactly the images were. The more she tried, the more she began to catch a migraine by the tragic event.

Tears managed to escape Heaven's eyes at the thought of the eventful night, but her tears were not of sadness. These were filled with anger and rage. Detective Crawford noticed the fluids spilling out of the sides of Heaven's eyes and felt compelled to console her. Initially, Detective Crawford and her partner agreed to let him handle the interview, feeling that Heaven would be more receptive to a man as opposed to a woman being as though she herself had played in a game dominated by men in the streets. Detective Crawford now realized that their decision and method was not the most effective one and not a good idea after all.

"The two of you must have been very close," Detective Crawford started out. Her words caused Heaven to snap out of her daze. "I have a twin sister, and she's my best friend. I couldn't imagine losing her," she continued, seeing that she had captured Heaven's attention. "My condolences to you for your loss, Ms. Jacobs. I understand that this is not the way that you're used to handling situations in life, and I respect that, but don't you want to see justice served and have your loved one rest in peace?" she asked in a passionate tone. She herself was becoming somewhat emotional just talking about the incident.

Heaven detected the sincerity in the detective's tone and felt that the woman actually did understand, to some degree, but still nothing or no one would make Heaven compromise her integrity or principles by involving the authorities in any street affairs of hers, or any affairs, for that matter. So many had fallen weak and sold their souls because they couldn't handle what comes with the streets and wanted out, or in many cases, couldn't do the time for the crimes they committed, so they became puppets for the system. Heaven knew that was not her caliber. She was cut from a different cloth, and despite the circumstances, if the situation were changed, she knew that Earth would have handled it the same and exact way.

"Thank you for your kindness," Heaven directed to Detective Crawford, "but like I said, I don't know anything. There is nothing that I can tell you that you don't already know," she ended in her most convincing tone, but neither Detective Saleski nor Crawford was convinced.

"Ms. Jacobs, you honestly don't have any idea or inclination who would want to do such a thing or why they would do it?" Detective Saleski was the first to say. "I mean, come on, Ms. Jacobs," he continued, "in your line of work, you don't have any rivals or people that may feel that you or Ms. Davis posed a threat? Maybe they felt the two of you were in the way or something? Are you, or was Ms. Davis, gang affiliated?" the detective asked in a semi-badgering manner. Detective Crawford felt that her partner was beginning to go a little overboard with his inquiries. Rather than interviewing, it was turning into an interrogation.

"Ms. Jacobs, you have my partner's card, and here is mine. If you think of anything that may be pertinent or of some use in our investigation, please don't hesitate to call us. Sorry to have disturbed you," Detective Crawford interjected, handing Heaven her business card. "Come on, Charlie," she added, grabbing her partner by the arm. Detective Saleski stared at Heaven for a moment, then shook his head. Heaven shot him daggers in return. He couldn't help but admire the tougher-than-nails persona Heaven was displaying, but the poor choice bothered him.

"Hope you reconsider," he dryly stated before following his partner out the door. As soon as the door closed behind them, Heaven placed the two cards together and tore them up. There was no way that she was going to allow the police—or anyone else—to assist her in her pursuit of justice. This was something she intended to do on her own.

Chapter Twenty-One

"Shell, how much is that?" Sonya asked as she separated the stack of bills she possessed in her hand according to their value.

"So far, it's nineteen grand, plus I still got all of this left," Shell replied, holding up a monstrous knot consisting of hundreds, fifties, and twenties.

For the past two weeks, it had been all business for Sonya and Shell. Ever since Heaven had regained consciousness and said what she had, they had gone back and had been hugging the block like no other. As of lately, they hadn't seen much of Le Le since her boyfriend had come home from prison. Both Sonya and Shell understood and were happy for their homegirl. They encouraged Le Le to spend quality time with her man while they held the block down and assured her that it would be there for her when she came back. It was Shell and Le Le who were actually the closest out of the three, but the incident with Heaven and Earth had drawn Shell and Sonya closer together in Le Le's absence.

"Shit startin' to pick back up since we been back out there, right?" Shell said in reference to the money flow on their block.

"Yeah, I was just thinking the same thing," Sonya replied. "Just two weeks ago, we couldn't even make a thousand dollars between the two of us. Now look."

"I know that block shit is crazy. Now, I see what Heaven and Earth had to go through when they first got this bitch jumping the way it was when we first came around here," Shell said.

"I miss them," Sonya sighed.

"Me too, *mami,*" Shell retorted in a similar tone.

"Damn, I can't believe Earth is gone," Sonya added.

Her eyes began to become mystified at the thought of the loss. It was Earth who had brought Sonya into the circle. Sonya was originally from New Brunswick, and since Earth's hometown of Plainfield was not that far, the two had traveled in the same circle before Earth had gone to prison. They had bumped heads at the Amboy movie theater, the rink out in Bergenfield, Echo Lanes bowling alley in Mountainside, and even the Jamaican Club out in Plainfield, which led to their acquaintance back in the day. Actually, after an intense evening/early morning in the

Reggae Club, partygoers would spill over into The Diner on Park Avenue in Plainfield. This was where you would find the hottest chicks and the brothers with the hottest whips posted up. This was also where you would go if you were trying to find someone to get your freak on with. That particular night, Sonya had been drinking heavily and smoking weed, and a group of dudes were there who intended to take full advantage of her condition, as they had in the past with others like her.

Despite having ridden up to The Diner with two of her girlfriends at the time, Sonya was left alone and found herself in a position that she was not coherently aware of or could get out of. That is, until Earth came to her rescue. Receiving backlash and practically being called every name in the book by the disappointed dudes, Earth successfully took Sonya up out of harm's way, returning her back to her so-called friends, but not before she smacked one of them and punched another in the face for their neglect and abandonment of their girl.

Weeks later, Sonya had tracked Earth down and thanked her for having her back after the incident was told to her. That day led to the two of them hanging out together for the remainder of the day. Before the day was out, they had found themselves up in a motel with Sonya embraced up in Earth's arms. That was the first and last time that Sonya had ever been with another woman and believed that would forever be Earth's and her secret as long as she lived. Shortly after, Earth had gone to prison, and when she came home, she bumped into Sonya down in Atlantic City at The Taj Mahal. After catching up, Sonya found herself joining the team that Earth told her about where she was one of the leaders. It had been on ever since.

"Sonya, you a'ight?" Shell asked, seeing the distraught state Sonya was now in. She couldn't have imagined the real reason behind Sonya's emotions.

"Yeah, I'm good," Sonya, replied. "I just can't wait for Heaven to come home, that's all."

"Me neither. This week's taken long as hell to end, and any other time, shit be flying; but don't worry, six days from now she'll be back with us."

"What do you think she's going do?" asked Sonya. "I mean, do you think she already knows or thinks she knows who did that shit?"

"If she do, she ain't sayin'. I guess we just have to see when she gets here."

"Who do you think it was?" Sonya asked, having her own suspicions.

"Really, it could be any muthafuckin' body, if you think about it," Shell replied.

"Look at all the shit we been in lately," she reminded Sonya as she began to run it down. "That nigga, what's his name? Twan, from Remsen with that shit that happened with Le Le. Them niggas could've found out who was behind that and got at 'em. Or how 'bout those two niggas that came around here that day we were shootin' dice? You remember the nigga you cut in the face, and we were shootin' at? Then that shit that kicked off up in Dolce's over that stripper bitch Earth use to mess with. That was that nigga Mustafa from up Elizabeth, and you know how they get down out there. And before that shit happened at Dolce's that day, I was up here baggin' up some of the work with Heaven and Earth, and they was talking about some nigga Black Rock that was telling Heaven at the club something about some nigga from South Trenton. They was sayin' how they had to find out who he was before he found them first. I should've asked what they was talking about, but you know how Earth used to act when it comes to a bitch being nosy."

Shell laughed at the thought of her fallen boss's temper. "Besides, that's the day Earth beat Le Le's ass, so after that, that shit went right out my mind 'cause I wasn't tryin'a be next."

"I feel you, girl, but out of all that shit, it gotta be one of them, or—" Sonya paused as if she had just discovered something.

"What if it wasn't none of them?"

Shell shot her a puzzled look. "Who else could it have been?" she asked.

"I don't know what made me think of this, but what about that chick from Plainfield Earth had been dealing with the past few weeks?"

"Who? The pretty, light-skinned one?" asked Shell, aware of whom Sonya was referring to.

"Yeah, what's the bitch name? Melissa, right?" Sonya shot back. "I mean, come on, Shell, don't it seem mighty strange that Earth start going back out there to Plainfield after all these years, and then, all of a sudden, this shit happens? Think about it. Not to be judging no chicks but as pretty as that red bitch was, she had to have a man or a girl, so what if some jealous ma'fucka forced her to tell him or her where to find or where to check? They probably found out she was cheating on them," Sonya rested.

"Wow," she expressed.

She was surprised by Sonya's theory, but at the same time, impressed. It had never dawned on her to entertain such a thought. But it did make sense to Shell. Sonya's assumption marinated inside her brain. "You know what, ma, you just might be on to something here," Shell added, becoming more convinced.

"I swear to God if that shit is true, I'ma go out to Plainfield and personally push that bitch myself," Sonya barked. She actually wanted it to be true because she needed someone to blame for the death of her partner in crime, and Melissa seemed like an eligible candidate.

"You know I'm with you all the way, *mamá,* but before we do anything or go flying off the handle half cocked, we gots to holla at Heaven and run it past her. See what she thinks, feel me?"

Sonya remained silent, and Shell knew what that meant.

"Sonya, you hear me? We got to holla at Heaven first," Shell repeated. "Just six more days and we can see what's really good. Promise me you'll be cool 'til then."

"Uh-huh," Sonya mumbled.

"Sonya, don't give me that. Let me hear you promise," Shell insisted. She wasn't convinced that Sonya was adhering to what she had said. After a long pause and hard stare, not to mention that Shell wasn't taking no for an answer, Sonya replied.

"Okay, I promise."

"That's my girl," Shell said relieved. "Now let's finish counting up this 'fetti so we can get out there and make some more," she added.

"You're right, let's do this," Sonya replied picking up the stack of bills she was once in the midst of counting, but rather having money on her mind at the moment, vengeance was the case.

Chapter Twenty-Two

At 7:30 in the morning, downtown Plainfield businesses were still asleep, at least for another two hours. All accept Melissa's favorite dining spot that she frequented every day at this time before she went off to her own nine-to-five in Newark. This had been her routine for years, even before she started working for Bank of America three years ago. Although she loved breakfast, she hated to cook it, so instead, she enjoyed the tasteful cooking at the hands of her favorite morning eatery. Despite this being her favorite, Melissa sat with a blank stare as she had for the past few days at the end table in Bill's Luncheon, waiting for the scrambled cheese and eggs, home fries, and wheat toast with a side of beef sausage. Ever since her lover's untimely demise, Melissa hadn't been the same. Just a week ago, she and Earth had been as happy as two lovebirds; now, her happiness had been replaced with sadness and pain. She had been an emotional wreck since the news, crying herself to sleep until her eyes became sore, and the first couple of days she had called out from work and buried herself in her own sorrow, restricting herself to her bedroom. She knew she couldn't go on like that and survive. Besides, she was sure that Earth would want her to be strong, remembering how she expressed to her how if she was going to be her ride-or-die chick, she had to be tough. Within days, Melissa had pulled herself together for Earth's sake and got back on track.

A smile appeared across Melissa's face as an image of Earth lying in her queen-sized bed with hands behind her head watching her lotion up after she had just finished showering flashed in her mind. She remembered how she asked Earth, "Do she like what you see?" And how her reply was, "Yeah, but I'd like it even better if you brought it closer to me." The thought of the passionate kiss the two had shared after that comment was a breathtaking thought. The way Earth pressed her lips gently up against Melissa's full, luscious ones melted her heart as Earth's tongue parted them. Melissa's head slightly slanted at the imaginary hand she envisioned being Earth palming the side of her face the way she always did, drawing her in closer to deepen their kiss.

Melissa could feel Earth reaching between her legs and inserting her two fingers slowly inside her. Her sex moistened at the thought. She inhaled as Earth's fingers toyed with her clit, then slid deep within the crevices of her wetness. Earth's kiss grew stronger, and the rhythm of her fingers increased. Melissa felt herself building up as she gyrated her hips into Earth's hand. The words, "make my pussy come," echoing in her ear through their lip-lock sent Melissa's body into overdrive. Her moans grew louder, and her pussy became wetter. She had reached her peak. The refreshing and pleasurable feeling was all too ready to escape, and Melissa welcomed it. She longed for the feeling, but her chain of thoughts was broken at the sound of the plate hitting the table. Standing over her was the waitress with her food. She stared up with an embarrassed expression written all over her face, hoping it hadn't told the truth of her thoughts. The waitress flashed an unknowingly smile and backpedaled away from the table before saying, "Enjoy."

Melissa looked around to see if anyone else might have been paying her any attention as she revisited one of her and her deceased lover's sexual encounters. She was thankful everyone seemed to be engulfed in their own meals and conversations. Melissa wasted no time cutting into her breakfast.

She couldn't help but notice the dampness of her panties. She shook her head and smiled.

Even in her death, Earth was still able to get her wet, she chuckled. She knew she had to scarf her breakfast down and double back home to change her thong and suit pants she was sure her juices had soiled. As she quickly ate, her meal was interrupted by the conversation taking place behind her. She was not particularly one to concern herself about another's business, but hearing the familiar name drew her immediate attention and interest.

"That bitch had it coming to her anyway," the female's voice behind her responded.

"Yeah, she had the game fucked up," another female voice joined in her best ghetto tone.

"I guess that night at The Diner, she didn't know who she was fuckin' with."

"Well, she a dead bitch now," the first voice started.

Hearing Earth's name and the mentioning of the incident she remembered transpiring at The Diner when she and Earth had gone up there for something to eat that evening made Melissa aware of who the three females were that were engrossed in the conversation. Her heart almost skipped a beat. Could it be? She couldn't believe sitting right behind her were the ones who had

taken her lover away from her, or at least had
something to do with it. Her mind went into
overdrive. She knew the females Earth had beef
with that night from the infamous hood rat crew
from East Sixth Street, so figured the killers had
to be some guys from the notorious drug block.
The more she thought about it, the more it made
sense. During the report of the shooting, Melissa
recalled the news saying someone had witnessed
two motorcycles carrying two masked men each
leaving the scene. Sixth Street was known for its
bike riders, as well as legendary for both toting
and busting their guns. To say she was speeding would be an understatement of how Melissa
felt at that moment. She was by far not a gangster, but the only thing on her mind now was
payback. She knew Heaven was still in the hospital, but her crew was still functioning. Melissa
made a mental note before the day ended she
would make a trip out to New Brunswick, but
first she had two phone calls to make; one to her
supervisor letting her know she needed to uti-
lize one other personal day, and the second one
to her younger cousin Mia who could assist her
in her personal business. Having lost her appe-
tite long ago, Melissa placed her normal ten dollars on the table, stood up leaving her unfinished
breakfast, and exited Bill's Luncheon.

Chapter Twenty-Three

Melissa sat on edge as she watched her younger cousin in awe loading up the two semi-automatic handguns. After she placed the call and met up with Mia at her Sandford Avenue apartment to fill her in on the situation and its details, Melissa was not surprised by her young thuggish family member's reaction. Although she knew Mia's main reason for agreeing to go through with what she intended to do was on the strength of the love she had for her, a portion of it also was out of the respect she had for Earth. Being a young gay female herself, not to mention an upcoming female hustler in the city of Plainfield, Mia was instantly drawn to Earth when Melissa had introduce the two. There was nothing remotely close to the attraction being sexual. Mia considered herself to be a good judge of character and dealt with people and situations based on vibe, and she had gotten nothing but good ones and had only heard good things from the streets, which confirmed her vibe when it came to Earth. Since then, the two had been keeping connected, unbeknownst to Melissa. There was no way her older cousin could have known that she held Earth in the highest regards and looked at her as a mentor not only as a female playing a man's game, but also the game of life. Earth had schooled her on so much and dropped so many drinks on her that her mind became intoxicated each time she thought back on them. As she loaded her twin Connors, all Mia could think about was the opportunity her cousin had just given her to pay damages to her fallen street sensei. After fully loading the four clips, Mia popped one in each weapon, switched on the safety, placed them back on the coffee table, then picked up the unlit blunt and lit it. She took a deep drag of the exotic substance.

"You want some?" Mia extended her hand as she exhaled the smoke.

"You know I don't smoke," Melissa declined. "What I want is for you to put some clothes on so we can go handle this 'fore I change my mind," she then said.

"Ain't no turning back now, cuz," Mia spoke, taking another hit of the weed.

"We ridin' today," she stated becoming amped at the thought. Melissa noticed the excitement in her cousin's light brown eyes as she stood there in a wife beater and boy shorts. Just a year ago, her cousin was attending Morgan State University in Maryland on a full basketball scholarship. Now, here it was, the long, natural, panther-tone tresses she once wore were replaced by a brush cut, her smooth caramel skin she used to envy and admire now appeared hardened and masculine. Even her shoulders had broadened. Her arms were more toned and her C-cups seemed to be a B size now. At five foot ten, dressed in men's wear, her younger cousin could easily be mistaken for a handsome man. Where had the college student gone? Melissa wondered, because what stood before her now was a street grade, one who had majored in gangsterism. As Mia disappeared into her bedroom and reappeared with her putting on work gear, Melissa could not resist the smile she now had plastered across her face at how much Mia resembled her baby Earth.

"What?" Mia asked, already knowing.

"Nothing," Melissa answered. "I'll be in the car."

"Right behind you, cuz."

East Sixth Street Park was operating full throttle on its evening routine schedule. Once the day care center across the street from the recreational playground had closed for the day, and as the night fell, it was business as usual. The park was legendary for its basketball games back in the day thanks to one of the blocks' fallen soldiers by the name of Gee Gee Brown who ruled the courts turf and had NBA potential had he not met with an early demise. Games played on the court could be compared to the Rucker games in New York. In memory of his name and ball handle skills, a friend of his by the name of Jabar had kept his legacy alive by starting what turned into the annual highlight at the end of each summer called The Gee Gee Brown Tournament. But on this particular evening, it was not the season of summer, rather the first sign of spring, and the players' heavy breathing up and down the court, performing crossovers, making layups, and jumpers were not participants of The Gee Gee Brown Tournament. They were hustlers. While they competitively engrossed themselves in a full-court game, others watched and cheered from the sidelines, some indulged in drug sale activities, and a few heads nodded to the echoing sound of hip hop blaring out of a parked car. Others stood around having conversations and doing their own thing.

Bug, NuNu, and Juanita were no exception
to the mini-Sixth Street bash, the block they
repped was displaying in the park. They themselves stood off to the side in a three-way cipher
passing the blunt of Sour Diesel and throwing
back shots of Patrón, compliments of their three
homeboys who intended to take them to Howard
Johnson's on Rt. 22 in North Plainfield and do
whatever they wanted to do after the basketball
game came to an end. Each woman that partook
in the smoking and drinking session anticipated
the upcoming rendezvous nearly approaching.
The more they drank and smoked, the hornier
and more anxious they became.

"Bug, you fucked Sha before. What he workin'
with?" NuNu asked, contemplating on whom
she would be sexing shortly. She had already
slept with the one named B and had performed
head on the other one named Reef when the two
shared a blunt of wet in his car late one night, so
she was eager to try the last of the two.

"Damn, bitch, you puttin' ya bid in on a nigga
already? How you know I didn't want Sha?"
Juanita jumped in before NuNu could answer
the question. She had actually sexed Reef on
numerous occasions and let him and B pull a
ménage à trois on her at the Ivory Towers in

Greenbrook after she tagged along with them for a night of bowling next to the motel. She too had visions of Sha blowing her back out for the evening, having already experienced his two street comrades.

"Both of y'all sound real stupid right now," Bug interjected. It was true she had been the only one out of her crew to have sex with Sha, but at some point, she had some type of sexual relations with all three of the men they had to choose from, both separately and all at once. In her mind, having all three holes filled by all three of the Sixth Street dick-slingers at one time would do her just fine tonight. She knew she was by far the freakiest of her crew and was proud of it. NuNu saw that her comment had gotten a rise out of her partners judging by the dirty looks that they were now throwing her way.

"Does it really matter who fucks who," she stated rather than asking the question.

"Before the night out, a bitch like me gonna suck and fuck every dick in the muthafuckin' room," she followed up with.

Both NuNu and Juanita looked at each other, then back at Bug with knowing expressions on their faces. They were three of a kind they thought as they all burst out into laughter, knowing Bug had spoken the truth. Between the weed, alcohol, and deep conversation they were involved in, Bug, NuNu, and Juanita's only concern now was when the real party would officially begin. They were so focused on what lay ahead of them once they reached their final destination for the evening that not even the pickle-green Mazda MX6 that slowly drove past could break their concentration.

"That's them bitches right there," Melissa pointed in disgust, the conversation she overheard earlier replayed itself in her head. Mia was more concerned about the extra bodies scattered throughout the park as she scanned the entire playground. Melissa unconsciously began to slow up as if Mia was going to just hop out right then and there and set it off.

Sensing the sudden slowness, Mia said, "Go around the corner."

"Right or left?" Melissa asked, reaching the corner of East Sixth Street and Richmond Street.

"Left and pull over," Mia instructed before she hopped out of the car.

"Turn right on Fifth and meet me across the street from Ben's old gambling spot, and keep the car running," she added, then exited the Mazda.

Chapter Twenty-Four

"Point game," Juanita heard B call out, indicating the next basket they made would end the game.

"About time," she bellowed.

"You can say that again," NuNu backed her up.

"I'm high as hell, and my pussy throbbin' right 'bout now."

"Girl, who you tellin'?" Bug joined in.

"I might ride one of them niggas' dick all the way to the 'tele."

Mia heard those words as she approached the three chickenheads who called themselves the hood rats. Although she enjoyed indulging in an occasional sexcapade with a chick from the hood, none of the three women was her type. In her book, they were lowest of the low, the bottom of the barrel. The hood chicks she fooled around with had style and class about themselves. It was chicks like these who gave the ones she knew a bad name. She was all too eager to rid the world of this caliber of women. Mia was surprised at how easy it had been to walk up on the females, but the closer she got, the more the reason became obvious.

She smelled the familiar fragrance even before she observed them passing the blunt back and forth. She knew weed had a way of making someone be off point, especially in a cipher, and that was exactly the case. For her, though, the substance enhanced her ability to function, and in situations such as the one she was faced with, it made her feel invincible.

Mia had gone undetected by the trio, and everyone else, for that matter, until she was right upon the three females. NuNu was the first to notice the new presence and nudged Juanita. Bug's back was turned as she became aware of company by NuNu's and Juanita's reaction, causing her to spin around.

"Can we fuckin' help you?" Bug asked in a sarcastic tone.

Both NuNu and Juanita let out chuckles. The weed caused them to hold the laughter longer than they normally would have.

"Can I smoke?" Mia asked in her best masculine voice.

"Nigga, we don't know you. Who you?" Bug spat, looking Mia up and down. Had she been thinking clearly and not under the influence, she would have noticed how out of place Mia looked despite the cool spring breeze. Everyone in the park area sported Polo-collared shirts, white tees, capris and baggy jeans with Air Forces, Jordans, Nike ACGs, and Tims, while the intruder wore a Black Label hoodie, black fatigue pants, and black Tims chukkas, and rocked her fitted low. Mia was pleased that her attire deceived the women into believing her to be a dude. Using the only name she really knew from the area, she replied, "Shamar my peoples." The mention of the money getter's name calmed Bug, but still she wasn't in the mood to be sharing.

"Oh, that's our dude," Bug replied admirably. "But no disrespect, we only got enough for us. Sorry, boo boo," Bug announced.

By now, NuNu and Juanita were both cracking up inside. Had they known the ending outcome of the encounter with the stranger, there would have been no room for laughter.

"Well, how 'bout I spark y'all up, then?" Mia offered.

Although they all were just about as high as the Mile High Club, they were not in the habit of turning down a free light up.

"What'chu got?" NuNu quickly asked, being the biggest weedhead out of the bunch.

"I got that shit that'll kill you," Mia answered, laughing on the inside at her own joke.

"This shit'll put you in a body bag," she couldn't resist.

"Light that shit up, then," Juanita churned.

That was Mia's chance. Without a second thought, she reached into her hoodie and delivered as promised. The first shot slammed Juanita up against the metal fence. Her eyes widened in horror at the sight of the handgun before the bullet tore into her flesh and lodged in her chest, but she was so in shock she was speechless. NuNu was the next to notice only a tenth of a second before the spiraling bullet opened up her skull, erasing any thoughts or memories she once possessed. The following two shots that rang out before Mia took flight found two separate resting places as they pierced the soft and tender flesh of Bug. The one that ripped through her neck quickly ended any cries for help or pleas she may have intended to emit, while the one that penetrated her abdomen instantly ignited her insides.

By the time the Sixth Street hustlers were able to take cover, retrieve, and draw their own weapons, and once they were aware where the shots were coming from and attempted their retaliation, Mia had already made it out of the park, letting off a barrage of bullets in the opposing shooters' direction as she fled. She could hear glass shattering and car alarms going off as the hailing bullets chased after her. Thanks to her athleticism, she made it safely back to the parked MX6. As she jumped into the passenger seat, her breathing alone alerted Melissa that it was time to get out of Dodge, and that she did.

Chapter Twenty-Five

Jersey Girl Strip Club in Elizabeth was flooded with ballers and generous tippers from all over, as usual, tonight, and although normally, she would be among the rankings of the dancers to capitalize off the night's atmosphere, Lite, rather Keya, was not her usual self that evening. Some of the best exotic dancers from the tristate area were in attendance. Top-heavy, petite-waist, corn bread thick, beautiful women of all shades with colorful designer outfits that left little to the imagination and six-to-eight-inch stilettos to match paraded around the establishment licking their lips and shaking their breasts, offering lap dances. Others propped their oily legs up on the bar's counter while touching themselves provocatively, inserting fingers into their mouths as they made their asses perform mesmerizing tricks.

The women on stage showed off their acrobatic skills, flipping themselves in upside-down positions and sliding down poles with no hands as some displayed choreographed exotic routine dances, consisting of full splits and placing their legs behind their necks. Meanwhile, Keya sat at the end of the bar in deep thought, nursing a Long Island Iced Tea in her work uniform, oblivious to her surrounding. The club was filled with the base from every strip club banger you could think of that added to the way the women gyrated their prized possession. The smell of her perspiration, Black & Mild cigars, and alcohol tickled her nostrils. A combination she had become accustomed to in her years of working those type of places. What she wasn't accustomed to, though, was how she was feeling at that very moment and had been, ever since she had received the disturbing news.

When she found out through another dancer that Earth had been killed, she felt as if a part of her had died along with her. Although they had ended on bad terms and their last encounter was nothing nice, still, there was no denying that Keya had loved Earth and had been secretly in love with her.

Despite what her mouth said and what her mind had thought, the last thing her heart wanted was for something to really happen to her ex-lover. A sense of guilt swept through

Keya's body. Ever since she had told Mustafa everything she had known about Earth, she regretted opening up her mouth, betraying the woman she loved. When she first heard of Earth's death, she nearly passed out thinking the worst. It had been almost a whole week since she had last seen or heard from Mustafa. She had immediately pulled out her BlackBerry and tried to reach him but to no avail. That had been two weeks ago today, and every day since then, she was unsuccessful. Believing he had been deliberately ducking her calls, Keya had taken that as confirmation that Mustafa was responsible for Earth's demise. Her thoughts were interrupted by the papers that almost landed on her drink as they fell to the counter right next to her. She looked up just in time to see the remaining stacks of bills from the pile of singles someone had apparently thrown up in the air. On any given Sunday, Keya would have received her cut of the green paper rainstorm, but tonight, she was unfazed by the normal club theatrics. What did catch her attention was what the deejay had announced thereafter.

"Shout out to my manz Mustafa, doin' it up real big tonight, makin' it thunder and all of dat for the ladies. This one's for you, playa," the deejay shouted as Jim Jones's track "Ballin'" burst through the club speakers.

Keya's eyes searched the faces that lined the bar. She knew the deejay could have been referring to anyone by that name, but a large stack of bills being tossed like confetti fit the Mustafa profile she knew. The two had actually met at the gentleman's club named Knockers in Plainfield before it got shut down after a female was struck by a stray bullet that paralyzed her from the waist down. It was there Mustafa had tossed $300 in singles at her during her solo performance on stage. Keya's eyes grew cold as she locked in on his presence.

He was surrounded by five of the club's dancers while an additional one made her butt cheeks clap in front of him cocked over on the bar's counter. She couldn't believe his nerve. She wondered how long he had been inside the club and whether he'd known she was actually there. He knew she worked at the establishment from time to time. Keya shot up, snatched her drink, and made a beeline over to where Mustafa seemed to be the life of the party tonight.

"Excuse me," she slid in between two of her two female colleagues closest to Mustafa. She knew they took offense but could care less. She was steaming, and her demeanor displayed it. If they knew what was good for them, they'd move along, she thought. Mustafa was so mesmerizingly focused on the dancer on top of the bar that he hadn't noticed the two females to his left had been replaced by Keya.

"What's up, Mu?" she spat, breaking his concentration. He turned in Keya's direction and instantly became irritated by the sight of her. His facial expression said it all. "Whaddup?" he replied before returning his attention back to the dancer on the bar. He grabbed a fistful of the second thousand singles pile and shoved them in the front part of the dancer's thong. Keya sucked her teeth in disgust. She knew he was intentionally trying to disrespect her and wondered why she had ever dealt with him in the first place. As far as she was concerned, their dealing had long been over. She had gotten more than enough out of him between keeping her hair tight, gear fly, and bills paid so that she had no more use for him. Besides, in her book, he was a mere three on the scale of one to ten in the bedroom department, so his services were no longer needed since she had found a ten outside and an eight inside the bedroom. Still, she needed to know for herself if he was the culprit behind the slaying of her loved one.

"I need to talk to you," she announced.

"About what?" he asked, never taking his eyes off the dancer.

Seeing that Keya had interrupted their cash flow, the other two dancers to Mustafa's right threw visual daggers and moved on. Wanting to see how he'd react, Keya blurted out, "About Earth."

"What the fuck about her?" Mustafa asked. His composure and demeanor remained the same as he answered.

"Don't play dumb, you know what," Keya shot back. She was looking for some type of reaction or something to indicate his guilt.

"You right," he let out a short laugh. "I'm not dumb. Fuck that bitch. She got what her hands called for," he ended with a smile.

"No, fuck you." Keya lost it. What little she had remaining of her drink was tossed in Mustafa's face.

By the time, he dried his eyes and regained his vision, Keya had already vanished into the dressing room, gathered her belongings, and exited the back door of the strip club.

Chapter Twenty-Six

As the hospital orderly wheeled Heaven toward the sliding doors, the closer she got to them, the faster her heart rate became. Heaven felt as if she was about to have an anxiety attack and knew the reason why. Almost three weeks had gone by since she had been cooped up in the hospital. Being confronted with the fear of leaving to return back to life, as she knew it, had her on edge. Although for the past few weeks she had longed to be discharged out of the hospital, Heaven was somewhat leery. She did not know what to expect once she was out, and this was unlike her. The incident that landed her in a hospital bed and her right hand in the grave still weighed heavy on her mind. Over and over, she had played the tapes and recapped the chain of events inside her head. When she was not thinking about it, she was having nightmares about it. Nightmares that involved her dead numerous times and caused her many sleepless nights.

Nightmares that she knew would haunt her for the rest of her life, or at least until she laid them to rest herself, burying them deep—along with the perpetrators. Heaven knew that she couldn't officially mourn her partner's demise until she had gotten to the bottom of what all had happened to her and why. And that was exactly what she intended to do. She knew that in the game, death and imprisonment were two strong options, just as she knew that Earth had known the same, and they both respected any and all that came behind the lifestyles they willingly and voluntarily chose for themselves.

"Are you okay, Ms. Jacobs?" the white preppy-looking orderly asked, breaking Heaven's chain of thought.

"I'm good," she replied.

As they reached, the sliding doors, the first thing Heaven noticed was Sonya and Shell leaning up against the black Tahoe with smiles plastered across their faces. The orderly continued to push Heaven through the glass sliding doors.

"It's OK, I'll walk from here," she announced to the orderly.

"Sorry, Ms. Jacobs, I can't allow you to do that. It's against hospital policy. We have to escort."

"Nigga, I don't give a shit what ya policy is. She said she good," Sonya interrupted meeting Heaven and the orderly at the sliding doors. Instantly, the orderly's eyes widened with fear as he released the arms of the wheelchair. Although he was no coward, something in the woman's eyes and the tone of her voice made the orderly uneasy. Whatever the case, he did not want any problems.

"Sonya, chill. He a'ight," Heaven calmly stated in defense of the orderly, at the same time feeling her soldiers concern for her. Ever since she had awaken out of her coma and gotten on their cases about handling their business in the streets and keeping their ears to the ground, Shell and Sonya had stepped their game up, and Heaven was proud of them both.

She was not at all surprised not to see Le Le waiting with Shell and Sonya, knowing the situation. Since Heaven had been in the hospital, Le Le had found out that she was pregnant by her boyfriend Monty, who had come home from prison. Le Le had been calling Heaven day and day checking on her. Though she appreciated Le Le's concern for her well-being, Heaven was never looking forward to hearing from Le Le, who sobbed throughout the entire telephone conversation. Heaven knew that Le Le had always been emotional, but that was the last thing she needed in her life right now. As of lately, Le Le cried over the little things. She cried about what had happened to Heaven and Earth, which was understandable, thought Heaven. She cried when she was informed of the pregnancy, and she even cried when she told Heaven that she was getting out of the game because her boyfriend thought it best with her carrying their child and all, which Heaven both respected and understood, wishing Le Le all the best. Heaven drew the whole ordeal up as Le Le's pregnancy being the cause of her heightened emotions.

Even that morning, Le Le promised to pay Heaven a visit through sobs. Though they were friends and comrades, Heaven had no desire to entertain the visit, if and when it came. Now that Le Le was out of the game, Heaven told herself that they really had nothing in common, knowing that things would never be the same between them, or anyone else, for that matter, after what took place. At this point, Heaven trusted no one but herself. Not even the crew, despite the unconditional love and loyalty they continued to display. How could she? she wondered to herself. Someone had tried to end her life and managed to take the person that she truly loved and trusted. Heaven rose from the wheelchair with that weighing heavy on her mind.

"I got it," she said as Sonya tried to help her get up. "Let's get up outta here."

With that being said, Sonya opened up the SUV doors, and Heaven climbed up into the backseat.

"Hey, *mami*," Shell greeted. "Where to?"

"Take me home," Heaven replied as she peered out the Tahoe's window. No other questions were asked as Shell accelerated on the gas pedal.

Chapter Twenty-Seven

"You want us to stay?" she asked as Heaven exited the truck.

"Nah, *mamá,* y'all go ahead and let me get some shit situated first. Just make sure you two are here tomorrow morning so you can bring me up to speed on what's been going on."

"You sure?" Sonya asked concerned.

"What did I say?" Heaven snapped. It was evident that Sonya felt that Heaven might have become soft, so she felt the need to be overprotective, but Sonya was far from knowing the truth. Heaven let her know it. "Make that your last time questioning me like that. I'm not dead, I'm still here, and I'm still me, so remember that the next time you open your mouth," she reprimanded.

"I'm sorry, Heaven," Sonya submissively stated. "It's just that—"

"No need to explain," Heaven cut her off. "I see y'all tomorrow," she ended as she made her way to her front door.

Heaven punched in the code to the computer-ized alarm system, deactivating her house alarm, which also unlocked the front door to her home. For a split second, an unidentifiable bad feeling swept through Heaven's body as she reached for the door handle, but she discounted the vibe that overcame her as she opened the door to her domain. All she really wanted to do now was to take a long, hot bath and collect her thoughts. Heaven was convinced the longer she stayed out of the streets, the colder the trail would become to finding Earth's murderers, and she couldn't let that happen. From day one in the hospital, she had already been contemplating her return to the streets, figuring out her most effective approach. She knew that the streets would be watching, and one false move could possibly end her up where her partner was, so she had already made a mental note to proceed with caution.

As the door opened, Heaven stepped in her lavish home and flicked on the lights. What she saw next caused immediate anger to arise. As Heaven continued to scan the living room, her blood pressure reached 190 degrees boiling as the thought of the violation that occurred played outside her head. Debris was everywhere. Someone had broken into her once-beautiful home and ransacked the place.

The African paintings Heaven had imported from Nigeria were torn off the walls, her plush carpet and butter soft leather living room set had all been cut up as residue of feathers still lingered in the air. Stepping through the confetti of her once-valuable possessions, Heaven made her way to the bedroom. She noticed as she walked past her kitchen that all the cabinets had been emptied and glass from broken dishes and old leftovers in the refrigerator were smeared and scattered on the floor. Heaven opened her bedroom door, and just as she had figured, her room had caught the worst end of the home invasion. It was obvious to her that this was no burglary, but, in fact, a robbery, and the violators had known exactly what they had come for. All of Heaven's designer clothes from leathers, furs, shoes, and jeans had been taken out of the closets and sprawled out on the bed and been vandalized. Judging by the smell of the room, Heaven knew that the liquid on her clothing was a combination of bleach and urine. Without having to even look, there was no doubt in her mind that whoever had come into her home had found what they were looking for, and she was right. The hidden safe containing 125 grand that she had built into her closet wall had been ripped out and removed.

As strong of a woman as Heaven was, nothing could stop the stream of tears that trickled down her face. She couldn't believe that what had taken place up until now had happened to her and Earth. The saying, when it rains it pours, came to her mind as she looked at herself in the broken bedroom mirror. She refused to let whoever had the audacity to bring beef to her and her partner's doorstep and violate to such extreme get the best of her, and she made a promise to herself that she would not allow her partner in crimes' death go in vain.

Chapter Twenty-Eight

Detective Saleski sat at his desk in frustration as he unsuccessfully tried to put the pieces of yet another unsolved homicide case together. He tapped the side of his forehead with his ink pen as he studied the mug shots and files of potential suspects, which he had all scattered about on his desk. Ever since he had been called to the crime scene and been given the case, he wasted no time trying to get a jump start on closing what he believed to be a drug-related incident. Although the case involved women, judging by their criminal history and his trust-worthy informants, the victims were no ordinary females. In his years in law enforcement, he had come across some females who were just as equally, if not more, ruthless as their male counterparts, so he had long ago stopped feeling remorseful or sympathetic to crimes that were fueled by, or the cause of, street violence, even if it was at the hands of a woman. He knew he wasn't going to get any cooperation or so much as a truthful answer from the Jacobs's victim even before he'd received the call from the hospital informing him that she had regained consciousness. He knew had it not been for his partner's presence, he would have used other methods to push the girl harder in attempts to back her into a corner and possibly trip her up into saying something he could go off. He made a mental note to do a follow-up alone that day, and the thought crossed his mind as he sat with a blank stare appearing to be looking at the lined up mug shots he had before him. Pictures of known gangsters from the projects and uptown areas of New Brunswick who had been through the system lined his desk. In addition to their government names were their street monikers, which he had highlighted. Nicknames like Rauf, Ali Born, New York, Infanant, Ali Quan, Shalik, Sup, Love, Sieffaldeen, Zeke, Bee Bop, IB, and many more took up 40 percent of the small workplace.

According to his colleagues, Heavenly Jacobs and Eartha Davis were no pushovers in the streets, so he was sure whoever was behind the incident was also somebody of strength in the underworld of the streets. In all of his sixteen years as a cop and nine years as a homicide detective, he had only failed at solving one case involving the death of a pregnant teen whose body was found in a Dumpster in the back of the housing project building on Tabernacle Way. A case that continued to haunt him to this day as it sat in the cold case files. He believed, according to his informants, that he'd never solve the case because the killer himself has been murdered by a family member of the girl who was also from the streets. Whatever the case, like all the others he had taken on, Detective Saleski was confident that this case would not go on his unsolved case record. He was brought back to the present at the sound of his name being called.

"Man, that case has you wired," his partner chimed, flashing a half smile.

"You know how compulsive I get."

"Yeah, well, if you don't eat, you can't think straight," she retorted.

"So are you coming to lunch with me or are you going to dodge me 'cause it's your turn to buy?" Detective Saleski laughed.

"I don't renege on promises or skip out on checks."

He snatched up his jacket after neatly stacking up the files and photos. Detective Crawford shook her head and walked off with her partner.

Chapter Twenty-Nine

Another month had passed since the incident occurred and still the debt owed for the death of Earth and the wounds Heaven had sustained had not been paid. A few weeks prior to Heaven's discharge from the hospital, Sonya and Shell had come close to being able to have good news for her upon her release. When Melissa, along with her cousin, had come out to New Brunswick about what transpired at the East Sixth Street Park out in Plainfield and produced the newspaper clipping to support the claim, they couldn't believe their luck. Although they were highly disappointed behind the fact they themselves were not in attendance when their comrade was avenged, nonetheless, they were grateful upon hearing and reading the aftermath, gaining instant respect for the young replica of their deceased friend and regretting even accusing and insinuating that Melissa may have been behind the ambush.

Their surprise for Heaven was immediately shot down when she informed them of the break-in and ransacking of her and Earth's homes. They were positive Melissa's cousin Mia had slain innocent women, knowing the girls could not have been behind the hit. Not after the description Heaven had given them of the conditions of both residences, but as the Maxima they had moments ago stolen glided up Route 1 North heading for Newark, they knew after tonight, either they or Heaven would be closer to cashing in with their lives on what was owed.

Chapter Thirty

Meanwhile, Heaven was traveling in the opposite direction on Route 1 South, headed for Trenton's South Side. She had been home nearly a month now and had done nothing but think. Since walking into the ransacked town house and discovering the same had been done to her partner's place, Heaven stayed at her second residence closer to town, no longer feeling her out-of-town home to be safe to rest, not, at least, until she addressed the culprits. Today, that's exactly what she intended to do.

Before she had called the meeting with Shell and Sonya, she thought long and hard about how she wanted to go about handling her business. Through her most trusted sources, she found out the whereabouts of two out of the three altercations she and Earth had been involved in just before the shooting. She was grateful for the information her peoples Nikki from East State Street had given her about the veteran stickup kid by the name of Blaze and what her homegirl

Rashida had told her. Coincidentally, the dude Original and his henchman King were from the Weequahic section just as Rashida was. There was no need to pursue the third matter a young girl by the name of Ciara, who was more so one of Earth's people, told her how the dude named Mustafa had been found in the bedroom of his Elizabeth home butt-ass naked. He had been stabbed to death. So, as it stood, Heaven had sent Sonya and Shell out to Brick City while she made her way out to the state capitol. The whole time driving, all she could think about was how the night would not end without justice being served.

Chapter Thirty-One

Money was flowing in abundance on the busy street of Leslie as fiends and addicts lined up the way one does at the check-cashing place on the first of the month, just the way he liked. Original smiled as he and King sat in the silver 745i overseeing their riches. Periodically, they would make their rounds to their cash cow block and park until they felt the need to relieve their workers of the wads of cash they had raked in for them. While others had different ways of conducting business, this was Original's method, one he felt to be effective. He believed his system to be foolproof because, while many of his workers had caught drugs or at times shooting cases, none were ever arrested with a substantial amount of his dividends. For the past thirty minutes, he and King had witnessed a few thousand dollars flow through the block and knew it was time to make yet another withdrawal from their workers' pockets. It was nearing seven o'clock, and the rounds they had been making since ten this morning had them well over fifteen grand richer than yesterday.

Original flashed his high beams. It was no secret; his workers knew the deal whenever they were alerted by the flashing lights of whatever whip Original drove. One by one, they made their way over to the passenger window where King sat and deposited the bulk of their earnings into the BMW. Judging by the stacks, Original was sure they had put him over his twenty Gs' quota he had for each day. He glanced at his watch.

"What's good, lord? What'chu tryin'a get into?" he asked King, ready to call it a day.

"It's whatever, beloved, why? What'chu tryin'?" King retorted, not having any plans for the rest of the day. Normally, they would shut it down and go their separate ways around nine or ten, but just like Original, King had noticed today's quota had been met, and then some, earlier than usual.

"I'ma shoot to Wendy's, then slide over this broad crib out in Montclair I been workin' on for the past couple of days," Original stated.

"Damn, you didn't beat that li'l thang up yet, akh?" King laughed.

"Man, I fucked around and showed the li'l broad my dick and scared her." King's laughter increased.

"I did that same bullshit to this li'l chick out in Irvington. It took me two months to hit that and a lot of runnin' my mouth. You know these young broads can't take no grown man dick."

"True," Original chuckled.

"But it's not going to take me two months; it's going down tonight," Original stated.

"Do ya thang, my G. Let's grab something from Wendy's, and then you can drop me off at my spot. I think I'm gonna call something up my damn self," King rebutted.

"That's what's up." Original started the luxury vehicle and pulled off. Unbeknownst to him, four car lengths back, another vehicle had done the same.

Chapter Thirty-Two

"Welcome to Wendy's, may I take your order?" the voice boomed through the drive-through speaker.

"Yeah, sweetheart, let me get two chicken breasts with cheese, ketchup, and mayo, and a large fries and a large coke," Original placed.

"Will that be all, sir?"

"Nah, hold up, ma. What'chu want, my dude?" he directed his attention to King.

"Let me get a number—" He never had a chance to finish his order. The combination of blood, brain matter, and glass that splashed across his face informed Original of the present danger. Before he had a chance to draw his weapon from his waistband and go into combative mode, his own blood and brain matter, minus the glass, sprayed his man King's lifeless face. A woman's screams could be heard as screeching tires burned rubber out of the parking lot and headed for the highway.

After quickly getting their prey's routine down, Shell and Sonya remained parked the last two times Original and King had pulled off and returned a half hour later. They were engaged in a smoke session of the exotic bud they possessed while they waited, but it was interrupted by what Sonya had noticed up the block.

"Look," she called out. When Shell looked, she observed one hustler after another make their way over to the 745i Original drove. Since tailing them, this was the first time they had witnessed this particular activity.

"They gotta be re'in up or somethin'," Shell offered.

"Yeah, that's what I think too."

Minutes later, their thoughts were confirmed. Seeing the BMW pull out, Shell started the Maxima.

"This is it, *mamá*, I can feel it," she relayed to Sonya.

"Me too."

They followed the silver beamer down Chancellor Avenue. When they saw them turn into the Valley Fair parking lot and pull into the Wendy's drive-through, they turned into the parking lot as well, only they kept going down the hill. Sure they had gone unnoticed, they made a U-turn and pulled over. They both drew their weapons and double-checked them.

"I'll take care of the driver; you take care of the passenger," Shell instructed.

"Gotchu," was Sonya's response.

Shell then drove back up the hill where Wendy's was located. She could see that Original's BMW was the only car in the drive-through. She pulled over to the right and parked in a space just a couple of feet away from their intended victims. Sonya was the first to exit the Maxima. Crouched down with weapon drawn, she scurried over to the 745i. Wasting no time, she rose up and let the Mac 10 loose into the tinted windows. Once the first shot cleared the window, Sonya saw the next three shots explode and open up the back of King's head in succession, spray-painting his man's face. The other six shots rattled his body. She caught Original attempting to reach for what she believed to be his weapon and aimed the Mac at his face, but she was too late. Before she could pull the trigger, she witnessed Shell's .44 revolver blow Original's brains out like an excited child when making a birthday wish. The screaming voice of the Wendy's drive-through worker let them know it was time to go. Both Sonya and Shell hurried back to the Maxima, hopped in, and made a mad dash out of the parking lot and onto Interstate 78 West.

Chapter Thirty-Three

The chill caught Blaze by surprise, so as he exited the Candlelight Lounge, he quickly drew his peacoat in and began buttoning it up. He was feeling nice after throwing back a few shots of Johnny Walker Black. The expensive liquor had warmed his insides as he sat at the bar, but stepping foot outside made him think about going back in and purchasing some shots of brandy. He shook off the notion and headed for his brand-new Cadillac Deville parked on the side of the establishment. Normally, unless he was out working, he would be in the house cuddled up with a young tenderoni around this time of night. At 11:20 p.m., Blaze knew it was way past his curfew; however, since his newfound wealth, he had been hanging out more. This night as Blaze semi-staggered his way to the Cadillac, he thought to himself, *You only live once*. Along the way, he fumbled with his keys, trying to hit the button on the disarming device. Not hearing the familiar deactivating sound, he stared down at the little black box, then banged it in the palm of his hand. He tried the button again, to no avail, so he stuffed the keys in his right pocket of the peacoat.

"Cheap-ass shit," he cursed to himself reaching the driver's door. Blaze strained to focus on the number pad on the side of the caddy door.

"What the hell!" he cursed again, expecting to hear the car doors unlock. Frustrated, Blaze located the luxury car's key and inserted it into the door. *This is what I get for my money,* he thought as he climbed into the Deville. He aggressively shoved the key into the ignition and turned it. Instead of the sound of his engine purring, he received silence. Blaze could not believe this was happening. *Somebody is going to get cursed the fuck out and possibly the fire smacked out of them,* he thought to himself, thinking about the thirty-five thousand cash he paid for the brand-new vehicle.

Knowing a little bit about cars, Blaze figured either a fuse had blown, or the battery wire had come loose. He was hoping for the battery because there was no way he could get a fuse this time of night, and he had no intention of leaving his whip in this particular area. Blaze reached under the steering column and popped the trunk. When he leaned back to reach for the door handle, he was met with a sharp object pressed up against his neck and a soft hand palming his forehead.

"Shit," he cursed under his breath, not wanting to believe he had just been caught out there. He could feel the warmth of the person who'd caught him slipping breathe as the words, "I hope it was worth it," rang in his right ear before the straight razor made a perfect incision from ear to ear. Heaven continued to hold a tight grip on Blaze's head as blood squirted out of his neck. She could feel the life seeping out of him until there was no more left. There was no doubt in her mind that breaking into the car and detaching the battery would be all the leverage she needed to snatch the life from this fat bastard. Her only concern was that he would notice the small back window broken out on the passenger side, but the instant smell of alcohol she had caught whiff of when he entered the caddy convinced her that he was too intoxicated to realize it.

Heaven wiped the bloodstained razor on Blaze's peacoat, then exited as she had entered the vehicle. With the exception of a few stray dogs and cats, no one was in sight as she cut through the bar's path and walked calmly back to where she had parked the car. Although she was almost certain Blaze was not the one behind her partner's murder, she was sure he was responsible for their home invasions. *One down and one to go,* she thought as she headed toward the highway.

Chapter Thirty-Four

Nearly six months had gone by since Heaven's escape from death and the loss of her partner Earth. In the months that passed, she had managed to regain her connect, rebuild her team, and build a new empire. The rumor mill on the streets had it that she had fallen off and couldn't hold it down or reign with the iron fist she once so easily had without her muscle and sidekick Earth. Heaven immediately cleared all the rumors and straightened the facts with the help of Shell, Sonya, and their newest addition to the crew, Mia.

Mia was a younger version of Earth from temper to sexual preference combined. They took it to any and everybody, male or female, who attempted to see just how thorough they and their block really were. Within two months and six shootings later, everyone within the New Brunswick and surrounding areas knew that Heaven and her female crew were a force to be reckoned with.

Throughout the course of them being back in the game, Heaven's trust for others was minimal. Everyone was a suspect as far as she was concerned, including her crew members. She had everyone under the microscope. Although she didn't want to believe it, the first thirty days after she was released from the hospital, she watched and listened to Shell and Sonya's every move and every word. After a while, it was apparent that they loved Earth just as much as she had. When Mia approached her about getting down, she even questioned her motives at first, although Heaven remembered Earth mentioning how she was going to put her down on the team and speaking about how gangster Mia was. Now, Heaven could see why Earth liked the twenty-one-year-old. Mia had expressed to Heaven how her reason for wanting to get down with her now was to help find the killers of her mentor and kill them. Heaven believed her motives to be genuine and embraced Mia, but they had gotten nowhere in that department. As much as the streets talked, there wasn't so much as a whisper about the night Heaven and Earth were ambushed.

Her only reason for agreeing to go out with her crew tonight was in search of answers or clues, hoping something or someone would jog her memory. Bored about the way she had heard the event being promoted on the radio and with flyers, she knew that everybody who was somebody would be at Le Le's birthday bash at the 40/40 Club in Atlantic City. Besides not seeing her since she'd been home and wanting to see her, Heaven wanted to see how people act and would react to seeing her. This would be the first time she had stepped out to an event since the incident, and she was looking forward to the evening. Heaven's cell phone went off. She peered out the blinds and answered.

"I see you. Here I come." She then hung up and made her way out the door.

"Hey, boss," Mia greeted Heaven, hopping out of the back of the 4.6, opening the front passenger door for her.

Heaven just nodded. Shell and Sonya spoke in unison once she was inside the Range Rover, both trying to read her mood.

"You mind if we smoke on the way?" Sonya asked out of respect, knowing how Heaven felt about weed. Once upon a time, she had smoked herself, but after the incident with her and Earth, she had given it up.

"I don't care."

"We bought you some Rémy," Shell followed up with raising a liter of Rémy Martin VSOP in the air.

"I'm good for now, y'all; just do y'all."

With that being said, Sonya switched the CD to Max B, passed a blunt she had rolled up earlier to Shell, and headed to the parkway.

Heaven woke to the sounds of laughter. "You see that white bitch face, tho," Sonya was still laughing.

"Yeah, I thought she was gonna ask for some the way she was staring at us," Shell replied in laughter as well.

"I thought her white ass was going to report our asses until she smiled when she handed the change to Sonya," joined Mia.

Judging by the strong smell of weed smoke, it was apparent to Heaven the extent of the conversation. She checked her watch, which read 11:30 p.m. She had been asleep for nearly an hour and a half. Ahead lay the Atlantic City casinos' lights illuminating the darkness as they traveled down the Atlantic City Expressway. Promotional billboards protruded on both sides of the highway in attempts to attract and lure in new and seasoned gamblers. Heaven admired the beautiful sight ahead. The last time she had visited the area was a year ago when she and Earth had come down to wash some of the money they had made back home. They each had gone from casino to casino, cashing in $9,000 per table. Heaven blackjack, Earth craps, both careful not to exceed ten thousand knowing that anything over that amount must be reported by the casino. The two used to travel down to A.C. two, sometimes three times, a week, to launder their drug money through the casinos, but this particular time stood out to Heaven.

It was a night to remember. Heaven and Earth had just left Caesar's and made their way over to Bally's which was another Harrah's Casino. Heaven was ready to go back home after unexpectedly losing fifteen hundred of the nine grand she intended to wash on blackjack at the hundred-dollar limit table. Earth had lost four thousand out of the nine she had laid on the table in less than half an hour, but unlike Heaven, Earth was determined to win all, and then some, of their losses back. She did that night; Earth won $42,000 on the crap table betting on the numbers five, six, and eight and six and eight the hard way. They had been given complimentary rooms in the past due to the amount of money they placed at the tables, but that night, Earth was given a suite fully equipped with a Jacuzzi and ocean view, along with a complimentary dinner. They took full advantage of the comps and left the casino before the sun came up.

Heaven noticed the blinking lights of the 40/40 Club sign off to her left as they approached the traffic light. The line waiting to get in nearly reached the next corner. As if she had read her mind, Sonya spoke, "Don't worry, we don't have to wait. We VIPs under your name."

Heaven nodded, but on the inside, she smiled. She was thankful to have the type of team she had. *Nothing less than the best,* she thought to herself. "Shell, pour me a drink," she requested.

"Pour me another one too," Sonya added.

"I'ma pour everybody one," she replied. She handed Heaven the first one, followed by Sonya's and Mia's. She then held her own drink up in the air. "To the hardest muthafuckin' chick I ever met in the game," she toasted.

"To Earth," Sonya and Mia both chimed.

"To Earth," Heaven and Shell joined them.

Everyone threw their drinks back, then began exiting the SUV.

"Boss, you good?" Mia asked Heaven. This was actually her first time stepping out with her team since she had become one of them. She had hung out with Shell and Sonya on separate occasions but never together, and she had never been anywhere socially with Heaven.

Focused and overprotective would be the words to describe Mia tonight. Although she didn't tell them, Mia knew Heaven's reason for coming out tonight wasn't to party, and neither was hers. She had already told herself and promised her cousin that she'd be Heaven's shadow up in the club and anywhere else they traveled, for that matter.

"Yeah, I'm good. Don't worry about me. Let's go have a good time."

Both men and women stared as Heaven led the four-woman pack to the front of the club. You could hear lips smacking, teeth sucking, and murmurs as they passed.

"Heavenly Jacobs, party of four," she announced.

The Ving Rhames look-alike in the all-black suit scanned the guest list, and then Heaven and the others. Heaven could see in his eyes he was a hater and the words that came out of his mouth only confirmed it. "I need to see some ID, but he can't get in like that, especially with no baseball cap." The "he" he was referring to was Mia. Aside from the black Yankee fitted, Mia was dressed like any dude that would have been granted access to the establishment. She sported a green, black, and white Polo-collared shirt, black Red Monkey jeans, and black high-tops Prada shoes, not to mention the twenty grand in jewels she rocked in her ears, on her wrists, and around her neck.

There was no doubt in their minds that the hater knew Mia was a female. Before anyone had a chance to dispute his words, a short, petite Hispanic female came over.

"What's the problem, Blue?"

"No problem. They're on the list, but he's not dressed right."

"I'm not a he," Mia spat, taking off her fitted.

"Relax," Heaven ordered. "A friend of ours is celebrating her birthday. Other than the fitted, my peoples isn't dressed any different than some on line," Heaven directed to the Spanish female, without having to scan the line. The Hispanic female then slid in front of the man she referred to as Blue. "I got them," she told him.

"Are you guys interested in buying bottles?" she asked. "I can set you up in your own area in VIP."

"Yeah, give us four bottles of Rosé," Mia was the first to bellow, pulling out a monstrous knot of cash. She noticed how all eyes were on them now and wanted it to be known that they were somebodies.

"You pay inside."

Heaven turned and shot Mia a look. Mia quickly shoved her money back into her pocket. She knew Heaven disapproved of flossing.

"Thank you, Ingrid," Heaven said reading the Spanish girl's name tag. One by one, they flashed their IDs and made their way past the velvet rope.

"Yeah, thanks, Ingrid," Mia followed up with, handing the girl her fitted along with a hundred-dollar bill. "Make sure nobody takes my fitted." Mia noticed the rainbow bracelet Ingrid wore on her left wrist. The two made knowing eye contact before Mia entered the club.

When Heaven and her crew stepped in the building, they saw the 40/40 packed, wall to wall. The sounds of the club banger "Dancin' On Me" by Ron Browz, featuring Jim Jones, had the body-infested club in a frizzy, the bar especially. Heaven noticed men and women climbing over the top of one another's backs to place their orders at the bar. Drinks were being spilled by occasional bumps as partygoers fought their way through the crowd of drunken and wild dancers.

"This spot is bananas," Shell managed to yell over Jim Jones's part of the song.

Just then, the Hispanic hostess Ingrid appeared.

"Follow me," she instructed.

One of the bouncers who saw Ingrid escorting the four-female crew parted a crowd of partygoers like the Red Sea and made a path for them that led to the steps of the upstairs VIP sections.

"Thanks, Beef," she smiled.

"Anytime, beautiful," he replied. "Ladies," he then nodded to Heaven and the rest of the entourage.

Mia watched as Ingrid's tight body sashayed up the steps, but her concentration was broken at the sound of Heaven's name being called. Heaven turned toward her left and saw Sharif from her hometown holding his drink up in the air as an acknowledgment of her being in the building and showing respect. To her knowledge, Sharif was good peoples, so Heaven returned his greeting with a wave. Instinctively, she scanned the other faces surrounding him. None stood out she thought as she continued up the steps.

"Would you like to be set up in the back in the A-Rod room where your friend's party is or somewhere out here?" Ingrid asked.

"We want to be back there," stated Sonya, glancing over at Heaven for approval.

"No problem. I'll have someone bring you out a table, and I'll bring you your bottles. Would you like anything else?"

"A pitcher of orange juice," Shell added.

"Okay, I'll be right with you."

As the Hispanic hostess faded into the crowd of people, Sonya led the way. As they approached the entrance of the VIP room, Heaven noticed

the banner overhead. It read HAPPY BIRTHDAY
LE LE. Burgundy and white balloons covered
them. In front of the elegant room sat a pool
table. Off to the right, there was a Ms. Pac-Man
video game and a mini seafood bar. Familiar
faces congregated in sections both standing and
sitting while others danced and hovered around
one of the many TV monitors protruding out of
the walls. As they stepped in the crowded room,
many heads nodded, even more faces smiled
and grinned in Heaven's and her entourage's
direction as all eyes focused on their presence.
Shell and Sonya gave acknowledging waves
while Mia disregarded them although she took
in all the faces. She was sure she did not know
any of the people and wanted to keep it that way.
For all she knew, Earth's killer was among the
smiling faces. Heaven nodded blankly to those
she knew and glanced at those she didn't.

"Le Le's over there," Sonya announced.

When Heaven looked over to her right, she saw
Le Le having the time of her life. A light-skinned
brother was holding a flute of champagne up to
her mouth as she sipped on the glass. Heaven
assumed it was Monty, Le Le's boyfriend, based
on how happy she seemed. She deserved it,
thought Heaven as she noticed birthday gifts
stacked up in the corner of the area they had on

lock. From what Heaven was told, Monty had come home and catapulted in the game during her recovery while in the hospital.

It was apparent to Heaven that he had no problem advertising his new wealth. He sported an expensive-looking maroon blazer with a black button-down collared shirt. Each earlobe was draped with sparkling carats, and a diamond necklace dangled from around his neck. As he fed Le Le the bubbly, Heaven could see an iced-out three-D pinky ring and a monstrous diamond bracelet dripping from his wrist. She noticed him adjusting his medallion after leaning over giving Le Le a kiss and hug. From where she stood, the medallion seemed to be a king's crown full of stones.

Even Le Le had an expensive look to her, not the tomboyish look she was used to seeing in her friend. From her ears to her wrists, her accessories were more than the average earrings, necklace, and bracelet sets one acquired from New York's Broadway Avenue costume jewelry spots. Heaven could spot the real a mile away, and Le Le was covered in it. Even what Heaven thought to be Monty's team was flooded with the latest fashion and jewels. She counted eight of them in total, each separated by a model-type female up under them ranging from the flavors of chocolate, caramel, and vanilla. In front of them stood more than nine buckets of ice containing two bottles of Rosé each. On the side of the buckets were bottles of Grand Cru and Grey Goose with cranberry, orange juice, Coke, and ginger ale as chasers.

As they continued with Sonya leading the way, Heaven noticed out of her side peripherals a body approaching to her right. Before she could even turn fully, Mia was on the job.

"What's good, playboy?" she asked with a stiff arm.

Heaven turned to see the Cheshire-cat smile appear on the man's face.

"Easy, baby girl, I'm family," the dressed-to-impress man said, throwing his hands up in the air.

Heaven couldn't help but grin to herself for the man's theatrics.

"He's good," she told Mia.

Cautiously, Mia removed her hand from the man's chest, and he sidestepped her and gave Heaven a hug.

"Damn, it's like that, cuz? Your security tight than a mu'fucka!" he chimed.

"You already know. What's up, Rome?" she returned the hug addressing her cousin Jerome by his nickname.

"True. Surprised to see you here," he then said. "I just came over to pay my respects and let you know it's good seeing you. I'm glad you're okay. That was some bullshit that went down. Earth was good peoples." He shook his head.

"Thanks, cuz," she replied. The sound of Earth's name made her feel uneasy inside. She scanned the room for a second time. She could see all eyes still remained on them.

"You know if you need me, I'm just a phone call away," Jerome offered, bringing her back.

"I'm good," she nodded.

Jerome threw his hands back up and smiled as he stepped back around Mia. "I don't want no problems," he chimed in a joking manner. Mia found no humor in his words.

"Mia, relax," Heaven advised.

"I'm good, boss," she retorted, breaking her eye match with Heaven's cousin.

Heaven shook her head. She knew it was no use; Mia would be on guard for the rest of the evening like a Doberman protecting its master. Everyone's attention was suddenly directed to the loud scream over the music.

"Oh my God," Le Le wailed, rising up from her seat next to Monty at the sight of her old crime partners. She literally flew into Sonya and wrapped her arms around her neck in a tight bear hug.

"Hey, sis!" Le Le kissed Sonya on the cheek, then drew Shell in and repeated the same actions.

"I miss y'all bitches," she admitted.

"We miss you too," they both agreed. Time seemed to stop for a moment as the three females stood embraced.

"Thank y'all for comin'," Le Le said, then unlocked the vice-grip hold she had around their necks.

"We wouldn't have missed it for the world," Sonya was the first to say.

"No doubt," Shell followed up with. "Look who else came out for you," she then said, but Le Le had already seen her.

Tears began to build up in Le Le's eyes at the sight of Heaven. This was the first time she had seen her since her release from the hospital. So many mixed emotions lightning bolted through Le Le's mind at the moment, but she managed to fight back her tears preventing them from breaking forth and pouring down her face. Le Le realized just how much she had missed the person who had put her on when she was down and out. She wasn't sure whether she should hug Heaven or not. She didn't know how well she had recovered and didn't want to inflict any unnecessary pain on her old boss. Le Le tried to muster up some words to say but was too overwhelmed at the sight of Heaven and couldn't get them out. As if reading her mind, Heaven leaned in and gave her a firm hug.

"Happy birthday, Le." Her words were all it took to break the water dam. Heaven could feel her shirt moisten as Le Le's body jerked in her embrace.

"I'm sorry, Heaven," she cried.

"You didn't do anything, baby girl. I'm happy for you," Heaven spoke into her ear in an understanding tone. "Live your life."

Le Le began wiping her face and smiled.

"Look at me. I'm a hot drunken mess," she laughed, trying to pull herself back together. It was no secret to anybody in the VIP room that an emotional reunion was taking place. For the most part, everyone knew the history of the parties involved in the scene, including Monty, which is why he remained seated and let the reunion play out on its own.

"It's your birthday, miss," Sonya broke the ice. All the women shared a brief chuckle at Le Le's expense, everyone but Mia. What had just taken place was before Mia, so she was not privy to the reunion. She had heard about Le Le through Sonya and Shell during their reminiscing times on the block or if they were just hanging out smoking. Aside from that, Le Le meant nothing to her. Le Le caught Mia eyeing her and wondered who the girl was. One thing was for sure; her appearance reminded her of Earth.

"Hello," Le Le spoke.

"Hey, wussup?" Mia offered a short reply.

Heaven smiled for the first time. "Le, meet Mia. She with us. Mia, this is our homegirl, Le Le," Heaven introduced them letting it be known to both of them that they were on the same team. Mia extended her hand, but Le Le declined. "Nah, we family," she said instead, giving Mia a hug. "If you're on the team, then you must be a thorough-ass ma'fucka," Le Le said in her ear.

"Absolutely," Mia replied, loosening up for the first time since entering the VIP room.

Just then, the Hispanic hostess Ingrid appeared with two ice buckets containing the four bottles of Rosé. Trailing behind her was a short Hispanic male with a table.

"Where would you guys like to be placed?" Ingrid asked.

"Put them in my section, right there," Le Le pointed over by where her boyfriend and his crew sat.

"No problem, miss," the hostess replied.

Again everyone laughed, this time even Mia.

"Whatever. ANYway," Le Le laughed, "I want y'all to meet my boo."

Le Le waved them on to follow her as she made her way back over to where she had been sitting.

She found her seat next to Monty and kissed him on the side of his face. "Boo, this who I'm always talking about," she announced giddy. "That's my girl Sonya, Shell, and Mia," she went down the line, and then paused. "And that's Heaven," she introduced last, putting Heaven in a class by herself. "Everybody, this is my fiancé Monty," she smiled excitedly, extending her right hand, revealing the three-karat platinum band ring on her ring finger.

"We just got engaged," she chimed, now grabbing hold of Monty's face and kissing him on the lips. He returned her kiss and then stood. "Pleasure," he greeted. One by one, he shook their hands.

"I heard a lot about you," he then said as he leaned over to shake Heaven's hand.

"I appreciate you holdin' my lady down while I was away, and my condolences," he added sincerely. His handshake was firm. Heaven returned his shake in the same manner and nodded as the two of them made direct eye contact for the first time. Heaven noticed how Monty's eyes possessed a certain type of hardness to them. The same type of hardness she and Earth had possessed in theirs. She knew it was the set of eyes one acquired from doing time in prison. Aside from that, Heaven could see that Monty was not someone to be taken lightly. His face told a story that only ended in death. There was no doubt in Heaven's mind that he was a cold-blooded killer.

"These here are my people." Monty began to introduce, breaking Heaven's eye contact.

"This my dude Pee, my manz Self, Shorty, the twins Ray and E, Fats, my dude Whip, and my cousin Murda."

Everyone exchanged head nods and what's ups. The one introduced as Monty's cousin Murda saluted them as his introductory greeting. The trophy pieces on the eight-crew members' arms all watched the scene in envy. Though they knew at the end of the night they'd be the lucky ones to bed the ballers they'd been playing close to all night, none of them had received nowhere near the amount of love the four females who stood before them were getting.

"I see y'all got your drinks already. It's food back there and more over there. Help yourself and enjoy yourselves," Monty then said.

"Thanks, we will," Heaven replied.

"I'm going to come over there and have a drink with y'all," Le Le bellowed.

"Well, you better hurry up 'cause me and Shell goin' to the dance floor out there," Sonya stated.

"I see ain't nothin' change," Le Le smiled.

"Monty, can I go over there for a while?" she turned and asked. Heaven happened to be staring in their direction when the question was asked.

"Sure, baby," he replied, but his eyes gave a different answer thought Heaven. The two of them made eye contact for the second time. Not wanting to read more into the meeting of their eyes, it was Heaven this time who broke the stare. She tapped Mia on the arm and started making her way over to where their table and bottles awaited.

The sounds of Drake filled the club as Heaven slid through the crowd of dancers that stood in the way of her and the restroom. As she made her way, she saw a small opening and sidestepped her way to the left. "Damn, pardon me," she heard a baritone voice bellow just as she felt the ice-cold liquid splash her arm. When she looked up, her eyes met with a caramel-complicated brother with light brown eyes and a well-groomed goatee. He was holding two drinks, now partially empty. "I'm sorry," she murmured apologetically.

"Nah, that was my fault. I should've been paying attention." He flashed a smile revealing pearl-white piano keys. Heaven leaned in to go around the six-footer, careful not to bump him again and spill anymore of his drink. She couldn't help but to take in a whiff of his scent as close as he was. The fragrance was foreign, but the freshness of it was breathtaking. Heaven shook the incident off and made her way to her intended destination. Moments later, she was making her way back through the crowd of partygoers, only to be stopped in her tracks by the familiar baritone voice.

"Excuse me," he cupped her elbow slightly.

Heaven paused.

"I know this sounds type lame, but have we met before?"

Heaven couldn't help but chuckle because his question did sound lame. She expected something more original from someone who looked and smelled the way this brother had.

"No, I don't think so," she replied before attempting to continue her navigation through the club.

"Jersey Gardens," he blurted out.

His words caught her attention. Jersey Gardens Mall in Elizabeth was once like a second home to her. She couldn't recall any guys trying to push up on her while she was out shopping because she wouldn't have given them the time of day, and if Earth was with her, it was even worse. But, apparently, the two of them had crossed paths at her favorite shopping spot before. She was curious to know when and how.

Heaven spun around and moved in closer to the bar where the caramel brother stood. She took a long hard look at him. He definitely fit the description of the type of men she was attracted to . . . tall, nice skin, well groomed, well built, and neatly dressed. He wore a white short-sleeved linen button-up shirt with peach checks, with peach linen pants, and a pair of caramel loafers that matched his skin. He sported a conservative platinum chain with a medium-size iced-out pendant of the letter "C" that hung down to his mid. He rocked what seemed to be a basic stainless steel watch, but Heaven knew it was one of the expensive brands in the Swiss or Cartier family. Despite him being her type, still, his appearance did not register. He stood there grinning as Heaven made her evaluation of him. Seeing that she could not place where they had seen each other before, he decided to jog her memory.

"The parking lot," he announced. Still, Heaven stood there clueless.

"You let me get your parking space," he continued further. Then, like magic, the day appeared in Heaven's mind. She smiled, remembering the flirtatious incident. Even then, the caramel brother caught her eye as she pulled out of the parking space and drove off. There was something vaguely familiar about him Heaven now remembered as she watched him through her rearview mirror standing there as she rode off. She hadn't given the encounter any more thought after that day and hadn't seen him since until now.

"Now you remember," he said reading her facial expression.

"Yes, I do," she held her smile. It had been awhile since a man had put a smile on her face the way she knew it was plastered at that moment. Overall, Heaven liked the vibe she was getting from the caramel brother.

"That's what's up," he matched her smile. "Well, since we never properly or formally introduced ourselves, I'm Calvin." He extended his hand. "But people call me Chill," he added. Heaven shook the extended hand.

"Heaven," she offered.

"Wow, that fits too," he complimented, earning another smile. *Very smooth,* thought Heaven.

"Is that your real name?" Chill asked.

"Kinda, it's Heavenly."

"Now, that's deep. Whoever named you was on point," Chill took the compliment a step further. He was instantly attracted to Heaven on what he thought to be their first encounter when he had accidentally spilled one of his drinks on her and their eyes had met. The first thing he noticed was her natural beauty. He didn't detect any major usage of makeup, and her short cut indicated it was all hers. What really stood out was the fact that she had sex appeal written all over her without being dressed provocatively or over the top. She definitely had style and class about herself, he thought.

"Thank you," she replied gracefully. "It was my mother."

Chill nodded. "Oh, where's my manners," Chill then bellowed. "Would you like a drink?"

"No, thanks," Heaven refused thinking about the drinks she had barely touched in the VIP room. "I have something already," she added not wanting him to think she was flat-out turning him down for some other reason. She was actually enjoying his company.

"Oh, okay," he replied understandingly. "Where are you sitting?"

"I'm back there," she pointed to the VIP room.

Chill knew what was taking place in the A-Rod VIP room because it was the reason he had come down to Atlantic City. Although he didn't really know or deal with the dude Monty for personal reasons, he and his boy Troy had come down to show face and see if they could come up on a nice female or two. He wondered where Heaven fit into the equation. He hoped she wasn't coupled up or with one of Monty's goons, because he hated to have to cancel one of their lifelines over a female. He had been learning about how Monty's crew had been running wild throughout Middlesex and Somerset counties, laying down the muscle and murder game. Chill was hoping they tried to come around his way with nonsense so he could make an example out of them but was glad they hadn't because an unexpected heavy cash flow began pouring into their block, and everyone knew that war and getting money didn't mix. "Are you here with someone?" he asked, hoping for the right answer.

"Someone's here with me," Heaven answered.

The look of disappointment on his face told her she had got him. "My homegirls are with me," she quickly stated ending the charade.

"You're funny," he smirked, knowing her response was made to make him believe she was with a man. Then, as if on cue, one of her homegirls appeared. It was Mia. "Yo, what's good? We been waitin' on you," Mia spat a little bit too aggressive for Heaven's taste. Heaven also noticed the visual daggers Mia was shooting at Chill.

"Who are you talking to like that?" Heaven's tone returned back to its normal authoritative manner. Chill didn't want to believe it but wondered if it was too good to be true. He thought Heaven's homegirl might have been her lover judging by the intruder's tone and ice grill toward him. It was one thing to beef over a female with a dude, but to beef over a female with another female was against his policy. He maintained his eye contact with the boyish-looking female as he wondered about Heaven's sexuality. Could she be bisexual? he thought, confident there was some chemistry between him and her prior to the intrusion.

"I didn't mean to sound like that," Mia retracted her words apologetically. Her ego was somewhat bruised from the way Heaven had just checked her in front of Chill, but she knew she had brought it on herself. She told herself to keep cool when she first spotted Heaven at the bar talking to the stranger, but her youthful mind, overprotective behavior, not to mention the fact that she secretly had a thing for Heaven, all contributed to her emotional outburst that caused her to be reprimanded. Seeing the confused look on Chill's face, Heaven could just about read his thoughts. "Why y'all waitin' on me?" she questioned, now agitated by Mia's interruption.

"Everyone's about to sing Happy Birthday to Le Le, and she asked for you," Mia replied in a more subtle tone. Any other reason and Heaven would have dismissed her. She would have resumed her conversation with Chill, but the fact that Le Le requested her presence, and it was her birthday, was a good enough reason for her to discontinue the conversation she was enjoying. After all, Le Le was still family and actually one of the two reasons why she had chosen to come to the club in the first place. "I'm right behind you," Heaven nodded. Mia turned around and vanished back into the crowd without as much as a blink of acknowledgment of Chill's presence. "I have to go," Heaven explained.

"I understand."

"Nice meeting you, though," she said.

"Yeah, definitely a pleasure," Chill agreed.

"Take my number before you go," he quickly added, right before Heaven was about to walk off. He was hoping she would initiate the exchanging of information, but she hadn't. If the female who had just interrupted their flow was her lover, he was sure she would have let him know, so he was definitely trying to see her or at least speak to her again. There was something about her that made her stand out above all, he thought, and he liked that. Heaven contemplated for a second. She did not come to the club to meet anybody, but she couldn't deny the vibe between her and Chill. Siding against the norm, she pulled out her BlackBerry.

"What is it?"

Chill called out his cell phone number as Heaven keyed it in. "Do you prefer Calvin or Chill?" she asked, not bothering to look up.

"Whatever one is gonna make you remember to call me," he replied smoothly.

Nice comeback, she thought. She smiled and locked him in as Chill. "Got you," she said, returning her phone back to her hip. A little disappointed that she hadn't called his phone right then and there, Chill extended his hand for a second time. "Enjoy the rest of your night."

"You too," she replied. Heaven then made an about-face and exited the bar area.

"Where you from?" Chill shouted over the music, forgetting to ask.

"Exit 9," Heaven turned back around and replied with a smile, then faded into the crowd. A puzzled look appeared across Chill's face. How could she be from New Brunswick where he was from, and he never has seen her before? He made it his business to know all of the best-bred and finest females in the surrounding towns of Exit 9. He was positive she was from somewhere in Essex or Union county, but to be from Middlesex County threw him for a loop. There was no doubt in his mind that prior to the mall encounter he had never crossed paths with her. As Chill stood at the bar in deep thought, out of thin air, the name of the female who he had just been conversing with appeared to him like the Angel Gabriel to the Virgin Mary. Chill didn't know the face but definitely knew the name and reputation behind it. He couldn't help but hold his head and chuckle.

Everyone was harmonizing the Happy Birthday song to Le Le as best they could while she stood in tears when Heaven reentered the room. All partygoers held up their preferred drinks as they sang while Monty held up his with one hand and Le Le's intoxicated body with the other. Judging by the off tempo sound of the singers, it was apparent to Heaven that mostly all in attendance had their share of alcohol.

The cake had been cut, and people resumed what they were doing previously. The VIP room was in full mingling mood. The night was winding down. It was after three in the morning by the time Heaven let her crew know she was ready to head back up to her neck of the woods. She had stayed longer than she had anticipated, and now it was time to bring the evening to an end. She signaled to Shell and Sonya who were engaging in a conversation with Le Le. She sided on, letting Mia know they were leaving on their way out seeing her engrossed in what seemed to be an intimate conversation with the hostess Ingrid from earlier at the entrance of the VIP room. Both Shell and Sonya caught the hand motion. They gave good-bye hugs to Le Le and hand waves to Monty and his crew before making their way over to Heaven. Le Le followed them over to where Heaven now stood.

"It was good seeing you, Heaven. Thanks for coming out. Glad to see you home," Le Le said as she hugged her.

"Anytime, baby girl," Heaven replied.

"Monty told me to tell you it was nice meeting you too." Then there was a brief pause, "And he told me to let you know that he got his ear to the streets," she added.

"Tell him I said the same and thanks." Heaven looked past Le Le over to Monty who was holding up his drink and gave a respectful nod as she did the same. She knew his message was in regards to the incident that had occurred with her and Earth. All night she'd been getting an earful of the same statements and comments and was appreciative, but nonetheless, she would have preferred something a lot more solid. The rest of Monty's crew threw either their drinks or hands in the air at Heaven to say their good-byes, while Monty's cousin Murda gave his signature salute. Heaven nodded to them all.

"Y'all call me and let me know you made it back safe," Le Le said, bringing Heaven's attention back to the small circle they had formed.

"We will, *mamá,*" Shell spoke for them. Again, they all hugged, then Heaven led the pack as they made their way out of the VIP room. Heaven received the same treatment exiting as she had when she'd first entered the room and handled it the same. She playfully bumped Mia from behind on the way out. Mia spun around, ready for confrontation, thinking someone intentionally tried to disrespect her. She smirked when she saw her boss standing there. "Make sure you hit me up later," Heaven heard Mia tell the Hispanic hostess before she walked off.

Atlantic City appears to be the city that never sleeps, thought Heaven seeing bodies continue to pour into the club as they reached outside. "I'll drive," she stated seeing both Shell and Sonya slightly stagger as they made their way to the valet. She refused to put her life in the hands of an intoxicated driver, no matter who it was, and Mia was not an experienced enough driver to be driving on the highway. Sonya started to protest until she nearly tripped over what she noticed to be her own foot. As she looked down, she couldn't help but chuckle to herself and passed the keys to Heaven.

Chapter Thirty-Five

Heaven navigated her way home down the deserted Parkway with Jay-Z's *Reasonable Doubt* album drowning out the snores of her three comrades. Heaven replayed the evening back in her mind. So many faces in one place it made it difficult for her to scrutinize them all; yet, she had been able to, at least those who filled the VIP section of the club. Nevertheless, none seemed to stand out or reveal they were who she was looking for. She had hoped somebody would make a false move and draw suspicion on themselves, but that was not the case. The only two people that actually stood out was Le Le's boyfriend's cousin Murda, who Heaven was sure she didn't know, and the caramel brother named Chill, who she had gotten acquainted with at the bar. She excused her thoughts of the young hustler Murda and unwillingly entertained thoughts of Chill. In the midst of it all, he had contributed to what little of a good time she had.

The conversation between the two hadn't been major, but his company was a breath of fresh air, she thought.

She had been on edge since the first day she was released from the hospital and hadn't taken out any real time for herself. She had been feeling guilty ever since that day and continued to question why Earth's life had been taken and hers spared. She promised herself that she wouldn't stop or rest until her sister in crime was able to rest in peace and dedicated all of her time and energy into following through. Heaven knew had the shoe been on the other foot, and it was Earth who survived, she would carry it no differently. For the first time in her life since the death of her parents, Heaven never felt so much pressure on her shoulders. The game was really beginning to take its toll on her. On the surface, she maintained her boss demeanor in order to run her operation, but on the inside, she was stressed.

The more she began to think, the more the idea to give up the game became appealing to her. She'd thought about getting out once she avenged her partner's death when she was laid up in the hospital, and now the thought resurfaced. The fact of the matter was, though she was doing a good job, she could not function on full throttle without her other half. Anger overcame her as the truth weighed heavy on her mental. Those who were responsible would pay and pay dearly, Heaven told herself.

Seeing the overhead sign reading Exit 9 two miles, Heaven's thoughts switched back to the guy named Chill she'd met at the 40/40 Club. Although he'd asked where she was from, she had never asked where he was from. If he was from New Brunswick, she'd have no way of knowing because she didn't get out much. Based on how most dudes from her hometown moved, she was sure he wasn't from Exit 9. He didn't even appear to be from NJ, she concluded. He had more of a New Yorker-type of style, she thought. Everything about him was natural, cool, and smooth she remembered as she revisited their conversation at the bar. He was definitely someone Heaven felt she wouldn't mind talking to or seeing again. With that being her thought, as she approached Exit 9, Heaven decided to give him a call.

Chapter Thirty-Six

Le Le's sleep was broken by the sound of a rattling noise. As she rolled over, she immediately held her hand up to cover her eyes from the sun that beamed on her face through the window of the bedroom suite. What little rays that seeped through triggered off the throbbing she now felt coming from her forehead. She had a splitting headache that had Advil written all over it. She knew it was credited to all of the alcohol she consumed the previous night, and now she was paying for it.

"Where are you going?" she managed to ask Monty despite the sharp pain continuously jolting through her head just as he was fastening his belt buckle.

Monty ignored her question. Le Le knew why. She knew he'd still be upset with her in the morning. The entire ride back to the casino's hotel and all the way up until the time they made it to their room, Monty was cursing her out and occasionally yoking her up each time he felt she wasn't listening. But the alcohol had gotten the best of her, and she was too far gone and feeling too good to care or hear what he was saying to her. His words were like that of the teacher on the Charlie Brown cartoon each time she tried to focus on what he was saying. She knew it had something to do with her drinking, but everything Monty said was inaudible.

"You heard me, where you going?" she repeated. Her words were slightly slurred.

"Take ya drunken ass back to sleep," he spit, not bothering to look up, slipping into his high-top navy-blue and gray Pradas.

"You still mad about last night?" she questioned. Monty's words had stung. "It was my birthday. I was just having a good time," she reasoned. Monty was not trying to hear her. He started to ignore her again but figured now was a better time than any, especially since it was evident that she hadn't remembered nothing he'd said to her last night.

"Ya drunk ass don't even remember shit," he barked.

"What I do?" she interrupted while trying to rewind the tapes of her party. In an instant, she began to sober up, and her headache suddenly ceased as she sat up in the bed.

She now wondered what she had possibly done that had Monty so upset, but the liquor had erased her memory for the most part.

"Just shut the fuck up, a'ight?" he cursed, irritated by her innocent role. "You don't fuckin' get it; it's not—"

"Get what?" she interrupted him again in a whining manner.

"You interrupt me one more time," he threatened, moving in closer to the queen-sized bed. "See, that's your problem. You talk too fuckin' much. You don't know when to keep ya mouth shut. It's not what you did but what you probably said."

Le Le was tempted to ask Monty who he was referring to that she may have said something to and about what but thought better of it. Instead, she sat there and said nothing as he went on. "I told ya ass not to go over there, but you wanted to be all up under that ma'fuckin' broad ass like you owe her something, or she ya ma'fuckin' man or something. Then you get over there, and I see you start runnin' off at the mouth and start cryin' and shit. That's when I came over there and got ya ass. On top of that, you were too fuckin' ripped to remember what you said to that ma'fucka." Monty shook his head in disgust.

At first, Le Le still had no idea what Monty was talking about, but as he continued, his words became loud and clear. And the memory of Heaven and her old crew attending her birthday party crept its way through the fog that was now hindering her memory. At the same time, Le Le also remembered how emotional she had gotten when she saw Heaven. The only thing she couldn't remember was the incident Monty was talking about. She remembered getting up greeting Heaven, Shell, Sonya, and meeting Mia, but she had no recollection of a one-on-one with her and Heaven at the 40/40. She understood why Monty was fuming the way he was now. At that moment, Le Le regretted drinking the night prior. The last thing she wanted was to jeopardize Monty, or her, for that matter, because of a slipup. She tried her hardest to focus as she racked her brain to recall her and Heaven's conversion, but to no avail. One thing Le Le was certain of was that there was no way she could have confessed to anything in front of Heaven and still be breathing, especially anything involving Earth. She had known the two long enough to know that one would lay their life on the line for the other as well as kill for each other. Again, regret swept through her body, only this time, it was about the alcohol.

Le Le had come to terms with her decision to set Heaven and Earth up when Monty convinced her to. It was a difficult decision for her to make back then because she had so much love for Heaven. Heaven was the one, above all, who was always there for her during the time Monty was in prison. No matter what, Heaven had always had her back, but it was Le Le's hatred toward Earth and her love that she had for Monty that overpowered her love for Heaven and made it easier for her to agree to betray her old bosses. Now, after seeing Heaven and her old team, she knew the damage had been done, and there was no turning back. She knew that she had chosen sides and was all in. The only thing she could do now was hope that she had chosen the right side and the strongest side, for her sake.

Le Le now turned her attention to Monty. She knew she had to say something to calm him down. Both, the expression on his face and the look in his eyes spelled murder. She knew he was a stone-cold killer. He had been one since she'd met him, but she was not afraid of him, nor did she think he would try to hurt her. However, for an instant, Le Le wished she had brought along her baby 9—just in case she was wrong.

"Baby, come here," she cooed as she crawled her way to the edge of the bed panther like.

Monty didn't make a move. Le Le reached out to him and pulled him closer to her by his button up. She looked up at him. "I didn't say anything out of the ordinary to her," she started. "It doesn't matter how much I had to drink."

"You don't know that," Monty replied dryly as he attempted to pull away from her, but her grip was too tight.

"Yes, I do," she answered. "There's no way that I would ever betray you for her or anybody else," she emphasized.

"I know that," he said calming. "But that alcohol had you loose last night, so there's no telling what you could've said to trigger something off in that broad's head. You said it yourself that she's a smart chick, so to be on the safe side now, I probably gotta have her and her whole crew wiped the fuck out," Monty stated.

"Well, do what you gotta do," Le Le retorted seductively while unfastening his belt.

"Chill." Monty made a failed attempt to push her hand away. All in one motion, Le Le had his jeans unbuttoned and his partial hardness through the slit of his boxers. Monty started to protest again, but the warmth of Le Le's hand wrapped around his dick caused him to side against it. Last night he was too mad to sex his girl although the liquor had him horny. Le Le took him into her mouth and sucked him to a full erection.

"Shit," Monty moaned, placing one hand on her head and the other on his hip. Le Le grabbed hold of Monty's manhood and licked around the helmet, then up and down the spine of his shaft. She then pulled his boxers down below his waist to expose the full length of his manhood and licked his sack. She knew that drove him crazy. Le Le sucked on Monty's testicles until she could feel his knees weaken. She then glided her tongue back to the head of his member and put him back into her mouth. Le Le began her expertise by deep throating Monty's pulsating dick.

"Yeah," he encouraged, now placing both hands on each side of her shoulders. The sounds of the slurping as Le Le performed fellatio turned Monty on. He began to sex her mouth as his thrust matched the rhythm of her lips. He wanted to replace her mouth with her pussy, but it felt too good to stop her. He could feel himself building up each time the head of his dick touched the back of her throat, and her tongue touched the bottom of his length. Le Le discontinued the deep throat session and focused on the top of him. She sucked vigorously as she jerked the rest of him with her hand. Monty's eyes were closed, and his head was thrown back enjoying the pleasure Le Le was displaying. Images of him pounding her from the back flashed in his mind as that familiar sensation began to emerge.

"Right there," he whispered just enough for Le Le to hear. Le Le worked her lips, tongue, throat, and hand even more at the sound of Monty's request. His nails began to dig into her shoulders as the inevitable took control over his body. "Aagh," he blurted out as juices exploded and sprayed the inside of Le Le's mouth. Le Le continued sucking until she emptied Monty's sex pistol. She swallowed every ounce of him until there was none left. Even when he had gone limp, she still continued to taste Monty's dick. She knew how sensitive it became after he orgasmed. She looked up and saw a look of satisfaction on his face. His words confirmed what she already knew. "Damn, you the best," he said.

Le Le smiled. "I aim to please." She slid back onto the bed and parted her legs so he could see the juices dripping from between her inner thighs. Her pussy hairs glistened from her own climax.

"My turn," she said, now rubbing her clit with two fingers. "Umm, I taste good too," she added, putting her two fingers into her mouth. "Don't you wanna taste?"

Monty's dick began to throb, but prior to her waking, he had other plans, and he refused to change them.

"Later," he answered. "I gotta go get this money."

Even if she'd wanted to, the disappointment on Le Le's face could not be hidden. Monty expected as much. He knew how turned on his girl became after performing oral sex on him. Any other time he would oblige her and bring her to three or four orgasms, and the two would lay exhausted, but business before pleasure he told himself. This was not the first time he had to step out in that type of situation, and he was sure it wouldn't be his last. He knew Le Le knew this as well.

"I got you," he promised, pulling up his pants and refastening his belt.

"You better." She tried to hide her disappointment.

Monty walked over to the bed and kissed her on the lips. "You already know," he said, then snatched up his cell phone from the nightstand.

"I'll just start until you come back to finish."

"Do that," he replied right before he exited the suite.

Le Le banged her fist on the bed in frustration as the door closed behind him.

"Yeah, cuzzo, where you at?" Monty asked as a sleepy Murda answered the phone. "I need you to meet me downstairs. We might have a problem," he informed Murda.

Chapter Thirty-Seven

"Hello," a hoarse tone answered the phone.

"Did I wake you?" Heaven asked. It was 9:00 a.m., and she wondered if it was too early to be dialing the number.

"Nah, ma, what's good?" Although he was seconds ago fast asleep, he was now wide awake. He recognized the voice instantly.

"I was just being a woman of my word," Heaven replied.

"That what's up. I'm glad you did."

"You sure I didn't wake you up?" Heaven asked hearing a lot of movement on Chill's end of the phone.

"It's cool," he laughed, knowing he had been busted. "I was supposed to be up anyway," he admitted.

"Since you put it that way," she smiled.

"Can you give me a minute?"

"You wanna just call me back?" she replied, figuring he wanted to groom himself.

"Ten minutes," he said. "Or less."

"Take your time."

Less than ten minutes later, Heaven's BlackBerry rang.

"So where were we?" were the words she was met with when she answered.

"You were counting sheep until I woke you up."

The two of them shared a laugh.

"You got that," Chill chuckled. "How long you been up?"

"Since around seven," she lied. She didn't want to let him know that she hadn't really been able to sleep at all and hadn't had a good night's rest in months.

"I see you're an early bird, huh?"

"You know what they say, the early bird gets the worm," she quoted.

"And so does the night owl," Chill added to the quote.

"I know that's right."

Even in the morning caught off guard, he was still smooth and sharp with his thoughts, Heaven thought to herself, and as before when they'd officially met at the club, she was enjoying his conversation.

"So, where you headed this time of morning?" he asked, hoping he hadn't sounded as if he was pressing.

"I'm actually on my way to this little diner out in Franklin on Hamilton Street to have some breakfast."

"I know the one you're talking about. The food there is decent. I ate there a few times."

"Would you like to join me?" Heaven boldly asked. When she first dialed the number, it was her initial intent to invite Chill to breakfast. She was not really a phone person, rather the face-to-face type. She liked to peer into the eyes of an individual when she conversed with them. It was a trait she had inherited from her father. "The eyes never lie" he used to say to her.

"That sounds doable," Chill replied. "I'm not too far from there, so gimme a few, and I'll meet you there."

"See you then," were Heaven's ending words.

Thirty minutes later, the two were sitting across from each other eating breakfast and enjoying each other's conversation. When Chill had pulled up, Heaven recognized the silver convertible 645i BMW. It was the same one she had given her parking space to at the mall.

When he stepped inside the diner and looked around in search of her, she couldn't help but remember and admire how well groomed he was at the 40/40 and just as equally standing at the entrance of the establishment. He could easily be mistaken for an actor, she thought. The hug they exchanged once he saw her hand up in the air and made his way over to her nearly made Heaven melt in his embrace. He wore the same alluring fragrance that had intoxicated her that evening at the Atlantic City nightclub, and the bear hug he gave her made Heaven feel as if she was smothered in it. She knew he was a street dude, and he knew a little history of her own street credibility.

The two of them indulged in general conversation outside of their current lifestyles. Heaven shared her childhood up until the time her parents had been killed. Chill shared the cause of the up-and-down relationship he had with his father, who had worked at the Newark Airport for the last thirty years and never missed a chance to tell Chill that he needed to get a job. He also spoke of the loving relationship he had with his mother prior to losing her three years ago to cancer. During intense conversion, they found they had more in common than they knew, like them both being their parents' only child. They exchanged views on what they thought and felt it to be like. They also both had graduated high school, Heaven in New Brunswick, Chill in Piscataway after being banned from New Brunswick schools due to his behavior. Neither had children themselves, and both were doing OK financially.

Morning turned into afternoon as their conversation caused time to escape them. It was a few minutes past noon by the time Heaven refused Chill the opportunity to pay the bill, and they made their way to their respective vehicles.

"I appreciate the breakfast," Chill thanked.

"My pleasure."

"And the conversation," he added.

"Another pleasure."

"The next one's on me. I think I just might let you taste some of my famous cooking."

His comment caused Heaven to burst out into laughter.

"What's so funny?" He knew why she laughed. That was always the reaction whenever he met a woman, and he made mention of his cooking skills.

"I'm sorry. I didn't mean to laugh like that," she apologized through chuckles.

"Yes, you did. It's cool, though. I guess I'll just have to show you."

"No offense but I'm not the TV dinner or Oodles of Noodles-type of sista," she joked.

"Damn!" he joined. "I guess I have to figure something else out to make, then."

"Okay, Chef Homeboy R-D. I see you're really serious. Just say when and where and I'm there," Heaven said sincerely.

"Tomorrow night. My place. I'll call you with the details."

"You have a deal."

"Anything special you like?" he asked.

"No, surprise me."

"Will do," he smiled.

Chapter Thirty-Eight

As she crossed the threshold of his living quarters, the aroma of something delicious smelling awakened her taste buds and caused Heaven's mouth to instantly water. Whiffs of a flavor-scented meal greeted her outside as she strolled up the cobblestone walk that led up to the two-story brick townhome with the only black door. She had no idea the attractive smell was complimentary of Chill's cooking but entering his home confirmed it. When he had first bragged about being able to put it down in the kitchen, Heaven concluded that he was merely trying to impress her, all the while thinking his experience did not exceed the microwave. How wrong she was she realized, knowing the herbs and spices she took in were beyond frozen dinners. She smiled at the thought. Chill caught it. He knew he had scored points with his master chef skills. During their conversation outside the diner the day before, he was sure she hadn't believed him when he expressed how well he knew his way around the kitchen. Her joke about Oodles of Noodles and TV dinners didn't count as cooking only added to how he had actually chosen to prepare his favorite meal for her.

"Let me take this," his raspy tone flowed with the smooth sound of the music, which filled the air, as Chill helped Heaven to relieve herself of the cropped chocolate-brown leather jacket. The color of her jacket complemented her skin tone, he thought. Heaven was so taken with the fragrances of the meal Chill had prepared that she just noticed the tunes of Maxwell's "Sumthin' Sumthin'" at a medium tempo surrounding the spacious one-bedroom. She took in the apartment for the first time as Chill opened the living room closet and hung her coat. For the second time within minutes, she was impressed. *This is truly a bachelor's pad,* she thought. Heaven also noticed that everything seemed to be neatly in place, from the CDs to DVDs. But what stood out the most were the expensive-looking panther-black leather living room set and the sixty-inch Panasonic that sat surrounded by an elaborate sound system.

On top of the flat-screen was a large framed picture that Heaven had a hard time making out, but gathering from the variety of artwork that was scattered throughout the apartment, she assumed Chill had a love or a passion for African art.

"Have a seat, I'm almost done. It's marinating right now," he offered, flashing her one of the sexiest smiles she'd ever seen in her life. His comment caused her to crack a slight chuckle.

She saw that he wore only socks as he walked around the house and realized it was due to the beige plush carpet the floor possessed.

"Do you want me to take off my shoes?" she asked.

"It's up to you. If you want to. It's not a requirement, though," he shrugged.

"I don't want to dirty your carpet," she admitted.

"Nah, you good," he grinned. "It's already dirty. It needs to be cleaned. They're coming to shampoo it this weekend anyway," he added.

"Oh, excuse me," she replied in a mock tone, but actually was impressed. Chill continued to impress her without even meaning to.

"You're funny," he said before disappearing in the kitchen. Heaven sat on the large sofa and nearly melted into the leather. She appreciated a man with taste, and Chill was full of it. Now directly in front of the enormous television she couldn't help but notice the video games he had stacked up on both sides. One pile obviously was for the Nintendo Wii to the right, and the others were for the PS3 to the left. She wondered if he brought his crew here to chill out and play video games. With that thought, Heaven started to think for just an instant that Chill was too good to be true. It never dawned on her that as fine as he was, and apparently well off and single, that he may have had some type of drama surrounding him, particularly ghetto groupie drama. Her thoughts were immediately broken by the base of his voice.

"Would you like something to drink?" he said popping his head around the wall that separated the kitchen from the living room.

"What do you have?"

He smiled. "I have Rémy, Grey Goose, Corona, Heineken, Pepsi, ginger ale, cranberry, and orange. Oh, and bottled water, of course," he ran down.

If he had added her favorite red wine by Taylor Fladgate to the list, she would have passed out in disbelief. Heaven loved a good bottle of red wine with her meals or when she was just relaxing, but she knew he couldn't be that good.

"Ginger ale is fine."

"Ginger ale and what?"

"That's it," she grinned.

"Come on, you have to have something stronger than that," he retorted. "I mean, I'm not trying to get you drunk or anything."

"Are you sure?" she teased.

"I don't have to do that." His face became serious in a sincere manner she noticed.

"I'm sure you don't," she passively stated. "You can mix the ginger ale with Rémy, but not too strong; more soda than alcohol."

Now it was Chill's turn to be impressed. He was a cognac drinker himself, but most women preferred white liquor to dark. It seemed they felt drinks like Hennessy and Rémy Martin were too strong for them to handle. Chill thought it took a certain type of woman to withstand the potency of the dark liquid.

"Coming right up," he said.

Within seconds, Chill returned with two glasses.

"Thank you," Heaven smiled accepting the drink.

"You're welcome," Chill nodded and sat next to her. "Dinner is almost ready."

"Smells good," she complimented. "What is it?"

"You said to surprise you," he reminded with a smile.

"I'm surprised that it smells so delicious," she teased.

"You still got jokes, huh?"

"No," she laughed. "It really does, though." She took a sip of her drink and set it back down on the footstool.

"Hold that thought," Chill chimed. She watched as he took a swig of the pure mahogany cognac before making his way back into the kitchen.

The sweet melody of India Arie's voice permeated the living room.

"Do you mind if I turn this up?" Heaven called out to the kitchen. The song was one of her favorites whenever she relaxed.

"Be my guest," the voice echoed from the kitchen area. Heaven increased the volume, then grabbed her drink and sat back down. She closed her eyes after taking another sip and enjoyed the smoothness of the lyrics. Chill had made her drink just right, she thought as the cognac flowed smoothly through her insides. She hummed along as India Arie's "The Truth" blared through the surround sound speakers, which hung from the wall over the couch where she sat.

She was so caught up in the rapture of the song that she was unaware of Chill watching her. He leaned against the side of the living room wall with arms folded. Now sensing his presence after his fragrance had given him away, Heaven's eyes opened.

"I'm sorry," she smiled apologetically.

"Nah, you're good. I'm the one who should be apologizing for disturbing you," he coolly stated. "You looked so at peace."

And that's how she felt. From the time she had been released from the hospital, she had been on a warpath that landed her down a dead end. All the work she and her crew had put in was for nothing, and it had her stressed. She was no closer to those who had violated her and her partner since the day the incident had occurred, which credited to her continuous sleepless nights. Now, here it was, she had easily fallen into relaxation mode in a complete stranger's home. At that moment, nothing else seemed to exist, and she wanted to savor the feeling.

"Dinner's ready," Chill offered. "Just relax." He stopped her seeing that she was about to get up. "I'm going to bring it to you." He disappeared and returned with a wooden foldup TV tray and set it in front of her. Like a waiter, he left and came back with a placemat, napkin, and silverware. Impressed would have been an understatement when describing Heaven's thoughts. After setting up the same for himself, Chill then returned with two plates and set one in front of Heaven, and the other on the tray in front of where he intended to sit.

"Enjoy," he grinned.

Heaven's eyes told it all. "Thank you," she replied admiring the delicious-looking meal.

The smell of the seasoned pink salmon served with yellow rice, peas, and corn tickled her nostrils, but the taste of the tender fish ignited her taste buds. Chill sat and proudly watched as she tasted what was his favorite dish to prepare.

"Mmm. This is sooo good," she cooed as she chased the seasoned rice with a small portion of the mixture of sweet and spicy corn.

"Glad you like," a modest Chill smiled.

For the next twenty minutes or so, Chill and Heaven enjoyed their meals through small talk.

The first to finish, Heaven leaned back onto the leather sofa.

A slight case of itus swept over her from the tasty meal that had filled her, but she fought it. Chill noticed and smiled. *Job well done,* he thought to himself as he removed the plates and table. He then returned and sat next to Heaven, only this time closer than before.

"Don't worry, I'm not going to fall asleep," she assured him seeing Chill staring at her.

"That's not what I was thinking," he corrected. Something in his tone sounded soothing to her.

"Well, what were you thinking, then?"

"What I've been thinking since the first time I saw you."

Heaven's eyebrows became one. "And what's that?" she asked puzzled.

"How beautiful your lips were," he admitted smoothly.

His straight face when he spoke aroused Heaven. She did her best to hide her reaction.

"Really?"

"Yeah."

"And?" she replied, not knowing what else to say.

"And now I think I want to taste them."

Chill leaned in to kiss her. The scent of the African musk oil he wore masked the aroma of the meal they had not long ago shared as he attempted to press his lips up against hers. Heaven gently placed her hand on his chest, stopping him from coming closer. They stared at each other for just a moment.

"Do You Feel Me" by Anthony Hamilton echoed in the silent space between the two of them. Heaven took a deep breath and released herself, allowing the softness of Chill's lips to meet hers. As she did, she could hear Anthony asking, "Do you feel me?" She could feel her heartbeat speed up and her special place start to dance.

Chill wrapped his arms around her waist pulling her closer. The aggressiveness of his embrace caused her eyes to open to find Chill looking her directly in the face. They stared at each other again for just another moment, and then Chill kissed her deeply. Heaven couldn't believe what was happening to her. Chill was kissing her like she had never been kissed before. He began to glide his hand around her breast, while his tongue continued to part her lips and dominate their kiss. It had been a long time since a man had touched her in the manner Chill was, and she welcomed it. The foreign feeling brought her entire body to life, igniting her insides and moistening her inner thighs. She inhaled at the touch of his hand caressing her nipple through the fabric. Chill gently massaged her mound as his mouth traveled from her lips to her neck. With his free hand, he began to unbutton her blouse, and then smoothly removed the shirt. His tongue trailed down to her exposed shoulder. Chill performed circular motions with his tongue on her collar while unfastening the laced bra. Free of the garment, Chill's hand had full access to the bareness of Heaven's breast. He toyed with the now-erect nipple, then replaced his fingers with his tongue.

Heaven threw her head back and closed her eyes, placing her hands on top of Chill's head as he assaulted her nipple. His free hand slid its way between her Seven Jeans and began to massage the warm area while switching his assaults on to her other nipple. Heaven's breathing increased from the pressure Chill was applying between her legs. She could feel her pussy getting wetter each time he caused the material to press against or brush across her clit. He then slithered his mouth down to her midsection and began to unbuckle her belt and jeans. Heaven opened her eyes and peered down at Chill who was staring up at her. His piercing brown eyes gazed up at her with lazy lids. Not knowing whether it was the room's temperature or the way his mesmerizing eyes had captured her, Heaven felt her body heating up. Light perspiration trickled down the middle of her smooth vanilla neck and glided down between her breasts, then disappeared under Chill's chin. Chill was met with the sweet smell of freshness when he exposed the top part of Heaven's matching lacy panties. She bit down on her bottom lip as he gently guided her out of her jeans and thong. As she slowly squirmed out of her clothing in attempts to aid him, her back instinctively arched itself from the anticipation of what was to come.

Chill had never been so attracted to another woman before. There had been many women before Heaven; however, there was something about her that had caused him to view her in a different light. Chill's strong tongue took on a life of its own and began to explore her inner wetness. He felt her body shudder as he tasted her. His tongue continued to explore her sex cave as she let out a passionate moan. She spread her legs wider as she felt Chill's hands slide underneath her, the tight grip of hands palming her ass caused Heaven's spot to release a flow like never before. Her kitten purred as he took her clit between his teeth and gently nibbled on it, sending a shock wave up Heaven's right side, causing her leg to stiffen, her ass cheeks to tremble, and her jaws to tighten up. Chill smirked at this as he continued to lick Heaven's glistening hole. His tongue stiffened and slid lower beneath Heaven until he reached his destination. Heaven felt his tongue flickering around her anus. The enjoyable pleasure he was performing on her had her in pure ecstasy. She could feel her pedicured toes curling as Chill's tongue sexed her ass. Just when she thought she couldn't take it anymore, Chill's anal lashing ceased.

He returned to her midsection and began kissing and licking her abs and sides. The gentle touch of his mouth and tongue relaxed Heaven's flesh. No man had ever made her feel the way Chill had her feeling at that moment. She had only been with four men in her whole life, and none could compare to him. His tongue game alone had her body in overdrive. What started out as a friendly dinner date slowly turned into an evening of passion. Heaven had no regrets. As if he had read her mind, Chill asked in his best Barry White tone, "You ready for this?"

She responded with a head nod and a seductive look to match. Chill took her by the hand and led her to his bedroom. The dimness of the room's light added to the intimate scene. He guided her now-nude body to the king-size bed. Heaven melted into the navy satin sheets. The sounds of Floetry's "Closer" could be heard coming from the living room while Heaven stared with lustful eyes as Chill undressed. When he removed the V-neck tee and wife beater, Heaven couldn't help but admire his toned physique. His caramel pecs, well-sculpted arms, and shadow abs added to the moistness she had between her thighs. But when he relieved himself of his velour sweatpants and boxer briefs, her eyes widened at what Chill intended to fill the condom with that appeared out of nowhere. It wasn't the biggest, but it was the biggest she had ever had.

Chill suavely made his way over to the bed. Heaven greeted him with parting legs. He guided himself inside her secret garden. She gasped for air as he entered her. Her body trembled for a moment under him as he slowly gave her all of the nine-inch length. She wrapped her legs around him as Chill filled her insides. The more he slow grinded, the wetter Heaven became. The tightness along with its wetness heightened Chill's attraction. The way her muscles contracted around his manhood was indescribable.

Heaven tried to match Chill's rhythm with each stroke, but every other thrust caused her to clinch the satin sheets beneath her as she let soft moans escape. She released the sheets and pressed her palms in Chill's chest signaling with her eyes for him to roll over on his back. All the while never losing possession of his tool as they moved into the new position, she straddled him. They locked eyes just then, and she could see that he was just as much into her as she was him.

She commanded her spot to grab hold of his dick and began to progressively ride it. Chill grabbed hold of her hips and met her downstroke.

As her pace increased, so did his. Heaven's moans grew louder as Chill deep dicked her with every inch of his tool from the bottom. She could feel the pressure from his hands on her waist as tears of pleasure formed in the creases of her eyes. She felt herself reaching yet a third orgasm and began to ride Chill's made-to-fit muscle like a wild woman. Chill felt his own self building up from Heaven's rapid pace. His toes now began to curl as he braced himself for the inevitable. It seems as if their flesh had become one as both Chill and Heaven erupted. The only thing that separated them was the condom Chill had worn. Heaven beamed as she lay atop of his chest, each of them out of breath with pounding hearts. Chill kissed her atop her head, then began to run his fingers through her hair. Minutes later, they both had fallen fast asleep in their rightful positions. That evening, a connection was made. It was the first of many nights to come for Heaven and Chill.

Chapter Thirty-Nine

Heaven tossed and turned as the face and voice of Earth invaded her dreams. This had been an ongoing occurrence since she had been released from the hospital. Each night, her subconscious revisited the last time she and her friend had been together, and she had seen Earth alive. The scene was always the same. She could see Earth as clear as day as her strong voice echoed in her ear. As usual, Heaven tried to fight off the disturbing nightmare but to no avail. Instead, she was forced to watch as if she were in the theater viewing a motion picture, and Earth starred in the leading role.

"I'll drive while you roll up."

"What? Girl, you buggin'! You know how I am about my baby."

"Bitch, ain't nobody gonna crash ya shit up. Besides, we only five minutes away from your crib. Gimme the keys and stop playin'. Heaven,

throw me the keys. I promise I'll do under the speed limit and even put on my seat belt."

Heaven began to perspire as the scenery continued. She could see Earth adjusting the radio dial to increase the volume of the Jay-Z track before pulling out of The Diner's parking space as she sat shotgun, rolling up the exotic substance she had been given in exchange for her Bentley GT keys. This was the same part of scene that would lead up to her jumping out of her sleep and waking in a cold sweat. Her sheets would be drenched, as if someone had thrown a pitcher of water on her, and her eyes would be full of tears. Her heart rate quickened, and her tossing and turning increased as the unforgettable sounds rang out.

"Brrrgaah! Brrrgaah! Brrrgaah!"

"Brrrgaah! Brrrgaah! Brrrgaah!"

Normally, the nightmare would have ended with the sounds of gunfire, but this time, it continued. Shots rang out in rapid succession and echoed in Heaven's ear as the bullets came crashing through the GT's window. It was as though she were watching from afar as the deadly metal penetrated her flesh. "No," she called out in horror to herself as she witnessed the attack on her and her friend from a safe distance. She wished it were a movie she was watching so this part of it could be deleted, but she knew her wish would not come true. Heaven now found herself in the passenger seat of the car losing consciousness. She could hear the engine of the coupe in full throttle. Before she could figure out why, the sudden boom and sound of the horn interrupted her thoughts. The front of the Bentley slammed into a parked car. Her body made a quick jerk from the impact of the accident. The seat belt prevented her from any further injuries, but she was in pain in addition to losing blood. With what little strength she had, she managed to peer over at her partner who she saw slumped over on the steering wheel. She squeezed her eyelids tightly, causing tears of anger to form in the creases of her eyes. Heaven felt herself weakening as her head rested on her right shoulder. Her vision became blurry, and she felt her eyelids getting heavy. Just as they were about to fully close, she caught a glimpse of a masked man positioned backward on a motorcycle. The last thing she saw before she passed out was the image in all-black making a salute gesture just before the bike sped off.

"Babe?"

Heaven was now breathing uncontrollably. The sound of Chill's voice caused her to shoot up in bed. He grabbed her by the shoulders and embraced her. He could feel her heart pounding like an Indian war drum as he squeezed her tightly. For a brief moment, Heaven was oblivious as to where she was, but the warm lips she felt pressed on the side of her face brought her back to the present.

"You were just having a bad dream, babe," Chill stated, rocking her back and forth.

"It was just a bad dream," he repeated caressing her hair. He had no way of knowing just how wrong he was.

"I know," she replied trying to calm herself.

"You good?"

"I'm fine." She hated lying to him, but she felt she had no choice. It was for the best, she reasoned.

"You wanna talk about it?"

"No." As far as she was concerned, there was nothing to talk about. After what had just been revealed to her in her dream, she knew her next move would be an action one. Her thoughts were interrupted by Chill.

"I'll be right back; I'm going to get you something to drink. Maybe you'll change your mind by the time I come back," he stated as he climbed out of bed.

Heaven flashed him a loving smile. Despite what he hoped, she knew she'd feel the same when he returned. She couldn't take the risk. Her mind was made up, and no matter what, not even the man she loved could change it.

Chapter Forty

As Chill paid the eight-dollar toll and crossed the George Washington Bridge into New York headed to the Bronx to meet up with his dope connect, he couldn't shake this morning's episode with Heaven. For the past month and change, things between the two of them had been as smooth as Shea butter, but still, Chill was certain there was a lot his new lady was holding back from him. After witnessing her sudden wakes during her nightmares on more than one occasion, he became accustomed to them. Like this morning, he would always offer the opportunity for her to talk about what the disturbing dreams entailed, but she always declined, and he never pressed the issue. She never spoke about the death of her ex-partner or the shots he had heard she had taken and the wounds he had massaged and kissed almost every night since the first time they had made love. The pact they had made not to bring anything from the streets into their bedroom made him respect her secrecy to the story only she and those involved in what happened to her could tell.

He had never met a woman as thorough and as strong as she was. That was one of the things he loved about her, but a part of him wanted to know everything and wanted to protect her in every sense of the word. With that being his thought, Chill decided to do a little homework of his own. As the thought crossed his mind, he was already contemplating on how he would handle things if, and when, he found out who was behind what he believed to be the cause of Heaven's nightmares. Knowing himself, he knew the only way to handle the culprits was to wipe them off the face of the earth.

His thoughts were put on pause by the interrupting sound of his cell phone ringing. He looked at the screen, which read "UNAVAILABLE CALLER." Normally, he didn't answer blocked calls, and people knew not to call him from one, so he was curious to see who this call was from.

"Yo," he answered. "Who's this?"

A surprised frown appeared across his face at the mention of the caller's name.

"Whaddup?" he asked, wondering what the call was in reference to.

"Nah, I'm not around," he stated. "Why? What's good?" he questioned quickly, becoming agitated by the caller. Chill pulled the phone from his ear and stared at it awkwardly at the caller's statement as if he was making sure the caller had the right person, then placed it back against his ear.

"A'ight, yo, gimme a few hours and hit me back. I'll let you know if I'm back in the area."

Chill ended the phone call. Had the caller called from another number he could have dialed back and asked how they had gotten his number. His thoughts of Heaven were now replaced with the suspicious call he just received. There wasn't anything Chill could think of that the person could have wanted to discuss with him in person that he couldn't over the phone. Whatever it was though, he would soon find out. Chill accelerated the Beamer, eager to conduct his business in New York so he could return back to New Brunswick and address the phone call.

Chapter Forty-One

Le Le activated the alarm of her brand-new cherry-red Honda Accord coupe with her mouth after parking in her assigned space in front of the newly built town house, which viewed the Commercial Avenue side of the three-story complex Monty had just purchased for her. She struggled with the half-dozen or so bags as she made her way to the flat level of where she resided. It had been an exhausting yet fun-filled day for her, consisting of pampering and shopping. Ever since nine this morning after Monty had given her ten grand worth of spending money, she had been out the door and off to the races. She started with her 9:15 manicure and pedicure appointment, finishing up just in time to make it to her 11 o'clock hair appointment at the Doobie Spot. After spending two hours in the salon, she had bounced from mall to mall on her mini shopping spree, and now both arms were filled with bags of the latest fashion designer stores in Short

Hills, Woodbridge, Jersey Gardens, Cherry Hill,
and New Port malls. She placed the bags she possessed on her right arm down in front of her door,
then retrieved the set of keys from her mouth.
She then punched in the security code number in the white box that sat off to the right of
the door. She sighed in frustration seeing that
she had typed in the code incorrectly due to her
haste. If it were up to her, she would remove the
box, but it was Monty's decision, and he paid
the bills, so it was not up for discussion.

The green light appeared after Le Le took
her time and punched in the proper digits to
deactivate the town house alarm. She was glad
because she now had to use the bathroom.
She rummaged through the key ring until she
located the right key. Once she opened the
door, she held it open with her left stiletto and
retrieved her shopping bags. Using her shoulder to push her way into the house, Le Le hurried to put the bags down, feeling the water
beginning to build up in her bladder. She
turned to close the door behind her before she
had a chance to realize that she was not alone.
Then the room went dark.

Chapter Forty-Two

Heaven watched from afar as Le Le exited her vehicle and made her way to her house door. It had been a long and drawn-out day for her following Le Le from venue to venue. Several times, she considered running down on her and abducting Le Le but decided against it, not wanting to take the chance of someone seeing anything. The entire day she had exercised patience despite the fact that her blood boiled each time she laid eyes on her ex-friend and thought of her betrayal. After all she and Earth had done for her and all they'd been through, she couldn't believe this was how Le Le chose to repay them. They say that you are only as strong as your weakest link, and Heaven knew that to be true, but never in a million years did she think that someone in her own camp would have been the one behind what had happened! Even when she was released from the hospital and felt everyone was suspect, she never really suspected Shell or Sonya, let alone Le Le. The thought of how Le Le deceived her enraged Heaven, but she knew in order to get the answers she needed, she had to use intellect over her emotions, something she had always preached to her crew.

Once Heaven locked in on where Le Le lived, she emerged from the side of one of the unfinished town houses and made her move. Due to needing an electronic card to enter the gated community, Heaven was forced to pursue Le Le on foot. Quickly, she found an inconspicuous parking spot off one of the side streets of Commercial Avenue and hopped the gate that separated the street from the property. Going unnoticed, Heaven cautiously cut through the parking lot headed in Le Le's direction as if she was a visitor of someone in the complex. The time it took for Le Le to enter her place gave Heaven ample time to reach her before she made it fully inside. Had she turned around rather than pushing her way inside her home, she would have seen Heaven a short distance behind her rapidly approaching.

By now, Heaven had her Glock drawn and down at her side. She quickened her pace seeing Le Le release her shopping bags to the ground.

Heaven now had the Glock raised up in the air. As Le Le spun around, Heaven came down on her face fast and hard, sending her crashing to the floor, instantly knocking her unconscious. Heaven stepped completely in, closed the door, then locked and dead bolted it behind her. She kneeled down, took Le Le by the hands, and dragged her into the living room.

Chapter Forty-Three

The splash of liquid slapping Le Le square in the face caused her to regain consciousness. Her eyes fluttered in attempts to refocus themselves, but the burning sensation from the liquid made it difficult. A foreign smell invaded her nostrils as she exhaled and choked on her coughs, all in the same breath. The taste of blood, snot, and the liquid seeped into her mouth, nearly causing her to vomit. She instantly recognized the unknown odor. The smell of gasoline heightened her senses and alarmed her of her imminent danger. Fear swept through her entire body. All she could think about was how someone had run down on her because of Monty. She knew of many cases how the loved ones of big-time hustlers were used as pawns in the game. Now, here it was, Le Le believed she had been kidnapped with the intent of being held for ransom.

She was no stranger to the streets, so she knew all she had to do was what she was told, and everything would be okay, she told herself.

Her only hope was that whoever it was wearing a mask was a stranger. If it wasn't, then Le Le knew that she was a dead ass.

"Please just wipe my face and gimme a phone. I'll call my man. I promise he'll pay whatever you want," Le Le pleaded.

A chuckled was offered as the response.

"I swear he'll pay," Le Le repeated blowing the fluids that continued to drip down her face into her mouth.

"Bitch, this ain't about money; this is about loyalty," Heaven growled removing the mask.

The fact that she felt partially blind enhanced Le Le's hearing, but she thought her ears must be deceiving her. She recognized the voice instantly but didn't want to believe who it belonged to.

She fought to open her eyes despite the pain she endured from the gasoline's residue. As she managed to establish vision out of her right eye, the image she saw matched the voice and was unmistakable.

"He-Heaven," Le Le's own voice cracked as she fought to establish vision in her left eye.

"All I wanna know is why, Le." The hurt was undeniable in her tone as Heaven said that.

Le Le's mind was racing a hundred miles a minute as she searched for a response. How could she know? wondered Le Le, unsure of whether Heaven was there for the reason she thought.

To play it safe, Le Le replied, "Why what?" in a puzzled manner, now regaining sight in her left eye.

"*Whop!*" The smack came from out of nowhere. The impact of the blow dazed Le Le and caused her to see images of stars and hear the sounds of bells ringing in her ears.

"Don't play on my fuckin' intelligence," Heaven snapped. "I swear on everything I love I'll kill your ass up in here," she threatened to illustrate how serious she was.

Le Le began to break down in tears. In a way, she was relieved that the secret she had been harboring all these months had finally been exposed. It had been a heavy load on her heart to bear from day one. It felt as if a ton of bricks had been lifted off her shoulders. She never meant for things to go as far as they had she told herself, but when she heard that Earth was dead and Heaven was hospitalized, she knew she was in too deep and couldn't turn back the hands of time. Now the gig was up, and the wall as she knew it came crumbling down. There was no doubt in her mind that Heaven was out for blood. Le Le knew the only thing that she could do now was to try to save herself.

"He made me," she blurted out through her sobs. "He got inside my head, Heaven, and had me all messed up. He told me he wasn't going to hurt anybody, and I believed him. I trusted him. He was my first love, and I was confused. I never meant for—"

"I don't want to hear that shit," Heaven silenced her. "Just tell me where the fuck I can find his ass." Le Le knew that the "he" she was referring to was Monty. "I don't know. He didn't—"

"What the fuck you mean you don't know." Heaven pressed her Glock up against Le Le's temple and cocked it.

"I don't know, Heaven, please!" Le Le screamed. She saw her life flash before her very own eyes as the sound of the bullet entering the chamber echoed and the steel rested on the side of her head. Urine had long ago cascaded down her inner thighs, and now it was followed by feces that fear had caused to escape her bowels.

"Bitch, you better think," demanded Heaven. She frowned at the foul odor she now smelled.

It didn't take Le Le long to come up with an answer. She knew her life depended on the next words that came out of her mouth. "His cousin Murda knows where he would be."

At the mention of Monty's cousin's name, Heaven's anger level rose. It was because of him she was able to put the pieces of the puzzle together. Now, she was already plotting on how she could literally kill two birds with one stone.

"Where can I find him?"

Le Le saw Heaven's eyes light up and knew this was her chance. She figured that if she told Heaven everything, her life would be spared. Deep down inside, she felt Heaven still had love for her and would acknowledge how remorseful she was. Le Le made a promise to herself that once this was all over with, she would vanish and never be heard of again.

"They have a stash house on George's Road. The address is fifteen, you know, next to Roe's house on the right."

Heaven knew exactly where Le Le was referring to. She knew who the woman Roe was. Everyone did. She was a street legend in her own right for many different reasons.

"Is he there now?"

"He should be. He's always there."

"Tell me everything and don't leave out shit."

Le Le began to ramble on, careful not to leave out anything. Heaven listened attentively as she studied Le Le. She shook her head when Le Le finished spilling her guts.

"Damn, Le."

"I'm sorry, I'm sooo sorry," Le Le cried.

"Me too," Heaven spat just before stuffing the rag she had been holding in her hand the entire time into Le Le's mouth. Le Le's eyes widened with horror. The yellowish orange flame from the lighter did a snake dance as it swayed from side to side just before Heaven set the cloth on fire.

"You should've kept your fuckin' mouth shut," Heaven sneered, setting fire to Le Le's gasoline-soaked Chanel tee.

Le Le's cries fell on deaf ears. That was Heaven's cue to evacuate the premises. By the time she made it to the door, Le Le's tied up body was in a full blaze.

"One down, two to go," Heaven murmured as she exited the way she had entered Le Le's town house.

Chapter Forty-Four

Murda was engrossed in an intense game of boxing on his Nintendo Wii. He bobbed and weaved to dodge the assault his computer opponent was launching on him, all the while with a blunt full of Kush dangling from his mouth. "Yeah, bitch," he mumbled through the blunt cigar as he dipped the jab coming straight toward him and began delivering his own attack on the skilled computer fighter. The computer energy level continued to decrease as the block figure seemed to be in a world of daze. Flashing lights illuminated on the screen with each blow Murda landed. He was perspiring profusely from the exercise he was receiving playing the intense game, but he wasn't going to stop now. He had reached the highest level possible on the game and was determined to outbeat the computer.

"Punk mu-tha-fuck-a," he emphasized with each punch he threw. Just as he was about to throw his infamous uppercut, the screen went blank. "What the fuck!" Murda barked, looking at the controller he possessed in his hands. He then looked over to see that the power was off on the Wii, as well as the fifty-two-inch flat-screen he was just seconds ago playing the game on. He quickly chalked it up to him accidently knocking the power plug out in the midst of the beat down he was putting on his opponent. He cursed himself for his clumsiness, knowing it would take him the rest of the day to reach the level he just had. Time he knew he didn't have, not today, anyway. He knew once his cousin Monty finished handling his business in town, the two would be New York bound to handle some more business.

Murda released the controller, took the blunt out of his mouth, and made his way over to the wall socket. He took a long drag of the exotic weed, then kneeled down. A confused look appeared across his face. "Man, what the fuck's goin' on?" he cursed. All of the plugs seemed to be intact. He checked to see if the red light indicating the extension cord was on. The cord's switch glared red. Not knowing for sure which cords belonged to which appliance due to eight plugs inserted in the sockets,

Murda began to push them all in tightly. He never got to check to see if he had solved the problem because the blow that was delivered to the back of his head turned his lights out and put him down for the count.

Chapter Forty-Five

Heaven knew the area she had just cruised past all too well. She was surprised yet grateful not to see the normal body traffic flowing that she was used to seeing around the small curved road. Instead, she observed an occasional dope-fiend and crack addict passing by in stride as if they were focused solely on their intended destination.

Heaven drove a short distance more up the block, turned onto South Ward Street, and parked. She then doubled back and made her way back to the intended address. By the time she reached the light blue three-family house, the street was cleared, at least the curved part, anyway. Down the street, Heaven could see images scattered going toward Troop Avenue. The fact that she could not see them good enough to determine their gender or race, she was sure the same applied on their end. With that, she faded to the porch of the house.

In no time, Heaven located the power box. All in one motion, she flicked out the blade she carried and pried the breaker box open. Le Le had told her that Monty owned the house, and aside from her, only he and Murda were allowed in the home, so she had no problem with killing all the power. Heaven smashed the fuses with the butt of her gun, then rerouted back to the front of the house.

The main door was unlocked, making it easy for her to walk straight in. She bolted in and put the safety latch on the entrance, then tiptoed her way up the flight of steps to the apartment where Le Le said she would find Murda. Upon reaching the top floor, she put her ear to the door. Heaven could hear someone she believed to be Murda cursing inside the apartment and knew the first part of her plan had been successful. It dawned on her that this was the first time she had actually heard his voice. All she knew was his signature salute, the same salute that had gotten her this far in her revenge. As reckless as she had considered him to be, Heaven reached for the door handle and slowly checked the knob. Despite how angry she was, it took all of her willpower not to let out a laugh at the young killer's stupidity. The cards were in her favor, she thought, as she carefully opened the door with ease.

With the door now partially open, she peered into the lavishly laced apartment. She saw Murda crouched down over by the big flat-screen and assumed the obvious. The smell of marijuana was heavy in the air as its fragrance met her at the door. Quietly, she entered the apartment as to not alarm him of her presence. Just as she was within inches of him, Heaven drew the crowbar she intended to jimmy the apartment door with. Having used the piece of metal before as an assault weapon, she raised it and expertly came down on the side of Murda's head.

Chapter Forty-Six

The sudden excruciating pain he felt instantly snapped Murda back to full consciousness, causing him to scream out in agony. His testicles were on fire—or rather, more like a four-alarm blaze—and he was in dire need of a coolant. Had it not been for the boom box Heaven discovered and retrieved from the bedroom, his cries may have been heard throughout the entire city. It hadn't dawned on her that knocking out the power would affect what she had in store for the young so-called killer. Busta Rhymes's latest CD was the perfect camouflage she thought to herself as the hip-hop artist's screaming type of rap style filled the room. Murda had a headache that had Excedrin written all over it from the blow he had suffered to the side of his face, and his sack felt as if it were covered with acid. You could literally see his veins pulsating on his forehead. He could smell and feel blood oozing out of the right side of his face, but not even his headache or the open wound he received from the blow could compare to the pain he felt between his legs. He inhaled and exhaled repeatedly as a means of withstanding the assault he was enduring. Fighting through the pain, Murda realized he was naked and tied to one of his kitchen chairs. He also noticed that the pad from the chair was put on the kitchen table directly in front of him. Someone had caught him slipping he knew. Whoever it was must've had a death wish he told himself. He cursed himself, knowing he had left the main door unlocked in case Monty arrived in the midst of him playing the Wii game. His focus on the video game caused him to lose focus of the bigger picture. Sleep and get crept on was one of the rules he lived by, and now it was one that was used against him.

"Ma'fucka!" he bellowed as tears leaped out of his eyes and snot shot out of his nostrils. The next blow delivered to his sack came out of nowhere, instantly breaking his chain of thought. His breathing increased, and his heart kept beating like a drum up against his flesh. He growled through clenched teeth, closed his eyes, lowered his head, and tried to shake the pain all in one motion but to no avail. He felt helpless, and now he knew why the pad to chair lay in front of him. Had it not been for Murda's willpower, he was sure he would have passed out again from the unbearable feeling.

The first hit brought him back to consciousness, while the second one nearly drained what little strength he had, but still he managed to hold on.

"You're fuckin' dead," he spat as he did his best to get a grip on the inflicting pain.

That was Heaven's cue. She stepped from behind the chair from which she had just orchestrated her torture methods and revealed her identity to him. Murda's eyes grew wide, and the muscles in his jaws stiffened. Out of nowhere, a grin appeared across his face. Unfazed by his facial expression as a mockery, Heaven saluted Murda with his own signature greeting the way he had done to her when they first met at the 40/40 Club.

"Ain't this a 'bout a bitch," he smiled, just before he spit out the blood that had filled his mouth.

Heaven expected as much. "You's a real gangsta, huh?" she retorted with sarcasm in her tone.

"Believe that, bitch!" Murda barked.

It was now Heaven's turn to smile. The open hole she had created by removing the pad from the kitchen chair that Murda now sat in and the way she had tied his legs apart gave her easy accessibility to commence her torture from any angle. Heaven leaned in and swung the towel she had tied in a knot at the end as if she was pitching a softball underhanded. The impact of the blow transformed Murda's tough persona into a childlike scream and forced him to lose his bowels.

Murda yelled out and spit flew from his mouth as he screeched, "You stinkin' whore." He was now breathing heavily, taking deep breaths as tears flowed down his face. Mentally, he tried to immune himself to the hurtful feeling as he attempted to regain his composure for a second time. But the pain was like no other he had felt before. Still, he gathered up enough strength to spit at Heaven and say, "You think you're gonna get away with this?"

"Like you thought you were gonna get away with what you did to me and my peoples, you cocksuka?" Heaven shot back as she hit him for a third time. It infuriated her to be in the same room with the actual person who had carried out the act of violation against her and her partner. There was nothing she wanted more than to spend the rest of the day torturing and making the young assailant pay for her loss and all the drama his actions had brought to her doorstep, but she knew time was of the essence.

"Fuck your peoples," Murda lashed out trying to get a rise out of her. He figured if he could stall her, just awhile longer until Monty arrived, the tables would be turned, and he could enjoy the pleasure of his own revenge for what Heaven was doing to him. Murda had already envisioned stripping the beautiful red-bone down to the nude the same way she had done him. He smiled at the thought of tying her to the same chair, conducting the same torture between her legs. He had even thought of violating her first in the vilest sexual ways for the pain she had caused him.

Heaven disregarded Murda's last comment. Instead, she picked up the crowbar she had laid on the carpet and approached him.

"I wonder what hand you used to pull the trigger," she stated rather than asking. With that, she raised the crowbar and came down with it. The hard metal smashed Murda's right knuckles. Again, he let out an agonizing cry which competed with Busta Rhymes's CD. Wasting no time, Heaven did the same to Murda's left hand. This time, he outyelled the rapper.

"You know you're gonna die, right?" she taunted. She then pulled her weapon from behind the small of her back. "You might as well tell me where I can find your bitch-ass cousin so he can meet you in hell," she added.

Murda noticed the Glock Heaven now possessed in her hand. All his thoughts and plans he once had began to fade. It didn't take being a rocket scientist to figure out he was a dead man. His only thought now was whether he should answer the question she was demanding an answer to. He knew there was a strong possibility that if he didn't, then his own death would go unsolved and unavenged, but if he did, then, at least, his cousin would have the heads-up and possibly see his would-be killer coming and get the drop on her. Murda quickly weighed his options. The latter of his thoughts seemed more appealing to him. For a tenth of a second, he felt like he was about to snitch on his cousin, but his conscience convinced him he was making the best choice, considering the situation and circumstances. Besides, he knew if he told her where Monty was, when she arrived at the scene, she'd receive a rude awakening.

"Times up, what's it gonna be?" Heaven asked, raising her weapon. She knew if she killed Murda without him giving her the information she needed, her chances of finding Monty would become slim to none. At least today, anyway, but that wasn't a chance she was willing to take. She placed the Glock up against Murda's temple. His eyes grew cold. He sucked his teeth as if he had something stuck in between them.

"He's at Feaster Park with—"

"Boom."

The shot entered his skull before he could finish his sentence. A few seconds more and his words would have prolonged his death, but since Heaven hadn't given him the time to finish, she would just have to find out on her own. Just as she had entered, she smoothly exited the apartment, off to her next destination. Her adrenaline was now at an all-time high as she got closer to avenging her partner's death.

Chapter Forty-Seven

Meanwhile, down the street around the corner, Monty was engaged in a serious conversation.

"Yeah, my dude, like I said, if the shoe was on the other foot, I would want somebody to pull me up. I don't want you to think I was tryin'a come in between you and your peoples, but when my peoples slipped it to me, I felt it was only right to give it to you." He tried to justify his reason for calling the meeting with the man who stood before him.

"Nowadays, chicks is more ruthless than some of the jokers out here," he added fuel to the fire he was sure he had already ignited.

The man listened attentively as Monty laid it on thick. He wondered what motives he had for giving him the information that was the missing piece to the puzzle he had been trying to solve for the past seven or so months since the incident had transpired. Whatever the case, he knew what was told to him was accurate, and although he was as calm as still waters on the surface, on the inside, he was bubbling like a volcano. Mixed emotions battled for supremacy in his mind, not knowing which would come out on top—Love or Loyalty.

"I know I just dropped some heavy shit on you, my G," Monty said, bringing the man back to the present. His facial expression let Monty know he was in deep thought. "But it's better to find out now than later, or never, and you'd be paying for it a different way. Chicks come and go, but you only got one life, ya dig?" Monty ended.

The man did not particularly care for Monty but could not deny that he spoke the truth. In the game they both played, they knew you could not allow feelings and emotions to dictate their better judgment. Trust was one of the most important rules of the game, and the man lived by those sets of rules. He knew if he couldn't trust someone or something, he had no problem walking away from or eliminating whatever it was, if need be. Distrust was a sign of betrayal in his book, and one of the penalties for that was death, but as the new information he was given played in his mind, he wondered if he had really been betrayed.

"But, yo, I'ma 'bout to get up outta here, my dude," Monty announced, breaking the man's thoughts for a second time.

The man nodded.

"I hope everything works out for you with that, tho." He then extended his hand. "And I know I don't have to say this, but I'd appreciate it if you keep me and my people's name up out of it," Monty added as the two of them embraced.

"You're right, you don't have to tell me that," the man retorted, taking offense.

"That's what's up." Monty knew he had offended the man but could care less. His only concern was that he had accomplished what he set out to do. Both men were about to go their separate ways, each in their own thoughts, when they were stopped in their tracks by the sudden presence of another.

Chapter Forty-Eight

Heaven cruised down the block once upon a time known as Macy's Boulevard. She couldn't help but to reflect back remembering how the particular hood had gotten its street moniker. Back in the mid-eighties and early nineties, Macy's was considered to be a place to shop for any and everything for those who had plenty of money and willing to spend it in order to frequent the legendary department store. Although there were different versions of how the area received its name, the story Heaven knew of was how old-school money getters such as Shalik, I. B., Wild Style, P-God, and some others, made sure, just like the department store, the notorious drug block had every product available for consumers. They saw to it that plenty of money was being spent for what they had for sale.

Heaven cracked a short smile after her brief trip down memory lane. She wondered where the days had gone, when hating didn't exist and there was enough money for everybody. The thought angered her because she knew at the end of the day, that was what all of what had transpired had been about, money, and now because of greed, Heaven knew the only way to put an end to the situation is by ending the life of the one behind it all: Monty. With that being her thought, she rode down the avenue. She noticed heads of hustlers spread throughout both sides of the street of Troop Avenue turning as she passed by Comstock and Hale Street. She recognized a few familiar faces that attempted to peer inside the whip she drove.

As she continued down the block, she saw someone who she was sure would recognize her, squinting his eyes, as if he wore glasses, to get a better view into the stolen Aurora. Heaven slightly dropped her head as if she was focusing on the radio station while driving past him. As she made her way toward the corner of Handy Street, she was convinced that she had gone unnoticed by the guy she had known by the name of Life. Between the light-tinted windows, the NJ fitted that once belonged to Earth she sported low, and the move with the car's radio, she was sure she had deceived him. He was one of the few money getters of the town and the only one from the block she drove down that she really dealt with, but right now, she was on a mission, and there was no room for error or mistakes, so she was glad he hadn't noticed it was her.

As she approached the intersection at the end of Feaster Park, Heaven waited for the ongoing traffic to pass. It was her intent to hook a left on Handy Street in search of the perfect parking spot until her mind was changed by what she saw to the right of her.

Heaven did a quick scan of the area and noticed that aside from what she was witnessing, the park was nearly empty where Monty and the unidentified person were located. She knew it was either now or never, unaware of how long Monty had actually been at the park. She made the right onto Handy Street and slowly searched for a parking space. As fate would have it, a burgundy Sebring pulled out of a space and sped off. Heaven wasted no time occupying the spot a short distance from where Monty and the man stood. Had she gone up a few more car lengths, she may have recognized one of the parked vehicles and questioned its presence in the area.

Heaven killed the engine of the Aurora and drew her weapons. She released both safety locks, then one by one, cocked them back, causing a bullet to lodge in each chamber of the twin sixteen shots. Before exiting the vehicle, she checked all mirrors and windows for stragglers in passing. Seeing that the coast was clear, she shoved her weapons back into their respective pockets of her down jacket and reached for the car door's handle. Out of force of habit, when she reached the sidewalk, she did another quick scan of the area. *So far so good,* she thought as she headed in Monty's direction.

As she neared, her adrenaline heightened, and her heart rate increased. *The moment of truth,* she thought. She was sure after this she would be able to sleep better, the nightmares would end, and her friend could rest in peace. Heaven reached inside her down jacket to retrieve her weapons. She had every intention on making both Monty and whomever he was indulging in a conversation with lifeless. Leave no witnesses behind was Earth's and her motto, and the rule applied now. Just as she was about to draw on them, Monty and the stranger gave departing handshakes and hugs, giving her first-time visual access to the second party. The sight of the unmistakable face over Monty's shoulder nearly took Heaven's breath away. She shook her head and did a double take, not wanting to believe what her eyes had just revealed to her. In an instant, her mind was overloaded with so many thoughts. Not knowing what to really make of what she saw, Heaven pulled out her two Glocks and beelined it over to the two intended dead men.

Chapter Forty-Nine

Monty was the first to see Heaven with the twin Glocks pointed in his direction. Instantly, he drew his .44 revolver despite her already having the drop on him. A surprised Chill drew his own .45 semiautomatic reflexively. At first, Chill had no idea of the identity of the person sporting the fitted and down jacket with weapons aimed at him and Monty. Upon the realization, despite the news just given to him, Chill lowered his gun, which he had locked on the NJ that sat atop of the fitted Heaven wore. Visual daggers were thrown in the triangle. Monty, Chill, and Heaven all stood stoned face. Each pair of eyes spoke volumes. In an instant, before any true clarity could be shed on the matter, the loud voice of a fourth party was the trigger that sent bullets flying. When the shots ceased and the park became silent, two people were left wounded while another lay where the individual once stood, fighting for dear life.

Chapter Fifty

The realization of what just transpired hours ago had yet to set in as Heaven sat in the bullpen waiting to be processed in the Middlesex County Adult Corrections in North Brunswick. Her bloodstained clothes began to stiffen as the cold air poured out the vents, attacking her from every angle like the arctic winds while she sat motionless on the hard steel bench, images of the incident flashed through her mind like those of a slide show while she watched them play-by-play. The first picture she saw was Monty and Chill together. It was that image that had sent her over the top and off the deep end. Betrayed would be the best word to describe how Heaven had felt at that moment after finding out Monty was behind the attack on her and Earth with the help of Le Le. Seeing these two men together left Heaven no other choice but to believe Chill was in on it. She cursed herself for not wanting to discuss the streets and know where Chill was really from in New Brunswick. It was evident to her that he was a part of Monty's camp the way the two were shaking hands and exchanging hugs. Her first instinct was to draw her weapon and let the bullets fall where they may, but her feelings for Chill overpowered her decision. The fact of the matter was, she not only loved Chill but also was in love with him. Guilt overswept her at the time. Had the shoe been on the other foot, lover or not, Earth would not have hesitated gunning down all parties involved.

The picture in Heaven's mind changed to the standoff between her, Monty, and Chill in Feaster Park. Four weapons were now drawn, one in Monty's hand, another in Chill's, and two in Heaven's. Both Monty's and Chill's weapons were drawn on Heaven. Heaven noticed Chill lowered his, recognizing her, while Monty's weapon stayed locked on her. The smirk on Monty's face and dazed look on Chill's confused Heaven, but his words put things back into perspective. The words, *"That was you who shot up Remsen,"* rang loudly in Heaven's ears. *He stated it rather than ask,* thought Heaven, remembering his tone and facial expression. For the first time, she remembered why Chill had looked so familiar, and the first time she'd actually seen him. The image of him shooting at them the day they gunned down his friend

Twan as they scurried up the block in the stolen Cherokee appeared in her mind. Heaven knew she'd never forget the love Chill once had in his eyes whenever he looked at her—that now was replaced with pain and anger when she didn't respond.

Heaven's own eyes transformed from warm to glacier ice cold when she asked Chill if he had anything to do with the hit ordered on her and Earth, and he chose to stand there in silence. *Had he answered, the outcome may have been different,* she thought. Everything could have been different.

Images of smoking guns appeared in Heaven's mind. Everything seemed to be happening so fast, she thought, yet it all had unfolded like a slow motion scene in a movie. The word *"Freeze!"* was the word that changed lives forever. It was the word that acted as the starter pistol that sent runners off and running in a marathon race. The same word which caused the shots to ring out.

The sound of gunplay echoed in Heaven's head in surround sound. Bullets spiraled and whizzed in the air at what seemed to be one mile per hour, lodging and ripping through any and everything, from trees, cars, to flesh. When the smoke was clear, Heaven sat cradling Chill, who had fallen from the impact of the first wild shot she had let off after being grazed by the one shot Monty let off that hit her. The other shot that plunged into him was from Monty's gun that continued to fire in succession. Heaven let off three of her own in Monty's direction as she saw him fleeing on foot. She was sure one of the three had hit him judging by the way she saw him holding his left arm as he vanished up the block. The tears of anger that began to form in her eyes made it difficult to see which way Monty had gone once he made it up Troop Avenue. But her mind was not focused on Monty as she raced to Chill's side. The final words he spoke before taking his last breath pierced Heaven's heart like thorns. "I didn't have anything to do with that," he uttered hoarsely. Heaven knew he was referring to the hit on her and Earth. She encouraged him not to speak with tear-filled eyes, but her request was disregarded. "I love you," were the words Heaven could never forget that Chill managed to say right before his eyes froze and his soul exited his body. His words had her in such a daze that she never noticed Detective Saleski standing over her, calling her name and ordering her to drop her weapon.

"Jacobs." Heaven finally heard her last name being called. The sound of the Middlesex County female correctional officer calling her name brought her back to the present. Unbeknownst to her, it was the third time she'd called her. Heaven stood up and made her way out of the bullpen. It had been many years since she'd been in the county jail, but although things seemed different, she knew the process was all the same.

"Don't I know you?" the brown-skinned female officer whose name tag read Brown asked as Heaven approached the desk.

Heaven shrugged her shoulders. She knew who the officer was. She was actually one of the ones who had treated her and the other female inmates fair, but she was not in the mood for a reunion, especially not this one.

"You've been her before?" Officer Brown asked, disregarding Heaven's nonchalant attitude. Being in corrections as long as she had, she understood. It always saddened her to see women, black women at that, come, go, and come back into the place she worked, especially those who were mothers. It was bad enough, thought Officer Brown, that the facility was overpopulated with black men who were fathers. She always thought about the impact having an incarcerated parent had on a child. She often questioned if both parents were locked-up, then who was on the outside raising the youth?

Officer Brown credited incarceration as being one of the main contributors to the demise of the young people and destruction of families. Which is why every chance she got, she preached and tried to educate and encourage as many men and women as she could to stay out once they got out. She was sure Heaven was one of the ones she had tried to reach in the past.

"When's the last time you been here?" she then asked, convinced that she had been.

Judging by Heaven's appearance, Officer Brown could see that she was no heroin or crack addict, but possibly a dealer or some dealer's girlfriend.

She had seen enough cases throughout the years come through to just about determine an individual's story. She had heard them all. She noticed the burgundy stains on Heaven's clothing for the first time. It was dried-up blood. She hadn't bothered to look at what Heaven had been arrested for, but after seeing the blood, thought she may have been in for stabbing or even shooting an abusive lover. For some reason, at that moment, Officer Brown sympathized with Heaven. Had she known the truth, she would feel differently.

"2000," Heaven answered as she followed Officer Brown to the corner of the room.

"You've been out for a long time," Officer Brown said. Normally, many didn't last nearly nine months, let alone years. She was now intrigued about why Heaven was there.

"What happened?" she wanted to know.

"Shit happened," Heaven replied dryly.

That was all Officer Brown needed to hear. She could take a hint. It didn't take a rocket scientist to tell her that Heaven did not want to talk about whatever landed her in the position she was now faced with. She immediately disengaged in prying but made a mental note to check her booking sheet to see why she was there.

"I understand," Officer Brown retorted. "Stand over there so I can take your picture," she then instructed. "You're not new to this. The quicker we get this over with and get you changed over, the quicker we can get you down to medical and on the unit, okay?"

Heaven did not reply. Instead, she just went through the motions as the officer took her mug shot, asked a bunch of personal and medical questions, fingerprinted her, and strip-searched her. Officer Brown then replaced her blood-stained clothes with a green tee and pants. The officer handed her a pair of flip-flops and a bedroll. Afterward, she attached a wristband around Heaven's left wrist with her photo, name, and inmate number printed on it before she escorted her down to the medical unit.

After what seemed like hours in the medical unit, Heaven was escorted to the female unit along with a young, slender, Caucasian girl. The clock read 11:43 p.m. Heaven could tell the young white girl was a heroin user. Her pale white skin, sore-infested forearms, and occasional nod while they sat in medical were a dead giveaway, not to mention the back-to-back vomiting and shakes. Officer Brown studied Heaven as they walked down the corridor. She couldn't believe this was the same female who had been charged with murder and attempted murder according to Intake. Furthermore, she couldn't believe this was the same female whose name she had heard so many times from many of the female inmates about being one of the biggest female kingpins in Middlesex County and one of the biggest drug dealers in New Brunswick. She shook her head in pity realizing how looks could be deceiving. The officer in the booth buzzed the door as they arrived in front of the female unit known as the Fox Trap.

"Name?" the officer whose name tag read Hankerson, asked, looking up from the clipboard.

"Jacobs," Heaven replied.

"Let me see your wristband," Officer Hankerson then said.

She jotted down the information from the wristband as Heaven held her wrist up in the air.

"Okay, first cell right there," she pointed. "Name?" she asked the white girl.

When Heaven stepped inside the cell, she couldn't help but sigh at the sight. Both of the bunk beds were occupied with bodies. Sleepy eyes peered up at her from the bottom bunk; then the inmate rolled back over and tossed the cover over her head.

Heaven set her bedroll on the desk. She then kneeled down and pulled the boat-shaped plastic bed from underneath the bunk. The top bunk occupant now turned over aggressively, agitated by having her beauty rest being disturbed by the sound of the sliding of the bed boat underneath the bottom bunk. Heaven paid her no mind. If she knew what was best for her, she'd turn back over, thought Heaven. As if she'd read her mind, the girl on the top bunk sucked her teeth and put her back toward Heaven.

Heaven tied one of the sheets onto the flattened mattress and lay down. She put her hands behind her head and stared up at the ceiling, eyes wide open. So many thoughts invaded her mind. She couldn't believe this was what it had come down to. She knew based on the type of life she lived that prison and even death were some of the possible outcomes if she ever got caught slipping, but didn't think either would be her final fate. There was no doubt in her mind that the charges she was in for were enough to make prison her permanent place of residency, or at least for the next twenty to thirty years. At that moment, she wished her life had ended the day her partner Earth's had. Although she would never kill herself, her thoughts made it difficult for her to fall asleep.

On top of that, the manly sounds of snoring and the foul smell of fumes from the two females passing gas added to what she knew would be a restless night. A bolt of anger shot through Heaven as the thought of Monty getting away appeared. The fact that she was able to land one out of the three shots she had fired at his fleeing body was not enough. She wanted every shot her twin Glocks possessed emptied into his flesh until he was dead and stinking. But that had not been the case. Instead, he had escaped death, and the man she loved was forced to embrace it. Chill's face replaced the image of Monty's. His lifeless body lay there in her embrace as if he were resting. For the first time, a tear trickled down her face. Then, another followed until they spilled out of Heaven's eyes onto her cheeks. She closed her eyes tightly and shook her head, trying to shake the image of Chill out of her mind, but it was no use. Uncontrollable tears took over her as her heart ached. She cried not only for the loss of Chill, but also for the loss of Earth and for the missed opportunity to make Monty pay. But most of all, she shed tears for the loss of her freedom.

Her nighttime tears soon turned into morning stains as she heard the click of the cell door and the sounds of running water combined with a flushing toilet.

"First tier trays up," Heaven heard the officer roar.

"You eatin'?" one of her cell mates asked dryly as she looked down at Heaven from the sink area.

Heaven matched her tone with her facial expression and shook her head. She then glanced over to the other bunk bed and noticed the bottom bed was still occupied with a body letting her know that the girl at the sink was the one who made the sound effects on the top bunk last night. Not being new to jail, Heaven was sure the girl had deliberately and intentionally made noise at the sink and toilet to wake her out of spite of being awakened in the middle of the night when she came in. Females, especially those in jail, were spiteful like that Heaven knew. She wondered if she'd have to make an example out of her cell mate while she was in there.

"Paula, get up; it's time to eat," the medium-height, dark-skinned female with bad skin and baby cornrows shouted to the lump in the bottom bunk.

"I'm good," a hoarse voice moaned from under the covers.

"Whatever," the girl shot back making her way out of the cell.

"First tier, let's go; last call for trays," were the words that boomed through the room when the cell door opened.

Heaven stood up and went to the sink. She held the cold-water button with one hand and used her other to splash water on her face, due to the fact that she had no washcloth in her bedroll last night. She saw how bloodshot her eyes were as she looked into the mirror. She snatched up the shank-proof fingertip toothbrush along with the clear toothpaste and brushed her teeth as best she could. She let out a chuckle at the unsanitary way the jail forced her to groom. She was drying her face when her cell mate reentered with her breakfast tray.

Heaven couldn't help but notice the morning serving before she lay back down. Her stomach turned at the sight of it. The facility called it Cream of Beef, but the inmates coined its rightful name as "Shit on a shingle" due to its resemblance to wet feces.

Heaven never understood how someone could eat a meal and enjoy it after calling it such a name. Her last six-month stay, she had never eaten the disgusting-looking meal and promised never to. The officer walked by, glanced in the cell, and slammed the door shut.

"So, what they got you for?" the dark-skinned girl asked with the same dry tone she had used when she spoke to Heaven about breakfast. Heaven was tempted to jump up and choke the girl until she regurgitated her breakfast, but instead, she answered, "Bullshit."

"Yeah, that's what they all say," the girl chuckled. Her remark got her more than she bargained for. Not expecting a response or a reaction, she was caught by surprise. Before she realized she was being deprived of oxygen, Heaven had her hands wrapped around her neck cutting off her air.

"Bitch, you got me twisted," snarled Heaven as she pinned the girl's head up against the cell window. Her words were deep and low enough not to alarm the officer but loud enough to wake the girl in the bottom bunk.

"Oh my God," Paula, the frail, half-Hispanic, half-Black girl hopped out of the bed in shock.

"Please," she begged on behalf of her friend Samantha, whose eyes seemed to be about to pop out their sockets.

"Whatever she did she didn't mean it," Paula pleaded.

"Nah, this bitch knew what she was doing," Heaven spat as she continued choking the life out of the girl. She pictured the helpless body being Monty as she applied more pressure to the girl's throat. She was already facing murder and attempted murder charges, so another one would make no difference she told herself. It wasn't until her name was called that she loosened her grip.

Paula tried to pry Heaven's hands from around Samantha's neck. Regardless of the situation, she refused to be labeled as a snitch, so she sided against banging on the door for officer assistance. When she looked into her cell mate's face and continued her plea, she could see that the newcomer had blanked out. What stood out the most, though, was that she had recognized the female stranger. Upon calling Heaven's name for a second time, Paula realized she had finally gotten through.

"Please, Heaven," she begged again, seeing Heaven hadn't fully released her hold around Samantha's neck.

Heaven was curious how the girl knew her. She released her death grip and shoved Samantha, causing her head to bang against the window.

Heaven walked to the cell door and looked onto the dayroom. The female officer was still at the desk filling out paperwork. Samantha bellied over, gasping for air. Paula rushed to the sink and got her a drink of water. "Thank you," she said to Heaven.

Samantha slowly sipped on the water as she regained the function of her throat, allowing an open passage for air. She regretted the façade she had displayed that caused her life to nearly end in attempts to intimidate her new cell mate—especially after hearing Paula call the girl's name. Being from New Brunswick herself, Samantha was all too familiar with the name Heaven and what she and her deceased partner Earth were all about. According to the streets, Heaven and her partner Earth were just as thorough and ruthless as any male hustler that was getting money. She had never had the privilege of meeting either of the two, but being the dopefiend and crack addict she was, she had spent enough money on their drug block and

navigated enough sales to Shell, Sonya, and Le
Le. Knowing all too well how the three female
hustlers got down, witnessing them all on different occasions making examples out of other
junkies and dealers who underestimated them
because they were women, Samantha was sure
her life had been spared by their boss. Silently,
she thanked her higher power.

Meanwhile, Paula was working up the nerve
to say something to Heaven to break the ice
and cut through the tension that filled the six-
by-nine cell but couldn't figure out what to say.
She could see the steam still mystifying overtop
of Heaven's head like a halo, while her eyes
began to darken by the second. Being kin to one
of Heaven's team members, Paula had heard
enough stories from her older cousin Shell to
know that had she had not intervened, life as
Samantha knew it would be over. She herself
wanted to join the all-female crew after watching
in admiration the type of love and respect her
cousin and the others received whenever they
entered a room with Heaven and Earth, but
Shell refused to bring her in. Paula knew the
reason, although she denied it. It was no secret
to the family, though. No matter how well she
tried to hide it, everyone knew she was sniffing
heroin, including Shell. Paula remembered Shell

saying that there was no way she would allow her kin's blood to be on her hands. Seeing Heaven in action made Paula realize the depths of her cousin's words. She knew her five-bags-a-day habit would have increased had she been around the drug with daily accessibility, putting her in a position to slip even further into addiction. Paula was sure her then twenty-two-year-old life would have ended before her twenty-third birthday came around had she joined their team.

Here she was now, at age twenty-five, sitting in Middlesex County Jail with a fifteen-bag-a-day habit and what would be her fourth charge. Tears began to well up in her eyes at the thought.

The silence was broken by the clicking sound of the door.

"Y'all got trays in here?" the female trustee came around with the trash can and asked.

Samantha just stood there plastered against the wall. She was hesitant, fearful of a repeat occurrence with Heaven. Not wanting to draw suspicion, Paula picked up the tray and walked it over to the trustee. The trustee sensed something was wrong as she noticed the facial expressions and demeanor of the three women. Regardless of the situation, it was none of her business, so she took the tray and moved on to the next cell.

"Where you know me from?" Heaven wanted to know as she studied Paula. There was no doubt in her mind that she didn't know the girl.

Her tone intimidated Paula. "Shell's my cousin," she offered as an explanation.

"Oh," Heaven nodded. She then took a second look out the cell door. The officer was still in the same position hovered over the desk. She was sure her attack went unheard.

"What time they let us out?" Heaven directed her words to Paula. Samantha had made her way back onto her bunk. Paula thought for a minute. "I think we go out at nine today because we went out before dinner yesterday. It rotates for us because we're on twenty-three-hour lockdown and one-hour rec until we get medical clearance," she answered. Things were different since the last time Heaven had been in the facility, so she was unaware of the new operations of the female unit.

"And in order to make a call, your peoples has to set up an account with Global Tel-Link. A lot has changed," Paula spat in disgust. She was among the percentage of inmates who couldn't reach out to their loved ones because of the new phone system.

"This place is messed up," she added in frustration. Heaven didn't say anything. Instead, she just listened as Shell's cousin babbled. Her eyes happened to look over at Samantha who she noticed was staring at her. "What's up?" gritted Heaven.

She was all too ready to finish what she had started if Samantha had felt froggy and decided to leap. Heaven kept her eyes locked on Samantha. Samantha chose her words carefully before she spoke. "I didn't mean any disrespect," she started out saying. "I was in the wrong. That was my bad," she confessed.

Heaven weighed up Samantha's apology. She had been in the game long enough to know when someone was trying to game her. Samantha's words were genuine.

"I respect that," Heaven retorted.

Instantly, the tension lightened, and the air cleared at the acceptance of Samantha's apology. Both Paula and Samantha were relieved for their own reasons. Paula, because she didn't want to be a witness or an accessory to a murder, and Samantha, because she wanted to make it out of the county jail the way she had come in . . . in one piece, breathing. It wasn't until Heaven had sat on the bunk bed that Paula and Samantha had lay back down. No one spoke anymore.

Heaven woke to the sound of the cell door clicking for the second time. She hadn't realized she had dosed off while sitting up. The excitement the night prior had taken a toll on her body as sleep overpowered her will to stay awake. She hopped up, splashed cold water on her face, gargled, dried her face all in one motion, and stormed out of the cell. She could hear the stampede of footsteps rustling down the steps of the second tier like a herd of cattle. By the time, she made it to the phone area, all five phones were occupied while other females waited in line. Heaven cursed herself as she looked around in search of other phones. There were none on the second tier but four others she knew she couldn't use. One was in a cage for any female who got into trouble and went to lock up, another was for a female who may have been deaf, and the other two were for females who had to be medically quarantined. Heaven shook her head as she watched the clock tick away at what seemed to be a rapid pace. She knew how time escaped you when you were up against it, especially in her situation. An hour was no time in jail when you needed to get something done.

The entire female unit was moving at lightning speed, thought Heaven. Women scurried to the showers, others huddled around the television, while women in red jumpsuits stood in a cipher congregating. Judging by the foreign appearance,

Heaven figured they were Immigration detainees. As she finished her observation taking in her surroundings, she noticed she too had become the observed. Sets of eyes locked in, glanced, and studied her as whispers and murmurs filled the dayroom. A couple of faces she recognized, while most she didn't. Either way, she was not beat.

The phone where she stood in line became free, and one of the callers in front of her hopped on. A total of twenty minutes had gone by since they'd been let out. Heaven sighed in aggravation. She had one more caller before her. She was tempted to jump in front of the female but feared she'd snitch on her. To her relief, she didn't have to because the phone became open again as the unsuccessful caller slammed the phone and stormed off in a tantrum after a three-minute failed attempt. Heaven crossed her fingers hoping the same for the new caller. The smile on the girl's face let Heaven know her wish didn't come true.

Heaven stood there steaming for what seemed like an hour as the tall, frail, white, dirty-blonde continued with her giddiness on the phone. Eight minutes had passed by the time Heaven was able to make eye contact with the blonde. She was sure her eyes had spoken volumes judging by the sudden fear that appeared on the blonde's face, not to mention the fact that she told whoever was on the other end of the phone she loved them and had to go. The blonde wasted no time getting away from Heaven once she ended her call. Heaven wasn't in the least bit concerned with the girl or any of the other females. She glanced at the clock as she dialed the only number she knew by heart. The clock informed her that she had thirty minutes remaining.

By the time Global Tel-Link phone system instructed them on the procedures to accept the call, nearly two minutes had gone by when she heard the familiar voice.

"Qué pasa, mami?" Shell answered happy to be hearing from her boss. "You good? What happened?" Shell bombarded her.

"I'm good, don't have too much time to talk or explain," Heaven spit out. "I need you to get in touch with Hassan or Bashir and tell them I need a bail ASAP."

"Already on it," Shell interrupted. "Left them both messages, waiting to hear back. Don't worry, we're gonna make sure you get out of there, no matter what," she assured Heaven.

"I know that," Heaven's tone dropped.

Shell caught it, "You sure you good, *mamá?*" she asked again.

"Yeah, this spot just fucked up and things just went fucked up," Heaven replied.

Shell knew what she was referring to, between the news and the streets. She had a clear picture of how things went down. "Why you didn't let us know something? You know we had your back," Shell had finally asked what was weighing heavy on her mind. That's what they all wanted to know.

"I don't wanna talk about it," Heaven answered, not because she was avoiding the question but because she knew the calls were being recorded and monitored.

"We'll talk, though," she then said. Shell understood.

"The girls send their love and said they'll see you soon." Heaven could hear Sonya and Mia in the background.

"I love y'all too. Let me get off this phone and take a shower."

"Okay. I'll see you when you get out tomorrow," Shell said.

"Hopefully."

"Nah, you're comin' home," Shell stated with confidence.

"You're right; see you tomorrow," Heaven ended the call.

"Excuse me, Officer Garace." Heaven approached the officer's desk addressing the nearest of the two female officers. She was sure she had mispronounced the officer's name she had read on the name tag. The stylish spiked-hair Caucasian officer looked up at Heaven. She was so preoccupied with the reading of her book she hadn't noticed Heaven's sudden presence. Her partner, an attractive sister, who was also engrossed in a book, her name tag read George, noticed Heaven. Officer Garace used an ink pen as a bookmark and closed the book. Heaven read the title of the cover. It was the book *Ride or Die Chick 2* by Earth's cousin. *How ironic,* she thought.

"Yes?" Officer Garace asked. Between her baby face features and soft-spoken tone, Heaven knew the officer couldn't have been more than twenty-three years old.

"Can I get a bar of soap?"

"Here you go." Being the closest to the crate that held the supplies, Officer George handed her a bar of soap. "Do you need tissue?" she asked Heaven.

"No. Thank you."

"No problem."

"And it's pronounced *Gracey*," the officer corrected Heaven before she walked off.

"Got it, Officer Garace," Heaven repeated before making her way to the shower.

Morning turned into afternoon, and the afternoon turned into the lights going out for the evening. As before, Heaven threw her hands behind her head and stared at nothing in particular while her cell mates lay soundly asleep.

Chapter Fifty-One

"Jacobs, come get your early-morning court tray," the midnight shift officer announced as she stood in the doorway of the cell. Heaven recognized the soft-spoken tone from earlier. When she opened her eyes, she saw Officer Garace standing there. She's definitely getting her hustle on thought Heaven, seeing how Officer Garace had just worked two shifts prior. The hustler in her made her think how much of an asset the officer could have been to her crew had they met on the outside.

Heaven made her way out into the dayroom and retrieved a breakfast tray consisting of boiled eggs, hot cereal, and bread. Just as before, the officer was reading a book by the Plainfield author. This time, it was his title *On the Run with Love*.

Officer Garace looked up and smiled at Heaven. "Good morning," she offered. Heaven nodded with a grin. Something about the officer's eyes made Heaven feel that she was older in a mature way than she had given her credit for being earlier. They appeared to be a set of eyes that had experienced more than she was willing to tell. There was no doubt in her mind that the officer either had played in the streets at some point or knew people who had.

"Abrams, Reed, Carmen," Officer Garace shouted. "Come get these trays if you're eating."

Heaven returned to her cell, woofed down her breakfast, and waited to be called out for court.

She was handcuffed to five females packed in the back of the Middlesex County Sheriff's van like sardines in a can. Luckily for her, she was the last female to be handcuffed and the last to enter the back of the vehicle. On the opposite side of the transporting van separated by a metal gate were six male inmates. While the men struck up frivolous conversations with the other women, Heaven peered out the back of the van's window as they traveled down Rt. 130 headed to the courthouse. Trailing a short distance behind was a Middlesex County Sheriff patrol car as an escort. All she could think about was getting bail so she could post it. She knew if the judge denied her, there was no telling when she'd see the streets of New Brunswick again—or any streets, for that matter. She had already told herself no matter what the ransom they give her, she intended to make bail, even if it meant going broke. She thought about the seven hundred twenty-five thousand she had stashed and the hundred-plus grand in product she possessed, and knew within the blink of an eye she would hand it all over for her freedom. From the house to the whips, she had already told herself she'd sacrifice it all, knowing that it was all replaceable and worthless without her freedom.

Once she saw the sign Livingston Avenue, she knew they were nearing the courthouse. Livingston turned into New Street, New Street into Kirkpatrick, then a right onto Paterson Street. The sheriff's patrol car blocked the intersection of Kirkpatrick and Paterson Street as the van backed into the garage of the Middlesex County Courthouse building. One by one, the females bailed out of the back of the vehicle led by Heaven. One would have thought it was the Super Bowl the way the bullpens full of male inmates stood and posted up against the cell bars, climbing on top of one another's backs catcalling, yelling, whistling, and cheering at Heaven and her handcuffed entourage that followed.

"Damn, that bitch in the front bad as hell," Heaven heard one of the men tell another. She was tempted to reply by saying the woman who gave birth to him was a bitch but kept her composure.

"What's ya name, ma?" another asked as she passed the next bullpen. Heaven ignored him and continued to follow the sheriff. She could hear some of the other females entertaining the attention the rude and disrespectful men were displaying. She was glad to be free of the metal bracelets and detached from the others. Heaven found her a spot in the corner to herself while the others congregated, speaking about their charges and hopes when their time to go before the judge came. Their conversation was interrupted by the first call that came from the bullpen of men across from them.

"Hey, baby," Heaven heard the slim, light-skinned girl scurry to the bars and answer. She couldn't help but hear the extent of the conversation. Within minutes, it was apparent to her the two jailhouse lovebirds were codefendants. Heaven shook her head and chuckled to herself. It didn't take a genius to figure out the boyfriend wanted the young female to confess to their charges they were being held for so he could go free. She thought back to the time when she was so naïve, or rather a sucker for love, as she knew the girl was. She was tempted to intervene but knew it wasn't her place or her business. Besides, she had her own problems, but she despised men like that girl's boyfriend. It was because of cowards like him that she herself was in her own predicament she felt.

"Heavenly Jacobs," the officer called out. Her thoughts were interrupted by the booming sound of her name being called.

"You're going up," the officer announced as he approached the holding cell.

The female who had occupied the bars brought her conversation to a halt and backed away so Heaven could step up. "Open up the inner female," the officer ordered.

"Outter," he followed up with as soon as he cuffed Heaven. Heaven's eyes remained straight-ahead as she was escorted to the elevator. She ignored the comments and statements bouncing off the walls from the jailed men.

Right as she reached the officer waiting for her on the elevator, she heard one guy say, "Yo, that's the broad Heaven that run them chicks on Seamen and Lee."

Heaven paid the comment no mind. She could feel the husky, black, bald-headed officer's eyes on her as the elevator climbed to its destination. Out of the corner of her left eye, she could see he was studying her. "Domestic case?" he asked.

"No," she answered dryly, annoyed by the stereotype. *If he only knew,* she thought. The white officer kept his eyes on the elevator's numbers. The elevator opened on the third floor. They all exited and made their way to the courtroom.

"Um," the husky, bald-headed officer moaned in a low tone but not low enough as he trailed behind Heaven. She knew there was not anything she could do about his behavior, but in her mind, she had pictured using his own weapon to blow both his big bald head and his little head off for the disrespect he was displaying.

"Sit right there," the white officer pointed, holding the door to courtroom 304. When Heaven entered, the first face she saw was Shell. Shell flashed her warm smile, and she returned it. Her lawyer offered a nod of the head from where he sat. Across from him was the prosecutor. On first sight, the tall, dark-haired, pale-skinned, clean-shaved-with-a-long-beak man looked like a dickhead racist to Heaven. The one look he did throw her way was one of disgust, she thought, with a smug expression on his face.

"All rise for the Honorable Judge Ferencz," the bailiff announced.

"Please be seated," the judge instructed.

Heaven had never heard of the presiding judge, but the red-faced-receding-hairline-Caucasian judge seemed to be a racist by the look of him, she thought. They all were, she figured. To her knowledge, Middlesex County was a prejudiced county, especially the judicial system. She heard enough stories and cases to know that there were two sets of laws in Middlesex County. The last time she was in, she had seen white offenders receiving slaps on their wrists for crimes that blacks and Latinos were routinely sent to prison for, despite their criminal records being similar, and sometimes, Caucasians being the worst offenders. Anyone from Middlesex County that ever had a brush with the law knew that whites were catered to and minorities were made examples of. Heaven knew her attorney had his work cut out for him.

"If I'm correct, this is a bail hearing," the judge stated.

"Yes, Your Honor, Muhammad Bashir for the defendant," Heaven's lawyer stood up.

"Michael Weiss for the Middlesex County Prosecutors Office," the prosecutor followed.

The judge skimmed through the papers before him. Heaven watched him carefully. By the way his eyebrows rose up and his eyes glanced over at her, she knew he had just discovered her charges.

"All right, Mr. Bashir, let's hear it." The judge extended his hand and gave Heaven's attorney the floor.

Heaven listened as her lawyer argued her bail motion. The prosecutor's facial expression changed with every argument while the judge remained motionless. When Attorney Bashir was done, the prosecutor stood with a stupid-looking smirk on his face. The judge offered the floor to him just as he had to Heaven's lawyer. The prosecutor argued that Heaven was a flight risk, based on the severity of the charges and her criminal history. He also threw in what was told to him by Detective Saleski stemming back to Earth's death up until when he'd arrested her at Feaster Park. Still, the judge remained like a statue as he listened attentively. After the prosecutor rested, the judge spoke.

"It is the court's decision after hearing both counsels that the bail request for Ms. Jacobs be denied."

Heaven expected as much after hearing the prosecutor's argument. Shell's eyes looked like Heaven felt as she noticed the pain in them. Shell managed to put on a smile for her boss as she stood. Heaven read her lips just before they escorted her out of the courtroom. Her words were comforting, but she knew it was over for her. As she reentered the elevator, Heaven was already wondering what type of deal her lawyer would be able to get her. Twenty years if she was lucky, she thought, unless they linked Le Le's and Murda's deaths to her. She knew the bullet from her gun lodged in Chill's body was enough to convict her of murder if she tried to take it to trial, and the testimony of the detective witnessing her shooting at Monty was more than enough to get her on attempted murder. The thought of it sickened her, knowing that the real culprit and one responsible for everything in the beginning had gotten away scot-free. Although she was no snitch, Heaven knew she would not be satisfied until Monty paid for what he had done—not with his freedom but with his life. Neither officer said a word as Heaven exited the elevator. The black, husky, bald-headed officer was still trying to digest the charges the fine-looking female was being held on.

Heaven was placed back into the female holding cell. She noticed none of the men made any comments as she passed. She also noticed none of the women had sat in the corner she had occupied prior to going up to the courtroom. All of the women stole looks in Heaven's direction.

Heaven caught the stares but paid them no mind. She brushed them off as the women simply being nosy. A short, brown-skinned female passed Heaven and made her way to the open bathroom area opposite of where Heaven sat.

She looked into the mirror, then took a sip of the faucet water. Heaven watched out of the corner of her eye, sensing there was more to the female's trip to the bathroom area than just a drink of water.

"Fuck them," Heaven calmly replied.

"I know that's right," the brown-skinned girl laughed. "That's exactly how I feel. They hate on me too," she added.

For the first time, Heaven looked in the girl's direction. Her short haircut and tomboyish posture were dead giveaways that she was a gay female. She didn't seem to be drugged out the way some of the other females appeared to be, thought Heaven.

"I knew ya peoples, Earth," the girl announced, seeing the puzzled look on Heaven's face. "That was my strip club partner," she chuckled as she traveled down memory lane in her mind. "She was good peoples," she then said returning to the present.

At the mention of Earth and strip club in the same sentence, Heaven realized the girl knew her friend. Despite the bad mood she was in, it put a smile on her face to hear someone speak about her road dawg in high regards. "Yeah, she was," Heaven stated.

"You probably don't remember, but we met before," the girl said. Heaven took a long look, but the face didn't register.

"Earth introduced us. We were at Jersey Girls in Elizabeth. She told you she was going to bring me on the team." Her voice dropped seeing all eyes were now on them.

Heaven had only been in the exotic strip club once, and the incident appeared in her head as soon as the girl mentioned where they had met. Heaven remembered the girl who at the time looked just as much of a male hustler as Earth had that night with her fitted, leather, and baggy jeans. Heaven recalled that evening Earth and the brown-skinned girl had made it rain with over five hundred-dollars' worth of singles for all shapes, sizes, and flavors of females. Although she couldn't place her name, Heaven remembered Earth campaigning and vouching for how thorough of a female the girl was as a hustler and when it came to putting in work.

"What's your name again?" Heaven asked.

"Anita."

"Yeah," Heaven nodded, not remembering.

"Did you ever find out what happened?" Anita asked, her tone now almost in a whisper.

"That's why I'm here," Heaven replied, not wanting to say too much.

"That's what's up," Anita stated in admiration. Earth had let it be known on more than one occasion how close the two were. Anita remembered how Earth would always say how she'd die or kill for her partner Heaven. Anita realized that Heaven fell under the same creed.

"They ain't got shit on me," Anita changed the subject sensing that Heaven didn't want to discuss her situation. "That punk-ass cracker Schuster said he saw me make a sale," she spat. Heaven shook her head. She knew the name of the infamous narcotic's officer. Paul Schuster was responsible for at least 95 percent of the drug arrests in New Brunswick. He had been trying to take down Earth and her for years but was unsuccessful. Heaven listened as Anita continued. "He didn't find anything on me and didn't lock no fiend up he supposed to had seen me serve."

Her story sounded like so many arresting stories complementary of Paul Schuster, thought Heaven. He had been accused of every unlawful way to arrest someone, according to the streets, that you could think of, from planting evidence to falsifying reports. Heaven felt among the fortunate that she and her crew had never been tangled up in the narcotics officer's web. She frowned and shook her head, realizing she was actually in the predicament she was in now behind another law enforcement officer who had a hard-on for arrests. Heaven still could not believe that Detective Saleski had been following her. She knew she probably wouldn't be in jail now had it not been for that. She sensed the detective was going to be a problem the day he had come to question her at the hospital about the incident with her and Earth.

She wondered how long the homicide detective had been trailing her. Since she hadn't been charged for murdering Le Le and Murda, that let her know that he hadn't been following her the entire day. Then it dawned on her. Maybe he hadn't been following her at all. Maybe he was already there when she arrived. It all made sense to her now. She drew the conclusion that Detective Saleski was not investigating her but a murder suspect, Monty, and she walked right into the line of fire.

She cursed herself at the strong possibility. Her thoughts were again interrupted by the boom of the officer's voice. "Abrams!"

"That's me," Anita informed Heaven. As she exited the bullpen, Heaven laid her head against the concrete wall and closed her eyes.

The sound of metal caused her eyes to spring back open. Her neck was stiff from the position she had dozed off in. Once again, the sheriff sounded off with roll call. Hearing her name, Heaven stood and stretched, then made her way over to the bars where she was handcuffed. With the exception of one, all of the bullpens were empty of the male bodies from earlier. Heaven wondered how long she had been asleep. She knew court ended at 4:30 p.m., so it had to be at least close to five. A total of six females and six males followed behind one another as the sheriffs escorted them to the transporting van through the underground tunnel. Just as before, Heaven was cuffed first, making her the last to enter the back of the caged vehicle. She noticed the sheriff's watch read 6:25 p.m. as he closed the back door.

Chapter Fifty-Two

Daytime had now been replaced by nightfall. The sheriff's van traveled up Joyce Kilmer Avenue headed toward Rt. 130 as the sheriff patrol car followed. Soft rock music filled the back of the van, compliments of the transporting officers being tuned into the New Brunswick radio station 98.3 as the males and females chattered. As before, Heaven gazed out onto the city's street through the back window in a world of her own. She could see silhouettes of bodies scattered throughout the all-too-familiar area as they passed both Comstock and Delavan Street just before they rode past Joyce Kilmer Park to her right. As the van hooked a left turn on to Stanford Avenue, Heaven was not surprised to see nearly fifty Mexicans gathered around the bodega while another twenty or so congregated in front of the car lot on the corner. The van came to a sudden halt within seconds after turning on to Sandford Street.

Heaven knew they were at the traffic light that sat off Livingston Avenue. She braced herself as the van accelerated through the light. As she peered out the window, she noticed the distance the sheriff's patrol car was trailing behind was more than usual, and thought it to be odd. She wondered why the vehicle seemed to be slowing down as she moved closer to the window. It didn't dawn on her that the sheriff's car had come to a complete stop until the van had pulled over and the light had turned red once again as the patrol car sat at the intersection. Between the darkness and the distance between them, Heaven could not get a clear visual down the street, but judging by the rapid movement of images, she knew something wasn't right. By the time she was able to focus her eyes and make out what was taking place down the street, her head was slammed into the van's gate from the sudden impact.

"Yeah, so my buddy convinces her to do both of us after the club is over, right?" the young Caucasian officer on the passenger side continues his latest wild excursion as they sit waiting for the light to change. The older Caucasian officer just shook his head and laughed the way he always did whenever his partner of three years shared one of his sexual excursions with him. Being a happily married man for twelve years and a proud father of five, he knew the closest he would ever come to taking a walk on the wild side again was through his partner's stories. "So we wait for her after the club closes, right, and we get her to the car," his tone increases. "And I shit you not, we don't even make it out of the freakin' parking lot before the chick reaches for my cock and starts blowing me," he bellows in excitement.

"In the front seat?" the driver asks as he chuckles.

"No, I'm in the back with her. My buddy's driving, but he can't even get the goddamn car started 'cause he's too busy watching her through the rearview. I mean, this chick is going to town, John," he illustrates with the motion of his hand.

By now, his partner is banging the steering wheel in laughter almost to the point of tears at the young officer's theatrics. As if reliving the moment, the young officer is so engulfed in his story that he doesn't notice his partner has ceased laughing. It took a few seconds to realize the sudden silence when he felt the warmness of some sort oozing down the side of his face. By the time reality had set in, it was too late. The young officer's own brain matter had sprayed the front windshield of the patrol car. Like the first shot that instantly killed his partner, he never heard the bullet that ended his life penetrate the passenger window . . .

"What the hell are those two assholes doing now?" the heavyset black officer sighed, pulling the van away just before the traffic light of Lee Avenue across from Livingston public school. He threw on the van's hazard lights and put it in park a few feet in front of the Puerto Rican store.

"They're always jerking around," his partner on the passenger side offered. He then leaned over to retrieve the CB to radio the patrol car. Had he taken a quick glance to his left first, things may have turned out differently. By the time he did come up with the walkie-talkie in hand and noticed something approaching out of the corner of his eye, the horsepower of the vehicle's engine was in earshot of him and well within striking distance. The last thing he saw was the shining lights just as they came on and the chrome crash grill, and the monstrous truck slammed into the driver's door. His partner heard his neck snap before his own head smashed up against the passenger window. The blow dazed him as his blood oozed down the side of his head. His only thought was finding the walkie-talkie and calling for assistance. That thought was interrupted by two shots that shattered the remainder of the passenger window and found a permanent resting spot inside his head.

Chapter Fifty-Three

The two gunmen rapidly approached the sheriff's patrol car from both directions. One from the left where they had been posted up waiting in the darkness, the other from the right on the side of the funeral parlor that sat on the corner. They were dressed in all black from head to toe, masked up in case someone saw something and wanted to share it with the authorities. As they reached the car, it seemed evident that the two officers were dead judging by the graphic scenery inside the patrol car. As an extra precaution, they unloaded the remaining shots of their silenced-equipped MP-5's into the sheriff's vehicle before they made a mad dash up the street, seeing that the second part of their plan had been executed. They could see the black Ford F-150 pickup truck slammed into the driver's side of the sheriff's transporting van. By the time they reached the back of the van, their partner had already made their way over to the passenger side of the vehicle. One of them watched as their partner pumped shots into the passenger's side while the other took a few steps back and aimed their weapon at the back door handle of the van. Two shots substituted for the key required to unlock the double doors.

Chapter Fifty-Four

Heaven was just regaining her senses when the back doors of the van flung open. The taste of blood invaded her mouth as it trickled down from her forehead and made its way down her nose and onto her lips. Cursing and yelling from a bunch of confused inmates filled the back of the van. When the two masked assailants appeared, the curses and yells from everyone were replaced with whispers and cries.

At least everyone except Heaven. A smile appeared across her face as one of the masked individuals spoke.

"I told you don't worry." Heaven recognized the voice immediately, remembering the words she had read from Shell's lips in the courtroom.

"Later for all that; let's get the fuck outta here," Mia barked, scanning the streets for any possible bystanders or unwanted vehicles, particularly police.

"Come on, let's go," Shell ordered.

Everyone listened and watched the scene as it was playing out, some in admiration while others in horror. The smell of vomit, urine, and feces began to fill the secluded van. Heaven rose up.

"Get these shits off of me," she raised her hands.

Anita, the girl who she had been conversing with in the bullpen, lifted up her arm in the air. Shell pulled out her nine millimeter and pointed it at the links that bonded Anita and Heaven.

The shot rang out separating the two of them. Heaven held her wrist, which was still handcuffed, off to the side of her. The next shot freed her wrist of the second pair of cuffs.

"Take me with you," Anita chimed. The look in her eyes spoke volumes to Heaven. Without hesitation, she took the nine from Shell and freed Anita's left arm. Anita hopped out of the back of the van. Heaven then emptied the remaining thirteen shots into the back of the female's side of the van. The male closest to the van's exit attempted to make a break for it, sensing he, along with the other male inmates, would be next—only to be stopped in his tracks by Shell's MP.

She then followed Heaven's lead letting off more than half of her second clip into the male side.

"No witnesses, right?" she turned to Heaven.

"No witnesses," Heaven repeated.

Mia, Shell, Heaven, and the latest addition darted to the F-150 SUV like Marion Jones, Jackie Joyner-Kersee, Gail Devers, and Flo-Jo in a four-way tie race. Sonya had already backed the pickup truck up from the side of the sheriff's van and pulled a short distance up the street through the light. Once everyone was in, she made the truck roar as she took the light on the corner of Remsen Avenue, passing Troop Avenue, then Commercial Avenue's light, which was green, until she reached George's Road.

Chapter Fifty-Five

"Honey, answer the phone," an annoyed Mrs. Saleski chimed shoving her husband in the back who was in a deep snore. Her annoyance grew as the unsuccessful shove went unanswered.

"Charlie," she barked in frustration, now upset that he was enjoying his rest while hers was broken by the sound of the ringing phone.

"Huh?" he shot up and managed to reply in between snores. It sounded as if he was choking.

"The phone," she bellowed as he rolled over in her direction. Just then, he heard it. He snatched up his watch agitatedly as he answered the phone.

"Hello."

His watch read 10:03 p.m. letting him know he had only been unconscious for an hour. Whoever was calling better have a good reason, thought Detective Saleski. Anybody who rang his phone knew that Monday nights was his day to catch up on his beauty sleep, especially since Tuesdays and Wednesdays were his days off.

"Sal, did I wake you?" the voice on the other end asked, already knowing the answer. He knew the detective's schedule like he knew his own. He couldn't help but chuckle to himself knowing he had just pissed his colleague off.

He and everyone else at the station got a kick out of lighting the detective's short fuse every chance they got.

"You know what you did, you little shit. Whadda ya want, asshole?" Detective Saleski asked, bothered by the call of the detective in his division. He yawned, stretched, and wiped the coal that had formed in the creases of his eyes all in one motion as he waited to hear what the detective he had a dislike for had to say. Whatever it was, he hoped it had nothing to do with him coming in tonight, because that was not going to happen, he told himself.

"Sorry for the bother, Sal," the detective's tone became serious. "But just thought you'd want to know there's been a breakout involving your girl."

Still half-asleep, the words, *breakout involving your girl* were not registering with Detective Saleski. As if reading his mind, the other detective continued.

"The Jacobs's collar you just made."

At the mention of his latest arrest, Heavenly Jacobs, Detective Saleski shot up in bed like a space shuttle at NASA. He was now wide awake and all ears.

"It's all over the news; happened a few hours ago. Four of ours, four female inmates, six males," he relayed in disdain.

"Are you fuckin' shitting me?" Detective Saleski spat as he searched for the television remote.

"I wish I was, pal. Turn it on and see for yourself. I'm down here now."

Like magic, the scene appeared on the detective's television as he hit the on button of his forty-two-inch flat-screen. His eyes widened at the image of Heavenly Jacobs's mug shot.

The entire time his wife had been listening to his phone conversation. The fifteen years they had been married she had never seen her husband so distraught over a case. She placed her hand on his shoulder.

"Honey, what's going on?" she asked.

"It's nothing, go back to sleep," he calmly told his wife, then rose up out of bed. "Jake, I'm on my way," he informed the detective just before hanging up the phone.

Holy shit was his only thought as he dressed and headed out the door.

Chapter Fifty-Six

The discomfort from his recent gun-inflicted wound to the shoulder had Monty tossing and turning. It had been the norm for the past few nights after his visit to the hood doctor. The painkillers he had been prescribed by the unlicensed practicing physician he had gone to didn't do anything to ease the pain. Instead, the pills had caused Monty to become sick to the stomach, so he discontinued taking them. He chose to fight the excruciating pain off naturally and was now realizing how difficult of a task his decision was. He didn't know how much longer he could take being cooped up in the rooming house either, which was one of his stash cribs, before he actually had to go see a real doctor at a real hospital.

He was sure the police were looking for him, either for what happened at Feaster Park or for questioning about of the murders of his cousin and girlfriend. He wasn't sure whether the police up at the park got a good look at him, or even knew who he was, but he was positive that they could link him in connection with Le Le because his prints, pictures of them together, and tons of other paraphernalia proving he lived there were available to the police. And the same at his cousin Murda's, not to mention they shared the same last name. The thought of how he had come to be in such a predicament angered Monty. Not only angry at the female responsible but mainly at himself for underestimating Heaven.

When he received the call from one of his soldiers who had found Murda's tortured and lifeless body tied to a chair, his question was answered as to how she had known of his whereabouts. After numerous and unsuccessful calls to Le Le and Murda, he could only conclude the worst. The description he had been given of the scene outside of their home was all the confirmation he needed about Le Le. When his lieutenant told him of the fire trucks, police, and a coroner's van surrounding the town house, Monty knew Le Le was dead.

He shook the two images of his deceased loved ones out of his mind and turned on the television to get his mind off his present situation. He flicked through channel after channel with nothing in particular in mind to watch, then stopped when he reached the BET station. He was just about to get into the latest Young Jeezy video when his mind did a quick backtrack. Subconsciously, he thought he had recognized something or rather someone a few channels back. His television slowly traveled backward as he pointed the remote at the screen. Four stations later, he could not believe his eyes. He increased the volume on the television as his mouth fell open at the photo on the television screen.

"So far, authorities have no leads as to the whereabouts of the suspects or the escapees. We'll have more as this horrendous story unfolds. In Jersey City, police are—"

"What the fuck!" Monty cursed as he switched to another channel. He turned just in time to catch the beginning of the story.

"We're standing outside Midtown New Brunswick, New Jersey. Earlier this evening, a Middlesex County Sheriffs inmate transporting van and sheriff's patrol car escort were ambushed on Sandford Street between Livingston Avenue and Lee Avenue. Sources tell us that this woman, Heavenly Jacobs of New Brunswick, may be responsible for the ambush, according to the police. Ms. Jacobs was arrested and charged with murder and attempted murder

after a detective witnessed her involvement in a gun battle a few days ago on Troop Avenue at Feaster Park uptown and was being held at the Middlesex County Adult Correctional Center in North Brunswick. Judge Ferencz denied bail to Ms. Jacobs earlier today, and our sources say that the decision may have resulted in the ambush. When police arrived on the scene, both the transporting sheriff as well as several males and females were found gunned down, a total of four officers and ten inmates.

"Sources also tell us that this woman, thirty-six-year-old Anita Abrams, may have been one of the escapees. If you have any information on the whereabouts of these suspects or leading to the arrest of those responsible for this heinous massacre, please contact 1-800-Crime Stoppers."

Monty's head was in a whirlwind. He rubbed his eyes and shook his head to make sure he wasn't dreaming. He did not want to believe what his eyes had just witnessed nor what his ears had just heard.

"This shit keeps getting better and better," he let out in insane laughter.

The news of Heaven's escape had him baffled. He had overheard stories and been told some by dudes who he had served time with, and then from his girlfriend, how hard Heaven and Earth played in the game. Up until now, after seeing and hearing about her escape, Monty had no clue of the depths of the stories. He himself had been in the game for over twenty years, catching his first murder at age thirteen, but even now, at age thirty-five, he knew he would have never had the guts or balls to orchestrate, or even *attempt* to go out, the way he heard Heaven had. For a split second, a sense of respect—followed by a flash of fear—jolted through Monty's body. Beads of perspiration began to form on his forehead, and his palms started to itch. He knew whenever these symptoms came into play, murder would result. The question now was—*whose* murder? A sense of dread swept through Monty for a split second. If there ever was any before, there was none now. He knew he could no longer underestimate the female who had disrupted his whole way of living.

"Damn," he cursed as he retrieved his cell phone.

Epilogue

The yellow, beige, and brown Winnebago floated down the New Jersey Turnpike. I-95 southbound was its destination. Sonya was in the front driver's seat navigating the mobile home with Shell riding shotgun. They had longed ditched the stolen F-150 and replaced it with the home on wheels. Sonya had purchased the latest getaway vehicle for cash from an elderly Caucasian family in Franklin Township, after discovering it in a Cars and Trucks classified magazine. After Heaven's lawyer informed her of the 30 percent chance of her receiving bail, Sonya immediately sprang into action. She was the one who had made the decision and came up with the plan to free her boss from custody. After all Heaven had done for her, there was no way she was going to let her friend rot in jail for what could be forever she told herself. None of the others objected.

Mia, Anita, and Heaven occupied the back of the home on wheels, along with enough guns and ammo to start another World War. Everyone rode in silence, each in her own deep thought, as the RV glided to the sound of Tupac's "All Eyez on Me," double CD.

"I ain't a killer, but don't push me, revenge is like the sweetest joy next to gettin' pussy," Tupac harmonized in his gangster and poetic tone.

How ironic, thought Heaven, how Tupac Shakur was the choice of getaway music. He was actually the nephew of the infamous Assata Shakur, who had traveled on the very same highway after her breakout and escape from the Edna Mahan Correctional Facility for Women in Clinton, New Jersey. It was the very same prison where Heaven had served time and met Earth. She had heard the classical and historical tale of the female Black Panther, whose real name was once Joanne Chesimard, on more than several occasions, and she couldn't help but feel like the woman now. She could only imagine being in a similar predicament that the lady she knew only by name and reputation had felt and thought, the way she was at that very moment traveling down the interstate with her team in an attempt to elude the law after her great escape. Although the situations and circumstances were different, she knew that the causes were the same—fleeing from prosecution by an unjust, racist judicial system and to avoid spending the rest of their lives imprisoned. For a brief moment, Heaven thought about relocating to Cuba, where she had been told Ms. Shakur had fled to and still resided. Had it not been for ego and pride, she may have considered going to the country that would make her free of extradition and prosecution.

Now that she was out, however, Heaven knew that she could not, and would not, rest or stop until she had finished what she had started, no matter how long it took. She was out for justice as well as blood—street justice, that is. She knew court would be held in the streets, with her being the judge, prosecutor, and jury. And when it was all said and done, death would be the sentence.

Heaven felt the mobile home slowing down. As she peered out the window, she grabbed hold of the AR-15 that rested on the floor, thinking the worst, ready for whatever. Immediately, both Mia and Anita did the same seeing Heaven spring into action. Heaven noticed the sign indicating the toll ahead and calmed herself. As they made it through the toll with ease, complements of the E-Z pass they possessed, everyone let out a sigh of relief. It was no secret that the New Jersey Turnpike was one of the scariest highways to travel on when you're doing something illegal. Aside from harboring two fugitives of justice and murders hanging over their heads, between the ten AR-15s, three MP-5s, sixteen handguns, a million-plus cash, and fifteen kilos of cocaine, they were traveling with enough contraband to land them each with five life sentences and the death penalty.

Heaven slid the curtain back from the RV's back window. She wanted to take one last look at her home state before making it a temporary distant memory. She knew the next time she set foot on New Jersey's soil, there would be hell to pay. As she looked up at the words NEW JERSEY, on top of the tollbooth, her thoughts lingered. The only thing on her mind at that moment was revenge, and at the end of her thought was the name Monty.

31901061075877